Praise for *The Gospel According to Blindboy*

'Mad, wild, hysterical, and all completely under the writer's control – this is a brilliant debut.'
KEVIN BARRY

'There is genius in this book, warped genius. Like you'd expect from a man who for his day job wears a plastic bag on his head but something beyond that too. Oddly in keeping with the tradition of great Irish writers.'
RUSSELL BRAND

'If you've ever witnessed (there's no other word for it) a Rubberbandits video you'll be anxious (there's no other word for it) to read this collection of short stories from one of the originators. I hesitate to use the word author as the experience is as close to reading a traditional short story as being burnt by a blow torch. Essential, funny and disturbing.'
DANNY BOYLE

'One of Ireland's finest and most intelligent comic minds delivers stories so blisteringly funny and sharp your fingers might bleed. In language so delicious you can taste it, we're shown holy and unholy Ireland: a land of lock-ins, nettle stings, stone-mad Cork birds, gas cunts and Guiney's jeans. No one is safe – we all have the unmerciful piss ripped out of us and there's no escape from the emotional gut punches, expertly dealt.'
TARA FLYNN

'Demented, dishevelled and deeply surreal – Blindboy Boatclub's book will shock and delight.'
IRISH INDEPENDENT

'It's not for the faint-hearted.
JOE.IE

'You won't be disappointed. It will take you to places unexpected.'
RYAN TUBRIDY

YOU

I WANT TO KNOW YOU
I WANT TO LEARN ABOUT YOU
I WANT TO FIND OUT ABOUT EVERYTHING
I WANT TO LOVE YOU
I WANT TO HAVE YOUR CHILDREN
I WANT TO FIGHT FOR YOUR RIGHTS
I WANT TO GROW OLD WITH YOU
I WANT US TO BE BURIED ON TOP
OF EACH OTHER WHEN WE DIE
I WANT TO MEET YOU AGAIN
IN HEAVEN
BECAUSE YOU ARE AN ~~ANGEL~~
ANGEL

The Gospel According to Blindboy

In 15 Short Stories

Blindboy Boatclub

GILL BOOKS

Gill Books
Hume Avenue
Park West
Dublin 12
www.gillbooks.ie

Gill Books is an imprint of M.H. Gill & Co.

© Blindboy Boatclub 2017, 2018

First published in hard cover 2017
First published in paperback 2018

978 07171 8100 1

Designed by www.grahamthew.com
Copy-edited by Ruth Mahony
Proofread by Matthew Parkinson-Bennett
Printed by Clays, Bungay, Suffolk

This book is typeset in 10.5 on 15pt, Sabon.

This is a work of fiction. Names, characters, businesses, places, events and incidents are either the products of the author's imagination or used in a fictitious manner. Any resemblance to actual persons, living or dead, or actual events is purely coincidental.

The paper used in this book comes from the wood pulp of managed forests. For every tree felled, at least one tree is planted, thereby renewing natural resources.

A CIP catalogue record for this book is available from the British Library.

RIHANNA UNIMPRESSED BY HER
NEW HAIRCUT THAT WAS ~~GIVEN~~
~~TO~~ HER BY THE ~~~~

Blindboy Boatclub is Ireland's foremost satirist and most original comedic voice, and one half of the Rubberbandits. Present in the art and theatre world with their movement 'Gas C**ntism', they represented Ireland at the Venice Biennale in 2015 and were the first entertainment act to headline at Shakespeare's Globe. Hit singles include 'Horse Outside' and 'Spastic Hawk', and popular television shows include *The Rubberbandits' Guide* and *The Almost Impossible Gameshow*. Blindboy also campaigns in support of a variety of social issues, including male mental health.

Acknowledgements

Helbo, Shontin, Jeff, Nack, Bop, Gad, Phile, Deag, Mr Chrome, DJ Willie O Dea J, Charlie, Cheesy

Preface

This is a book of Gas Cuntist short stories, each from the perspective of a different character. I've been writing for 17 years in some shape or form with the Rubberbandits, whether it be writing TV scripts, writing the outlines to prank phone calls or writing songs. But this is my first time writing words on paper as the sole medium.

With songwriting, you create music and production that tugs and sways at the listeners' emotions. You set a tone and a feel that influences how the lyrics are perceived, which is great craic, but the listener is handing a lot of control over to the artist.

With television and video work, you use a lens to literally represent on a screen what the viewer will see. If I film a garden shed, for instance, everyone experiences the exact same garden shed as I intended it to be perceived. There's very little two-way engagement; the artist commandeers the viewer's imagination.

But with pure writing, just words, it's a very participatory experience. I can describe a garden shed in as much detail as I like and you, the reader, will still see a different garden shed in your mind's eye, based on your own experiences and interactions with garden sheds, and your acquired emotional relationship with garden sheds throughout your life. Positive, negative or indifferent. With the written word, no two people experience a story exactly the same way, because you, the reader, participate creatively.

The following stories are like scripts, or song lyrics, and you are the director of how they will appear and how they will sound in your head theatre. Unique to just you: no one else will experience what you experience. That seems fairly fucking class to me.

P.S. In the spirit of Gas Cuntist socially engaged art, this is also a colouring book. Each story is punctuated with a drawing that you are invited to colour in. There is also a lot of blank space for you to contribute and expand on the drawings yourself. Tweet them to me @rubberbandits.

YURT

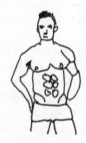

IDEAL MALE MAN

Contents

HOLLYWOOD ACTOR GARY SINISE
HE'S AT A FUNERAL
DRESSED INCORRECTLY

SCAPHISM

The way the bottom of his jeans used to soak up the piss from the floor of the jax would bring on that metallic taste on my tongue that I get before an epileptic fit. Every fucking Thursday after darts. He'd have those navy denims that you get in Guiney's, with all the unnecessary stitching around the thighs and the arse. They made him look like a giant toddler with a dirty nappy. Every Thursday, lads. Fat Macca and Ernie Collopy would be going head to head in a vicious tourney of darts. It was always the two of them in the final. Ernie would have went professional if it wasn't for women and liquor. Fine men.

Without fail though, this other fucking eejit would be over for his first drop of Harp. He'd drink it in this servile way, where we could all see his teeth through the pint glass. He'd drink his pint like the pint was telling him to drink it rather than him telling the pint to get drank. Then off to the jax he'd go, and come back out with an inch of piss on the boot-cut cuffs of his Guiney's jeans. I couldn't go near my porter, because I'd be transfixed by the cuffs of his pants. I'd watch a centimetre of cold piss on denim creep up and darken his trousers. Capillary action: the ability of a liquid to flow in narrow spaces without the assistance of, or even in opposition to, external forces like gravity. I'd stare at that exact definition on the screen of my Samsung, to try and achieve a sense of control over the situation.

By 10.15 p.m., he'd be on Harp number two, and a pack of scampi fries would be ordered. 10.25 p.m. and he was back into the jax for his second piss. Two inches of dark wet navy up his leg at this point, lads. Other people's piss, he's wearing the feculence of every man in this pub up his fucking leg. Get different trousers, man ta fuck. The heel of his black leather Gola tackie would sometimes trap the bottom cuff of the pants leg, so he'd be standing on the end of his own pants. It would squelch, there'd be grains of sand on the soggy denim, from fucking where? No sand in the jax of this pub.

By 11.20 p.m., the third piss would be had. He'd be half-cut, leaning against the bar, belly hanging out of the cardigan. And the piss, boys, the piss would be six inches up his shin. Capillary action, sucking up piss, contradicting Newtonian physics. He never even noticed, and that's what would hurt the most, he didn't even know what was happening to his own leg. Art Naughton and Julie Slattery would notice, coz I'd see them staring, but they'd just fall back into their sherries. I'd try to catch their eyes, maybe get some backup, sort this out. A mutiny. But no. Cowards.

At 11.45 p.m. or thereabouts, the piss would be threatening his upper shin. That's when the taste of metal would arrive in my mouth, like I'd licked a nine-volt battery, followed by a burnt almond sensation and finally bad eggs. When the room would lose its place in time and shapes no longer made sense, that's how I knew I was having the epileptic fit. I'd come around after, and Packie Willie the barman would have tonic water and ice for me with a slice of lemon in it. All that citrus and effervescent quinine would see me right and bring me back. Every Thursday, lads, swear to fuck, every Thursday.

No one took notice anymore. No one knew why I'd droop into a fit, no one talked to me about it. No one knew it was because of that stupid bollocks and the capillary action of the piss on his floppy Guiney's denim. At 12.10 a.m., she'd come in off the night shift, Anne, and stroll over to him. He'd have the Grand Marnier and sparkling water waiting for her at the bar-top, and she'd lean in and fucking kiss him, and the leg of her Garda uniform would rub off the shin of his capillary-action piss-pants. Every Thursday.

When Anne came in, it meant the doors got locked and Art Naughton and Julie Slattery could take out their pack of Major and smoke indoors like it was 1985. Packie Willie would turn on the Sanyo behind the counter with the six-changer disc tray. Deacon Blue, Jimmy Nail, Showaddywaddy, Prefab Sprout, Thomas Dolby, The Style Council, The Communards, Wham, Kajagoogoo, the solo efforts of Lamar from Kajagoogoo. He'd start dancing with his elbows, and the belly over the belt, and the top of his arse on show, squelching piss-britches on the wood floor that had eight generations of varnish and was black. She'd dance alongside him, with one of Julie Slattery's Majors sticking out of her mouth, clapping her hands like Daryl Hall, looking at him into the eyes. Acting like myself and herself hadn't been married for eighteen years.

I'd sit up, looking at the screen of my Samsung. The battery would go at three, so I'd read the back of a packet of King crisps. At around 5.30 a.m., we'd all clear out. Barney Shanahan would collect them in the taxi, and I'd walk home. Every Thursday, lads. In the winters, I'd walk home in the pitch black, not a hint of light. I'd click my tongue like a bat, that way I'd hear a lamp-post if it was near. The sound would bounce back at me. When it's November dark, the slip on the ground underneath, you've to dance with it or it'll crack you open. The cold has such bitter presence that you can feel your way through it, it has rises and lumps. You can sense the lukewarmth of a hedge, the trail that a panting fox leaves, a little band of clammy air that you can grab like a rope and use it to drag your way up a bóithrín. In the summer, it'd be bright, I hated that, there's too much pomp and show to summer mornings. When it's winter and dark, you can get properly acquainted with your journey. You get its honesty, you get to know its fears, its intentions. There's areas of the Limerick countryside that can't be trusted purely on grounds of personal integrity. These are where people fall into ditches, or drown in bogs. The area charms that person into their death, it's never accidental. I've walked them all with no eyes.

I'd arrive back to the cottage at around eight in the morning. No keys, I'd leave the hall door wide open to confuse the tinkers. That's when I'd be able to relax and have the first drink. I'd be away from the pressures of the pub and the piss-britches. I keep the bottles of Tyskie on the window where they'd be cold. This particular Friday morning, I couldn't find the opener. I scanned my belongings to see which one I was willing to risk breaking to open the cap off. Not my Samsung, not the remote, not my lighter, fuck it, it's my only one, not Anne's hair straightener that she never collected. So I ripped the curtain-pole off the wall. Seven foot long, some fulcrum on it. I jammed the bottle of Tyskie in between two cushions on the couch with a heavy encyclopaedia holding it in place, and opened it with the curtain-pole from the other side of the room. Popped off in two seconds, lads, what did I say? Fucking fulcrum. I haven't got a master's in physics for nothing.

I had a fine lump of smelly sock hash that I got off the Costellos from Pallasgreen. Hums like black pudding when you burn it into the Rizla. I continued with the Tyskies until *Judge Judy* came on the television. She was talking to young ones who couldn't stop spending money and getting into debt. I'd been meaning to ring Anne's piss-trouser boyfriend for the best part of two years. I'd been meaning to tell him that I hoped himself and Anne would have good fortune in all their future endeavours. The Samsung was charged, and something about this particular episode of *Judge Judy* gave me the courage to ring his number, so I fucking did, lads.

The phone was ringing, he answered, he was talking to me. I was going to tell him about the epilepsy, tell him how silly it was that I'd be getting fits over his piss-pants, and how I'd get so upset when himself and Anne kissed while dancing to the solo efforts of Lamar from Kajagoogoo. We'd all laugh about it. Maybe I'd call over for dinner some night. Fuck it, maybe I'd dance with the two of 'em next Thursday. I'd smoke Julie Slattery's Majors too, and clap like Daryl Hall with Anne and high-five himself. We'd all head back to their gaff in Barney Shanahan's taxi, drink Grand Marnier, have a devil's threesome, why not? Breakfast, dinner and toast.

But I didn't. I told him that I'd developed stage three cancer of my oesophagus and needed to clear the air. I asked him to meet me by the river in Plassey where we could fish for perch together. In fairness to him, he had no qualms about this and felt fierce sorry for me. I don't have stage three cancer in my oesophagus at all though, lads. I left the house with an open Tyskie in either fist. I'd no fishing rod, so when I made it as far as Castleconnell, I dropped into the Spar for a ball of twine, a naggin of Huzzar for the rest of the journey, a litre of milk and a squeezy bottle of honey shaped like a gay bee. At Castletroy, I found a branch of oak and inserted the twine onto the end of it. Threw it over my shoulder. At the University of Limerick, I asked a girl to give me one of her earrings. She lashed it straight over, not a bother, fair play to her. I put that on the end of the twine like a hook. I had the bones of a fishing rod on me, lads.

When I got to the bank of the Plassey River, he was there. Daycent enough rod he had too, got it in Aldi the last time they had a fishing sale, not that bad at all. Big welcoming smile on him, as I got closer, he doled out his fat hand in friendship. When I could smell his breath, I wrapped the twine around his neck and didn't stop pulling until his eyes closed. He lay flat on the sandy Plassey riverbank, sleepy boy. Gorgeous evening. There's a pond a small bit upriver, with stagnant water, near a little island, very quiet. I carried him up into my arms, pure cradling like, and went there. I tore the fucking ridiculous Guiney jeans off him, first port of call, and lobbed them in the river where they'd never give me another fit again. I found three old logs, hollow boys, great for floating. One under his back, tied his fat belly to that, one above his head with hands bound, and same with the feet. Getting great mileage out of the Castleconnell twine. Gas-looking cunt, balls naked, tied up to the logs, like a bachelor at his stag do in Liverpool. Some craic.

He woke up when I was rubbing the picnic honey all over his balls and arse. Roaring and shouting he was, so I started pouring the honey down his throat, we wouldn't get disturbed that way. Flaked a litre of milk over him too. This is the best bit though, lads. I gently floated him out into the middle of the pond. Logs doing their job at buoyancy, feeling proud of myself. Very still water, so it was nice and calm. There he was, drifting out, not one move on him. Eyes up to the sky. Mad bastard. It was midday, so the horseflies were having a great time with the honey all over his goolies.

Now, I know what ye're thinking. What class of sick bastard comes up with this type of stuff? Who'd do this to their ex-wife's new lad? But they've been doing this for years, especially to adulterers. It's called scaphism. Perfectly legitimate method of execution. Look it up on yer Samsungs. The Persians invented it. The flies will bite as he floats on the pond. The longer he floats, the more he'll shit and piss. This will bring more flies. Give it a day, and they'll lay their eggs. The maggots will hatch, and he'll still be alive, floating gently on his back. All tied up. The underside of him will get nice and putty-like in the water, and fat pike will take schkelps out of his calves, trying to eat the worms. Maggots eating into him too, only the soft wet bits though, like the mouth, the dick, the eyes, the nose, the ears, the arse. The maggots will accumulate so much that they'll cut off blood flow, causing early gangrene to set in.

Don't blame me, lads – blame the ancient Persians for inventing the slowest and cruellest method of death known to humanity. You'd think methods like that get lost in the flow of time, forgotten in barbarism. But they don't, because time doesn't flow, it creeps capilliarily up the universe's leg, ignorant of Newton's laws, slow and unnoticed by the weak, bringing the dark stain of retribution with it. I gaze up at the heavens, and they gaze back, in boot-cut jeans and black leather shoes.

- DONT GET ASH ON MY NANS CARPET

DR MARIE GAFFNEY

Speciation, learning, instinct, guilds, ecological niches, island biogeography, conservation, phylogeography – these are the categorisations that concern me in my research. My specific area of interest is vocalisation. Last year I chaired a conference in Malta on the syringeal function in the roseate tern. My PhD interrogated cultural heterogeneity among populations of this species of songbird and its geographically specific correlation with human dialects. Every scientific field of research contains these 'big' words and phrases that we simply don't use on a daily basis to order a coffee or speak to our neighbours. In my area, avian research, we use these big words like a mechanic would use the names of their tools to speak to another mechanic – they are simply tools that help a community to communicate meaning among each other. But if I'm not speaking in a language you understand, well, then I can't communicate what I mean to you. So I'm gonna drop the big words because effective communication happens in the language of the receiver, which is kind of what the next twenty minutes will be about.

My name is Dr Marie Gaffney, and I am an ornithologist from University College Cork, in Ireland. I study birds. This year I'm honoured to say that I was awarded the Nobel Prize for Medicine or Physiology. In this TED Talk, I'd like to take you through the work over the past sixteen months that lead to this achievement.

Humans and birds have evolved alongside each other over millions of years. We share a commonality in that our two species both use complex vocalisations to communicate within our communities. But what most don't know is that we communicate between our species too. When birds sing, we experience this as quite soothing and calming, whether it be the long chirps of a robin or the more melodic song of thrushes. When we hear these sounds, they make us feel happy, make us pause and take note of our other senses, such as smell or sight. When I'm out having a walk through a park and I stop to hear birds sing, I naturally take a big deep breath, and I notice the colours of the leaves or the angle of the sun, I smell the dew, the flowers, the grass.

Birdsong instantly takes us to a very meditative, mindful and contemplative state. This is no coincidence. Our brains evolved a symbiotic relationship with bird vocalisations. For our early ancestors, not only was birdsong nature's alarm clock, but the sound of birds kept us safe. When the birds stopped singing in the trees, it meant that a predator was near. The birds would go quiet to protect themselves and our brains slowly evolved to react to this. Even today, one of the first lessons that our militaries receive in field training is to stay on guard when the birds are quiet, as it could mean a hidden ambush. When birds don't sing, we sense an eeriness or creepiness. This is our brains and nervous system telling us to be on high alert. We've all heard the myth that the birds don't sing in Auschwitz. But when birds do sing, we feel safe, we can relax, chill out.

Birdsong also keeps us sharp and pepped up, in the positive sense, not like we're on edge – it makes us feel alive and ready to tackle work. I mentioned nature's alarm clock. Well, humans are diurnal, as opposed to nocturnal. Interestingly, our diurnal behaviour evolved alongside birds – our brains wake up when stimulated with avian vocalisation. Birdsong works because it's stochastic, made up of lots and lots of random sounds. Its rhythms don't repeat; there are no patterns. And the human mind is obsessed with pattern. Stare into some big fluffy clouds long enough and you'll convince yourself that you see shapes of people and things. We attribute meaning to random coincidences. We create geometric balance in our art, fashion, our architecture. Our aesthetic values centre around balance, geometry and pattern. Some say that our existence itself is entirely random chaos and so we invent the idea of a creator, God, just to tolerate the ambiguity of meaninglessness and uncertainty. But we won't get into that today. We strive for pattern. Our engrossment in patterns is necessary for recognising other humans' faces and remembering and categorising them as friends, lovers, family, enemies etc., which makes our ability to recognise patterns quite a complex cognitive function and one that is necessary for such a social animal as the human.

But birdsong undercuts our pattern-recognition capabilities. It's too random – we can never find the patterns, which is why it keeps our powerful brains alert and awake. My good friend

Dr Tungsten Gulp, who is an evolutionary musicologist in the University of Berkley, California, posits that music evolved because of humans' frustration with the random nature of birdsong. He suggests that we rationalised and altered birdsong into the categorical patterns of geometric melody, rhythm and scales that we call music. But my work over the past 42 months, ladies and gentlemen, isn't in the area of how the vocalisations of birds impact humans – that's a very well-researched area. My work is quite the opposite of that.

The city of Cork in Ireland is a place that I have called my home for the past eleven years. It's where I researched my PhD and it's where I work, in UCC. Soon after I moved down from Dublin, I began to notice that the birds of Cork were especially agitated and aggressive in their behaviour towards humans. Crows in particular fly from buildings several times a day and attack the people of the city. I initially assumed that I was just being hyper-observant of the behaviour of birds, considering that ornithology is my area of study. This changed, however, one morning on MacCurtain Street. I had just gotten my coffee and began to scrutinise the behaviour of three Brent geese. Their feathers were puffing, and they were cackling and displaying signs of aggression. However, they were three females and there were no male geese present, nor were there any chicks, which made this aggressive display particularly out of character. They directed their attention towards two men who were unloading coal from a lorry. The engine of the lorry was particularly loud, so the men were shouting over it to be heard. They were arguing about the price of shoes. As the men returned to the van, the three Brent geese made a beeline for the cabin, which had open windows. All three geese began to attack the men in the cabin of the lorry as it drove off, pecking at their faces and flapping their wings. The lorry then bashed into a wall at the bottom of MacCurtain Street, narrowly missing the River Lee. Two of the geese fled into the river. I rushed towards the accident to see if I needed to ring an ambulance. Sadly, one of the geese had died in the crash. The men were unharmed.

'Are you lads OK?' I asked.

One of the men, whose face was black from coal, replied, 'Third time in a fortnight, ma'am. The birds in Cork are stone mad. They must be from Limerick or something.' He gestured at the other man, who was throwing the dead goose's body over the wall and into the river below. 'His brother was nearly choked by a wren who flew into his mouth last week as he cycled back from the bookies' office.'

I returned to my research office, rattled by what I'd seen. I was most definitely spotting a pattern of bird aggression in the city of Cork, but could not understand why this was happening. My first instinct was water pollution, as Cork Harbour has many factories that could cause an excess of mercury to find its way into rainfall and ground water. Heavy metals are known to injure the avian brain, which could possibly explain excessive aggression in Corkonian birds. However, my theory was dashed when I began to search the local archives for bird attacks in the city of Cork. There were several a year as far back as the local papers would go, which was 1778 and therefore far pre-dated the arrival of mercury into the Cork water supply. In 1817 the Lord Mayor of Cork was killed by a heron. A hurler was blinded by an osprey in 1868. Seagulls caused several injuries at a communion party in Blackpool in 1925. There were too many incidents to list here. When I searched hospital records, I found thousands of bird attacks, dating back centuries. When I contrasted these attacks against records for the rest of Ireland, the results were dumbfounding. Outside of Cork, there was maybe one incident every ten years, which would be considered completely normal within ornithological circles. There was most definitely an epidemic of bird attacks in Cork city, and Cork city alone. I tested every possible angle – diet, air quality, elevation, habitat – and came up empty-handed.

Then, one night, I was listening to recordings of the song of a speckled wren. I have a piece of software that analyses and categorises bird-call. It measures tone, frequency and rhythm, and extrapolates this into an algorithm. Remember what I said earlier, about what the human brain couldn't do with birdsong? Well, my software does what the human brain can't, it analyses the stochastic patterns of a bird's song, and extracts algorithms from it. While I was working, the radio was playing in the background. It was local DJ Neil Prenderville, and he had a caller on who was complaining about young people setting fire to his bin. As the song of the wren played over this caller, my software began to behave abnormally, and the fan of my laptop got overheated. The software crashed. I immediately shoved my dictaphone to the speaker of the radio and recorded the man who was talking about the bins.

The next day, I brought this recording to the much more powerful computer in the UCC ornithology department. I ran both the song of the wren and the caller from Cork complaining about the bins into the analytical software, and my suspicion was confirmed. The Cork accent contained identical random tones to that of birdsong. For those of you here who are not Irish, I need to explain the Cork accent. It is highly unique.

Cork people sound like they are singing when they speak – not in a pleasant way, but in an arbitrary, discordant way. It has been described by a colleague as tonally similar to a baby with adult lungs, crying for his nappy to be changed while simultaneously complaining jealously that his friend has received a bigger ice-pop. My dear friend Dr Barrington Talent, who sadly passed recently, gave what I think is the most accurate description of the Cork accent: 'It is like a scolded Alsatian whimpering on the roof of a car that passes from your right to left at such a speed that the Doppler effect is apparent.' It is, as you may have gathered, a strange accent.

I presented my hypothesis of the Cork accent's relationship to birdsong to my superiors and a research trial began immediately. One of the conveniences of working in a university. We tested a sample group of 250 people from Cork city and analysed their speech. I was correct. But what was even more interesting was that we found that in the way that birdsong is relaxing to the brains of humans, the Cork accent, with its erratic, rising and dipping nasal tone, is highly irritating to the brains of birds. It seems to interfere with their means of communicating with each other. Birds use call to warn of danger, to find a mate, to protect their territory and to let others know that food is nearby. They depend upon the ability to communicate through vocalisation for basic survival. This system almost completely breaks down when a Cork person is nearby. The proximity of a Cork person is a highly irritating experience, which causes the poor animal to defend itself aggressively. To put it in human terms, imagine trying to conduct your daily business while another person incessantly follows you with a party horn and points it directly into your ear. You'd feel like hitting them, wouldn't you? This is what it's like for a cormorant or a rook when they hear a Cork person talk about why the Cork Jazz festival is proof that Cork is the most cultured city in Ireland, or why the English Market is better than anything offering similar wares in Dublin. Birds cannot stand Cork people. I published a paper on my findings, and it was received warmly in the ornithological community. But it was not this research that got me the Nobel Prize.

So the Cork accent is annoying to birds. Great, I thought. Pretty interesting. But ultimately, this discovery didn't improve the lives of birds or humans. The research was published in many Cork newspapers, in the 'In Other News' section. But unanimously the people of Cork agreed that they would rather keep their accent and continue being attacked by birds than 'give some bitch down from Dublin the pleasure of changing our culture'. I gave up, and went through a period of depression. My greatest study was pretty much just an interesting fact, with no useful applications.

I returned to research to investigate the declining numbers of spotted flycatchers in Ireland. The spotted flycatcher is a small brown bird, so called because it eats flying insects and its juveniles have a breast-pattern of brown spots. It's one of Ireland's migratory species, and makes a yearly round trip to Africa. Since 2003, the numbers in Ireland had been declining rapidly. Researchers in Maynooth discovered that this was as a result of the growth in population of a mosquito species that carried a parasite which attacked the livers of the spotted flycatcher. Global warming in Ireland was most definitely responsible for this. The birds were eating the mosquitos and succumbing to the parasite. This parasite was reducing the population by as much as 5% each year, and its effect appeared to be growing exponentially, meaning that the spotted flycatcher would most definitely become extinct in the next fifty years. Not only would this be very sad, but it would be detrimental for the Irish ecosystem, which relies on this bird to control the insect population. The Maynooth researchers discovered it was possible to administer a prophylactic to the bird, which would cause its liver to reject the parasite. This could be delivered via water, either through drinking or bathing. However, the spotted flycatcher is an elusive and incredibly swift bird, so catching one through traditional means would be quite difficult and depletive of resources and manpower. The Irish ornithological community was banging its head against the wall.

One day in the canteen of UCC, I was having some small-talk with my colleague Dr Liam Flag, who is a professor of engineering. I was telling him about the spotted flycatcher and he was telling me about his current research. He was investigating alternative methods of propulsion and fuel, in particular an idea for powering an engine using the vibrations created from sound. I was highly intrigued by this, I thought it was an excellent example of outside-the-box thinking. I said goodbye to Liam and went back to my office to rack my brains about liver parasites.

Then a flash hit me, in relation to Liam's sound propulsion research. What if there was a vehicle, not one powered by noise, but that generated noise? Cork noises? I thought, if the spotted flycatcher is so difficult to catch, then why can't I make them come to me? I immediately called Dr Liam Flag with my idea and we soon got to work on sourcing funding for the proposal, which was not difficult. I began to identify the areas in Ireland in which there were known habitats and populations of spotted flycatchers. They were to be found in most of Ireland below Mullingar, in wooded areas.

I then examined the spotted flycatcher's call, and evaluated this sonically with the accents of some test subjects from Cork. The Cork accent counteracted the flycatcher's song only when conversing about certain topics. This was to be expected. Gannets, for instance, are only enraged by the conversations of Cork people when they speak about architecture. The topics that were found to trigger an emotional reaction in the spotted flycatcher were: giving tips on which horses to put money on, speaking about the importance of Cork nightclub Sir Henry's influence on the Irish music scene, complaining about how sick your dog is, and listing out the sizes and types of drill bits available in a hardware shop. I recorded such conversations, and played them back to some live spotted flycatcher specimens that were being kept in a cage in UCC. The birds only showed mild irritation, which was quite disappointing. I was not giving up, however, so I brought three live Cork people into the laboratory and asked them to speak freely about the aforementioned topics. The flycatchers became incredibly aggressive and tried to break free from the cage, attempting to attack the human specimens. This was something I had overlooked in my initial research. The ear canal of a bird doesn't respond as readily to recorded sounds. The voice of an actual Cork person is a necessary factor. If this wasn't the case, a crow would fly down your chimney any time Ronan O'Gara was on television.

I took this research to Dr Liam Flag, who began to design a vehicle. Behind me are some photographs of the Cork Man Bird Van. As you can see, the vehicle is heavily armoured. Liam was inspired by the design of security vans and riot vans. The front cabin seats two people, and the windshield and side windows are protected by a substantial metal cage. That's where Liam and I sat throughout the expedition. But things get really interesting when you look at the back of the van. As you can see, it has very thick metal plating with no holes. This was a titanium–aluminium alloy, for strength but also to remain lightweight. It was imperative that the vehicle remained light, to minimise refuelling. Jutting out from the top are four wide-mouthed sound cones, which are essentially modified trombones. If you look at the cross-section of the van in the next slide, you'll notice four barefoot Cork men standing upright, with their heads tilted back towards the ceiling. Their necks are tied to the belts of their trousers using rappel cord. Just above their mouths are the openings of the trombones. It is into these receivers that they spoke. Their voices were then acoustically projected outside the van, with a more significant increase in volume than usually afforded by the mechanics of the human voice box, achieving twenty decibels at various stages of measurement. This was very impressive, considering there was no electronic assistance boosting the signal of their voices. The four Cork men stood barefoot on a metal hotplate, which was turned on at irregular intervals to keep them talking and prevent them from falling asleep.

On this slide is a map of the journey we took around Ireland. As you can see, we essentially circumnavigated the country, in a clockwise direction starting at Cork and ending in Waterford. Doing this gave the amplified sound of the Cork men's voices an audible circumference of several hundred miles to reach the ears of spotted flycatchers. Our journey was also influenced by the locations of the largest electrical pylons in the country as marked on a map given to us by the Electricity Supply Board. There was a reason for this. We timed the journey for early September, because this was when the spotted flycatcher population were congregating in large flocks on telephone wires and pylons across Ireland, getting ready to make their winter trip to South Africa. We were fully aware that once they heard the Cork accents attuned to their specific frequency, the flycatchers would become highly irritated and attack the van. Our plan would hopefully attract as many flycatchers as possible. The journey began at 6 a.m. in Douglas in Cork city.

Cork Man Number 1, Oliver Kenny, was instructed to talk about how sick his dog was until we reached Galway. If he stopped at any point, the hotplate was turned on to a high temperature. His pre-prepared statement read as follows: *My ould dog is pure sick, sir, I don't know what's wrong with her at all. She's been turning away Pedigree Chum. Feel her neck, boy. Feel it. Can you feel a lump under her neck? That wasn't there last week. My poor ould dog, boy. She's after getting up a load of sick across the road, boy. Over therela. Watch it over therela, go and look into it, beside that manhole cover, watch it.*

Mr Kenny delivered this in an incredibly whiny and annoying timbre, with a slowly rising tone. His words travelled far and penetrated the countryside in his shatteringly shrill amplified Cork brogue. After thirty minutes of broadcasting this statement continuously, there were several hundred flycatchers in pursuit of the van. We travelled at a speed of 120 km/h and could not stop, or else the birds would envelope the van and halt it. By the time we got to Galway, we were met on the road by a motorbike with a fuel tank. Borrowing from the practices of commercial aviation, we re-fuelled via a hose, while still moving.

Cork Man Number 2 then took over the duty of recitation. Bart Flaherty began reading his paragraph about Sir Henry's nightclub: *I was there when Nirvana played, boy. I met my old doll there. Sonic Youth played as well. My ould doll got a photo with Dave Grohl, boy. Krist Novoselic asked for her number too. You'd never get that in Dublin, I swear. 'The Ball and Chain', you ever hear of that? It was a New Jersey acid-house song from 1993. Its real name was 'Make This Love Right'. But we called it 'The Ball and Chain' in Cork. And the song was so popular in Cork that they changed the name to 'The Ball and Chain', because of Cork. And it went out of print on vinyl. And the lad who made it was called Romanthony – he's dead now, but he used to mention Cork in interviews even though he was a black lad from New Jersey, and he played with Daft Punk. Pure Cork, boy.*

This particular speech was delivered in a very superior fashion and succeeded in encouraging at least 15,000 spotted flycatchers to follow our Cork Man Bird Van. Several of the birds were swooping down on the van at this point, trying to gain access to the Cork men contained behind the steel plating. Unfortunately, this had the unintended result of some birds receiving injuries and one going underneath the van's wheels entirely, so the decision was made to increase the speed to 160 km/h. We required a refuelling in Athlone as we traversed the midlands at ferocious speed, with 23,000 spotted flycatchers in aggressive pursuit. Several car accidents arose as a result of the expedition, and I feared for my life at times. The Cork men were getting tired and angry. We'd been travelling for six hours, and their feet were covered in blisters from the hotplate. When they protested, Dr Flag inserted a coat hanger through a square of wire-mesh on the front cabin and poked it into their ribs, so that they were made aware that they had no choice in the matter. To increase morale, they were each given 50 ml doses of Tanora to drink.

Careering through Cavan, Mr Robert Foley, Cork Man Number 3, read his statement, which was about drill bits: *What type have you? I've a Black and Decker, boy. My uncle has a JCB one – I thought they only made machinery but they make drills as well. You should see his masonry bits. He's got a box of counterbores too. He used it on drywall. He's got a spade bit for wood, boy. He gave me a loan of his auger bits too. I'll leave you have 'em for a few weeks if you pay me before you give 'em back. Wait till you see his plug-cutters.*

By that point, there were over 100,000 spotted flycatchers chasing the Cork Man Bird Van. It was still daytime, but the sky was entirely black from the gigantic swarm that loomed above us. We reached the home stretch, having crossed the midlands, when we arrived on the east coast, in the town of Drogheda, travelling at 180 km/h. Our next destination was Waterford.

Cork Man Number 4, Mr Barry Collins, situated himself under the mouthpiece, the hot plate turned on to full as his feet hopped up and down, and delivered the final soliloquy, which was about backing horses: *Wally's Favourite Spastic, she's not bad. Won four last Derby. I'd back her for twenty. There's a few others for the 4.15 that'd grease your palm though, boy. There's Gideon's Retreat, Fuck my Spanish Husband, Salary Dandy, Portion Party, Jeffery Archer's Far-fetched Car Park. Any of them are fine. Oh, and Guilty Fashanu too. You'll buy me a Murphys if one wins, you will?*

This was repeated approximately 64 times, and was successful in riling the remaining flycatcher population of Ireland. We reached Waterford with a quarter of a million birds in tow.

UCC scientists waited in a large field outside Tramore, accompanied by a number of fire engines. The fire engines' tanks were filled with a diluted mixture of diethylcarbamazine and thiaben-dazole, which are anti-parasitic medications. In this slide, you can see that we grounded the Cork Man Bird Van in the centre of the fire engines. All four Cork men began reciting their prepared speeches, simultaneously, one last time. This drew the gigantic bird flock into a bitter frenzy. They began attacking the heavily armoured van. The hoses on the fire engines were turned on, dousing every spotted flycatcher in anti-parasitic medication and eradicating them entirely of any risk of liver parasites. The Cork men were instructed to cease broadcast, at which point the birds left for their South African migration. They will return next summer, immune to the liver parasite and thus capable of controlling the Irish mosquito population.

It was for this work of conservation, for saving the Irish flycatcher, that I received the Nobel Prize. Thank you, ladies and gentlemen, you have been a wonderful audience. Enjoy the rest of the TED Talks.

ALL THESE MOMENTS WILL
BE LOST IN TIME LIKE
TEARS IN RAIN

DRACO

My dear associate Deccy Badbuzz has a cat who once got caught in the space between a coal bunker and a concrete wall. It was one of those old bunkers from the '70s, when people used more coal. The Saudis figured out that they could knock the chess-pieces off the board by refusing to sell oil to the rest of the world. It caused a fair bit of hassle. Most Irish homes started to freak out about the price of fuel and upped their coal consumption. That's the reason Deccy had one of those big grey metal jobs out his back garden. It was due to his grandparents overreacting to the events of the Arab–Israeli conflict of '73.

It was about the size of three washing machines stuck together, but a bit more stout in its vertical projection. Its odour was rusty and coaly and it sounded like Cú Chulainn coughing when you closed it down. You'd never stick your hands in it fully due to spiders. If you didn't cover the lid with old sacks, the rain would corrode away at it, and little holes would form. In the summer, wasps would violate those holes and start making their small paper nests that look like counterfeit Chinese sliotars. Of course because you'd never go near a coal bunker in the summer, you wouldn't really know – there'd be no need for a fire. In the hot months, the wasps and spiders would battle it out inside, big spiders, wolf spiders and hard-men spiders like false widows with skulls on their backs. The wasps would always win, and you'd sometimes hear the whisper crackle of dried-out spidery exoskeletons when you threw the coal in the stove come September.

You judge the severity of a wasp problem in a coal bunker not by the number of tickets sold at the door, but by the smell and the dirt on the tarmac underneath the nest-hole. Wasps don't have humility like bees, they eat meat and fish and all sorts. And they stick their arses out of the nest to take shits, which smell like homemade bottles of ammonia from a country hardware shop. I found this out the day Deccy's cat got caught in the gap between the bunker and the garden wall. The cat was named Tiesto. He was tortoiseshell in pattern, one of those cats that look like marmalade and Nutella spread over a slice of white pan. We first heard an unmerciful howling, then a deep grumbling that rose in pitch at uneven increments. When we took a gander at the commotion, we were accosted with the coal-bunker stench of the wasp shite.

Poor ould Tiesto was caught bad. The entirety of his body was down the back of the bunker, with his little head mashed up against the side of the wall, and one paw stuck under his chin. The available exterior of his fur was crawling with wasps. Wasps have a novel way of selecting the areas on a victim to sting: they only attack dark areas. They had concentrated themselves on the black and brown areas of Tiesto's tortoiseshell coat.

Deccy was in bits, because he was fiercely fond of Tiesto. Without one thought, he galloped towards the back of the bunker and grabbed Tiesto by his head, dragging him out and holding him in his arms. The wasps frenzied at this new attacker. Tiesto was still being stung, and worse still the suffering creature in his ecstatic pain began to sink his claws deep into Deccy's cheek and lower lip. The cat hung from Deccy's jaw, as they both received innumerable stings. Blood ran freely from Deccy's wounds, down the cat's arms and into his mouth, and the cat licked the blood between bawls. There was a very gentle empathy to it in fairness, a frantic union of fraternal agony.

All of this happened, I should say, because Tiesto was incredibly overweight. Deccy was also overweight. Ould Dec was pure fond of greasy chips from Donkey Ford's takeaway inside in town. Gorgeous salty chips fried in old cheesy beef fat, 50p battered sausages, and not those big yokes they have up in Dublin that feel like biting into a condom full of dong. Proper small soft Sheahan's breakfast sausages dolled up in fluffy batter. Pink Limerick pork, sliced from Sarsfield's arse. Square cod that burns your leg with hot oil through the bag. Batter burgers with red sauce. Garlic mayonnaise that transubstantiates translucent if you don't give it a prompt quaff, and grated fake amber cheese that melts like God's spit. Deccy fucking loved it, and so did Tiesto. Deccy wouldn't go near the chipper without ordering double for the cat. Tiesto was about the same size as an A3 office printer, and as heavy as Sunday morning hangovers. Deccy had to groom him with his ma's hairbrush because the poor lad couldn't lick himself anymore. His sleeping breath was a broken kettle that huffed out squeaky steam through a buckled nozzle and would ruin the quiet bits in *Breaking Bad* when we were watching it with a few joints.

After Deccy pulled the cat from behind the bunker, we hopped on the back of his Kawasaki Ninja motorbike. It had a tiny engine but looked pure fancy. Deccy's ex Stacey did a PLC in Art and she painted a green dragon on the side of it that looked like it had the gawks. Deccy tucked the suffering cat into his racing jacket, which made him look heavily pregnant. I sat on the back seat, smoking a John Player, with my arms around Deccy's leather Tiesto-filled belly. We booted it down the road in the direction of the vet's clinic near Johnsey's shop in Killeely, and hauled the cat into the emergency room. The vet had a mullet haircut and began to administer antihistamine injections to Tiesto, who had gone into shock from all the wasp stings. Rod Stewart was on the radio, singing that song 'Do you think I'm sexy?' I was feeling fair nervous for the poor cat and distracted myself by imagining that Rod Stewart was singing 'Do you think I'm cunty?' and the music video was him dressed as a racist-looking minstrel drinking cans in the Sistine Chapel while vandalising a Caravaggio with a golf club.

Tiesto was handed back, worse for wear but alive. The vet suggested to Deccy that he put him on a draconian diet or else the misfortunate character would die of a fat liver. Deccy didn't know what this meant, but didn't ask either in case it made him look thick. He assumed that a draconian diet was what dragons ate when going about their daily business. After scouring the internet, he came across an article about pet dragons and their fondness for dragonfruit, that mad-looking morsel you get in Asian markets for about three quid a pop. They look like glamorous red testicles with class designs and flames on them, and their insides are emulsion-white with little black seeds. Open one up and it's the dessert-bowl of a man who's gone apeshit and put a load of pepper on his custard. You'd never think they were named that because dragons ate them but fuck it, they are and all. Tiesto was fed nothing but dragonfruit for a fortnight, until he eventually got so sick from the scutters that he died. We buried him behind Donkey Ford's in the cemetery of Saint John's Church, in some Protestant prick's grave, lad who died in 1874. Deccy was heartbroken. He took a bread knife and scraped Stacey's green dragon with the gawks off the petrol tank of his Ninja, as a mark of respect. All the boys bought him a pint when they saw that.

After this experience, I couldn't stop thinking about that word 'draconian'. It would pop up in my head at odd times. So I said, fuck that, and went and learned what it meant and where it came from. Turns out there was a Greek lad called Draco. He lived in Athens 2,700 years ago and was the first person to write a law down on a sheet of paper, or whatever craic they wrote on back then. Athens squeezed out the origins of modern democracy from its arid gant. *Demoskratia*, the people rule. Before Draco, laws were oral, passed around by mouth like fairy-tales, open to interpretation and bent out of shape to suit each individual case. If some gomey robbed the door off your house or something, you could just fabricate that the punishment was to have him killed and made into a door, and no one could prove you wrong. This oral law was mostly exploited by the aristocracy. They'd use it fuck over people less wealthy than them, or to start blood feuds between themselves. Draco sorted all that out, he evened the playing field. He enacted the first homicide and manslaughter laws, and he introduced a council of magistrates. Granted, nowadays we look back on Draco's laws as being pure harsh. They weren't too far off sharia. If you robbed your neighbour's apple, the penalty was death. If you owed some cunt money and couldn't pay it back, you became their slave. Shitty circumstances indeed. That's why we use the word draconian these days to refer to something that's strict or unforgiving. That's what the vet meant when he said 'draconian diet' – it had nowt to do with dragons.

Draco's laws were toned down eventually by a lad called Solon, who is considered to be the father of western law. But without Draco, there'd be nothing. It's hard to think it, but the man who'd have you killed for robbing an apple was considered a hero of his time. The people of Athens adored him. Why? Because his laws created a culture of certainty – a harsh certainty sure, but they removed the existential anxiety of ambiguity. If there's one things humans crave more than the ride, it's a sense of certainty. We hunger for it. Which brings us to how Draco died. The people of Athens loved him so much they held a testimonial for him in 590BC. It was on a small island, called the theatre of Aegina, and thousands gathered, unreal fanfare, like a Rod Stewart concert. Draco arrived by boat. Back then, the highest expression of respect that you could give a person was to take off your jacket and your hat, and throw it on the worthy party. So the audience did that, loads of them, fucking their hats and coats at Draco, for about an hour. The clothing encased him, the pile growing larger and larger, until it was nothing but a hillock of fabric. Draco suffocated and died from jackets. They buried him on the spot.

- Why must we carry our past trauma on our shoulders?
- In case someone takes a photo and it gets retweets.
- Wow thats really profound
- I know. We are so absorbed in our egos ~~by~~ nowadays thats what I meant by it. Its an art statement.
- I got that, thats why I said it was profound
- Dont get uppity
- Jesus Christ Eamon

TEN-FOOT HEN BENDING

'm running my fingers through Eimear's pearls. They feel cold on my collar and I count them slowly like they're rosary beads. Sitting on this bus makes me feel a trepid power, like I'm riding on the back of an angry wild bull. I hadn't left my room in the evenings in 105 days. The time before that, it was 78 days. The weird thing with anxiety is you create this map in your head that keeps tabs over where you can and can't go, it helps you gain a sense of control. For me, it started a couple of years ago in first year, during a lecture on early medieval history. Our lecturer, Susan, was going over a slide about the economics of feudalism, when all of a sudden, I just felt this belt across my face. And then a sensation of having a thin layer of clothing ripped off me in one go, like a medical gown. I didn't feel naked or anything, just, like, imagine you were in a public place wearing a long gown, and then it just got pulled off. That feeling, of being vulnerable and tiny, with everyone looking on in disgust, worse than disgust, looking on in pity, feeling relief that they weren't in the position you were in. Exposed in the middle of O'Connell Street, with everyone examining and judging and finding out, no escape. That's what it felt like for me in that lecture theatre.

I was five seats in, on the seventh row. Everyone around me was just carrying on, listening to the lecture while my face dripped cold. My heart was belting in my ribs, I was like a cat trapped in a coal bunker, trying to get out. I couldn't breathe. I was drowning in people, suffocating in how OK they were with the universe. My thoughts dangled over a fantasy of humiliating myself, raw, uncooked, exposed, dirty, public. What if I got up and tried to escape? I needed to run from the feeling, but if I did that, would they all stare and think I was mad? I could taste the bland, oozing saliva rushing around my tongue and convinced myself I was ready to puke on everyone. I just focused on that saliva relish and imagined puking uncontrollably on everyone sitting around me. Down Conor's collar, on the nice fringe of that girl who listens to Jeff Buckley who I've never even spoken to. And then everyone would jump up, startled, horrified, and it would just be me in the spotlight, sitting like a freak on my own. They'd be almost sick themselves because they'd be inundated in my puke, the private intimate contents of my stomach, and their faces would be so disgusted, because my chunder and bile would be on them. In their hair and eyes. Then they'd look at me, me like a rabbit in their headlights, with that disgust, that offence and horrified anger that you direct at someone who's guilty.

This shit just played out in my head as real as if it was happening. It felt as if it was. I felt sheer and utter terror, terrified that I'd just lose control, and paralysed that I was trapped in that lecture theatre. Rubbing my palms together, scared that the person beside me could hear my breaths. Then it just kind of faded. As quick as it came, for no reason, it just went away. And I went back to normal, with this great sense of relief. It was so horrifying, I just pushed it away. By the time it had passed, the lecture was over. I left with Ella and Cian as if nothing had happened. We went to lunch, they spoke about being out in Costellos the night before, who drank what, how much, who shifted who, and we laughed. I didn't think about what had happened in the lecture theatre. I didn't want to talk about it, I didn't really want to acknowledge it in my own thoughts.

I went home that evening to my mum and dad, I drank tea, I watched a good documentary about the Aztecs on Discovery. The feeling crept back though. The next week, I was in Susan's lecture again. She recapped on some of the bits about feudalism. Her computer for the lecture had this loud fan, and that's what set it off. Not the same turn of events. But the memories of terror, of sitting in that room, and never ever wanting to feel that feeling again. Low-key PTSD. Of course, then I started worrying, oh no, what if it's going to happen here again, the exact same thing? The sweats, the breaths, the pictures in my mind. It came from nowhere. I didn't control it. And that was when shit got nasty. It's not the panic attacks that fuck your life up. It's the fear of when and where the next one will happen. So I stopped going to Susan's lectures. My terror was drawing out the mental map of where I could and couldn't go. I stopped going to that lecture theatre. If I stayed away from there, I was safe.

Or so I thought, until it happened in Boots when I was buying deodorant. A bad one. I don't know what triggered it. I think it was a smell of lavender but it was the same experience. I got the fuck out of Boots. I ran down the street, and found a strong solid wall to lean against. When your brain is on a roll like that, crowds are the worst. You cannot control your mind, every idea is paralysing. Your brain reboots itself, over and over and over, each time it sucks breath from your lungs and blood from your knees. Resting against the wall, I started to scan the buckets of people in Limerick city centre. I pained to contemplate how each one of them had their own thoughts, and how they all had families who also had thoughts, and how I couldn't possibly fathom how all these people were all thinking thoughts when I was there trying to control my own thoughts. Their faces were smudged unrecognisable by the fingers in my head. All their thoughts jumping out of their ears, like wifi signals, their eyes blinking lights, everywhere. All this activity trying to drown me in the notion ocean. There's no unbothered spaces. Their thinking climbed down my neck-ladder and filled my insides like I'm a sleeping bag.

A hand grabbed my arm really hard. It was the security guard from Boots.

'Where the fuck are you going with that?' he screamed.

I looked down and saw that I had accidentally ran out of the shop with the lavender bottle of Dove deodorant. Lots of people on the street stopped, to watch me getting caught shoplifting. I tried opening my mouth to let them know it was an accident, but I couldn't form words. I don't mean to be insensitive, but I sounded like a deaf person sounds when they try to talk. Maw maw maw urrr oooo. All these faces, whispering, judging, 'she's been shoplifting'. Then, to my right, there was this older lady with dyed-black hair, and she looked so disgusted with me, so disapproving, like I'd hurt her. That's when I felt that light just wave across my face and I went out like I was on a vet's slab.

The rest after that is so hazy. I was in the security office of Boots. I think the security guard had his arm around me and took me back there but I can't be sure. They were really nice, the security lad and the manager. My dad came to collect me. I felt really safe then, but also fairly useless. I got into my dad's car and asked if he'd get me some nice cakes, Black Forest or something, and he did. That evening I was back in my room, with my smells and my things. My TV, my laptop, my bed, my bean-bag, my books. And if a panic attack happened, at least I knew I could do it there, on my own. And my parents would be downstairs all the time, if I needed an ambulance or anything. I asked my mum and dad if I could take a few weeks out of college, and they said ya, because they were really scared about what had happened in Boots. But they didn't ask what the problem was.

I felt so safe in my room, so controlled. It was like a big womb that had no expectations of me. I began to stay in my room as much as possible. I enjoy my own time anyway. But the more I did that, the more threatening and frightening the outside became. I never ever wanted to feel the way I felt that day outside Boots, never again. That feeling was the worst I'd ever felt, hands down. I felt powerless, I felt incapable, and useless. I didn't feel nineteen, I felt like a baby, not an adult. That feeling burned itself on to my brain so bad that not leaving the house felt normal. On the occasions when I did have to leave the house, I'd focus only on my breathing. I'd breathe deep into my nose and feel it expand my lower stomach like a ball, that's how you get the most oxygen to your brain. If there's lots of oxygen, then the bad chemicals like adrenaline and cortisol can't cause the fear to attack. I bought a little digital metronome. It keeps this tempo'd beat with a click-click sound, it's for piano players to learn rhythm. I'd put earphones in the metronome when I left the house, and time my breathing, deep, measured and rhythmic. I wore big baggy hoodies to hide my body, and to stick my hands inside to hug myself. I began walking with my head down, looking only at the ground. I couldn't risk looking up, and meeting someone's eye. I'd cry if that happened. I wasn't ready for the cameras in their eyes. I wasn't ready to see all their thoughts, when I was struggling to control my own.

When you get that far down with anxiety, you grow angry and bitter. You want everyone to go, to leave you alone. You pray someone won't try and talk to you. You hate them for their ability to walk down the street without needing a metronome to breathe. For their happiness. It's because they are stupid, they can't see the pain and complexity I see in the universe. If they could, they'd be overwhelmed by it too. That's what I told myself at least. It's tiring, it was so tiring. I'd venture to town, only to get a book or a DVD or a CD, some piece of art that I could scurry back to my room with and enjoy there in that warm hug of safety. That's what made the trips worth it. But it was tiring. You don't notice how much breathing takes out of you when it's autonomous, but when you breathe deep to a metronome, you're fit to collapse at the day's end.

The further into this lifestyle I slipped, the more shame I felt. I felt shame for being a freak, for not being normal. Conor or Eimear would ask me out on Tuesdays, where the normal thing to do was get yoked up and dance. But I'd make so many excuses: 'I have work to do', 'I think the dog is sick', 'I think I'm getting a chest infection', 'I'm giving up drink because my uncle was an alcoholic and I've been told to watch it, it's genetic', 'I don't like using the jax in nightclubs because there's an African lady in there to dry my hands and it makes me feel racist'. All lies. My friends just thought I hated them. Eimear in particular took it very personally. She'd heard about the time at Boots, her sister knew the security guard. Eimear told people in college that I was always stealing, and that I stole pearl jewellery from her room when I used her bathroom once. That totally wasn't true, and it fucking hurt real bad. Ok maybe it was true. Sometimes I steal things, I don't know why, I just do. But I wasn't letting anyone else know that.

But I didn't hate my friends, not them. I hated their ability to go out and enjoy themselves with the lads. And here I was, a baby, a toddler, a useless, worthless freak with no possibility of having a future. The shame hits hard, the shame of being incapable, and then the sadness comes on. It starts off like this pang of regret, which feels like something really disappointing has happened but you can't think of what it is, and that makes you even more sad, because you feel sorry for yourself that you're this sad but can't think of the rationale for being sad. I'd cry for no reason, cry for what was inside me, cry for not being able to feel, cry for what wasn't inside me. Crying for feeling too much, but not being able to label whatever it was I was feeling. I'd see my shadow cast on the wall, and get confused that I wasn't able to tell the difference between me and the shadow. I'd stare at my hands, and they wouldn't feel like they were part of me, they'd feel like they belonged to someone else, so I'd hide my hands behind my back in case I saw them. And this caused me to cry too.

As weeks passed, that sadness took everything. Worst of all, it took my enjoyment. My island of pleasure, my room, my books, my music, it took my ability to enjoy those things. It took any plans for the future. Every morning I'd wake up, and my first thought was this little hopeful glimmer, for just a moment. Then it was smothered by the blackness and smashed with the morbid hammer. It became impossible to imagine never having that blackness. I forgot what happiness felt like, I forgot the reasons why I ever felt happy before. I lashed out at my parents. I slept a lot. Sleep was all I had. With sleep, you can switch off and rest. Thank fuck I had sleep, because some others don't have that, but I did.

No matter how bad it got, I never wanted to end myself. I'd think about it, but there was this little voice of preservation inside me that said no, ride it out, stick with it. That's what I did. I thought about cutting my ankles with a razor, when I got real numb. To feel something. But I didn't, because it would have hurt my poor dad too much if he knew. No matter what, I knew my mum and dad really loved me, that they weren't lying. I truly believed that, and it's what got me through. One night I just exploded in tears. I cried and I hugged them in the kitchen, I begged them to help me, please do something to help, my life is so painful. And they did. They arranged for me to see the counsellor in my college, whose name was Alan. He was really kind, and looked like a poodle. He just asked questions, he didn't talk. Which felt great, because I was finding my own answers through his questions. He'd ask me what the anxiety felt like, to describe it, in detail. 'What's it like to be frightened like that?' he'd enquire. He'd never ask anything that had a yes or no answer. And he didn't give me advice either. I'd go through it all, the thoughts, the feelings, that time in Boots. It felt safe to think about it, and to hear myself talk about it out loud. That room was safe. Sometimes we'd even laugh. We laughed about how I spoke like a deaf person when I got caught shoplifting. I hadn't laughed in so long. I didn't tell him that I deliberately stole the deodorant though.

Each week we'd go deeper. I'd talk about my childhood, and we'd go further and further still. 'You mentioned feeling useless and like a baby. Can you speak about why you'd feel this way?' was another one. And I'd rant, I'd answer these questions, and he'd just smile and listen, with no judgement. Every session, I'd have a revelation about myself, about my feelings, and it would give me such hope. I'd feel normal for like a day. Then the blackness would come back, but I knew, because I felt better after sessions with Alan, that the blackness wasn't permanent. This made it a lot easier and less devastating.

Alan wrote to my tutors and explained my troubles, which really helped with project deadlines. I was beginning to feel like me again. In summer we had to wrap up the therapy, after the semester ended, but I was free to return in September. The great insight that I had gained was that I was scared of standing on my own two feet. I didn't feel capable of being a proper adult, who could rent a house or drive a car or get a job or a boyfriend. Alan had a hunch and probed me about my childhood. I had an older brother who died when he was four. Gus. I don't think about it much, to be honest. He's just this picture of a smiley little boy with curly hair and fat fingers waving with a red ball under his other arm that's always been above the mantelpiece. He died when he drank a bottle of caustic soda in the garden shed that my dad had left in a 7Up bottle for cleaning drains. I don't remember Gus, but I know from speaking to my neighbours that it hurt my parents bad. My dad blamed himself, and my mother blamed herself. I was only two, but that was my earliest experience. The adults in my life were in deep grief and regret when I was just a tiny baby. Babies don't understand this stuff, but we pick up on emotions and fears. We learn how to react to threats through those early years. Babies have huge empathy, and we learn our emotional boundaries from how our parents react to things, like big sponges, and sometimes the water is dirty. That's how Alan put it.

My parents both over-parented with me after Gus died. Everything was a potential danger that could hurt or kill me. I wasn't allowed get a bicycle in case I fell. I wasn't allowed to leave the house in case I got hit by a car. If I wanted to go on a school trip, I was talked out of it, but my parents would do something really nice, like buy me tonnes of books or video games to make up for it. As I got older, it was the same for the Energizer teen discos in Mungret. I couldn't go, but my dad would buy me something cool in HMV, which made it OK. I wasn't unhappy, I was very happy. But I slowly began to learn that I needed protecting at all times. That I couldn't risk doing what the other children did in case it killed me. The older you get, the greater the impact of that message, particularly when you get to fourteen or fifteen, when you should be taking risks and testing boundaries. I never did. I was always made to feel completely safe, so long as I never took any risks. When that's the lesson handed to you by your parents, you just accept that reality. The problem for me was that when I hit nineteen, when I went to college, my friends were renting, cooking their own meals and talking about going on J1 visas and getting summer jobs in California, and it threatened the fuck out of me. It was too far from where I was at emotionally.

I didn't know that it threatened me. Instead, it threatened me unconsciously. When the unconscious is threatened, it finds a strange way to act out. For me, it was anxiety attacks. I understand that now. But just like a sponge that gets soaked in dirty water, I can squeeze it all out and soak up new clear water now that I'm an adult. Alan introduced me to cognitive behavioural therapy. It's a type of self-help that taught me that my thoughts influence my emotions, which then influence my behaviour. Basically, my anxiety and depression aren't caused by lecture theatres or going to Boots. They exist because the way I think about these things is flawed. The way I think about myself, my future and the world is flawed. It's flawed because my autonomous reaction is fear, which is what I've learned and it isn't objective reality. If I can change my thoughts around these things, from flawed to rational, I can be happy. If I get a negative thought around my future or my capability, I treat that thought like a scientist would. If Conor from college goes to Tesco and buys carrots and meat to make a stew, I don't say to myself, 'God, I could never do that, I need Mum for that, that's so adult of him.' I say to myself, 'Where's the evidence that I can't do that? There's none. Just because I've never done it doesn't mean I can't.' Then I quietly go to Tesco and buy carrots and meat, and I cook my own dinner, to prove to myself that I can, that I'm normal and capable. I identify my negative thoughts, my belief that I'm weak, then I test it with my behaviour.

That's what I'm doing right now on this bus. I'm nervous as fuck, I'm regulating my breathing, and I'm fucking terrified of getting a panic attack. This is the first bus I've ever been on on my own. Ya, I know, I'm twenty-one in August. But public transport is a real trigger for me, because there's nowhere to hide. I'm here, on a packed bus, and I've handed all control over to some driver who I don't know. The thoughts jump into my head.

What if I puke up? What if I just start screaming, and everyone stares? This time, I don't tell myself how awful it would be. I say to myself, 'So what if that happens? So fucking what?' Ya, there's a small chance I might get sick on myself or on someone else, or maybe get a leg cramp and have to stand up and walk up and down the aisle and draw attention to myself. But so what? Maybe I might even have a panic attack, but it will pass. It won't be nice, but it will pass. What's the worst that can happen? Some strangers will look, some might feel sorry for me and may even help me. But that's it. I can handle that, on the slight chance it happens. I can clean sick off myself, maybe buy a new T-shirt. It wouldn't be pleasant, but it's not death either. The idea that it would be this horrible, shameful, life-threatening ordeal is not reality. That's my earliest childhood memories talking, and they don't define my reality, because I'm an adult now and I have complete responsibility over how I react to my environment.

And with these thoughts, this rational-thinking process, my fear subsides, then my fists clench and I feel power. I feel like I've just stood up to a bully, and they backed down. That's what anxiety is, it's a bully, it's the bully in your head that knows exactly how to hurt you the most. Well fuck that, I deserve happiness, because I'm a good person. This is what it feels like to grow. I'm a flower reaching towards the sun, and that sun is the best version of me possible.

The bus rumbles on out past the Two Mile Inn Hotel, a poorly designed 1970s structure in the shape of a pyramid bent in the direction of Shannon airport. I press my forehead against the cold glass and watch the summer grass and hedgerows blur past in a collective olive smudge. I grit my teeth, to feel the vibrations of the engine and the road shaking inside my skull. I mentally scan my body. My denim pressing against the worn sponge of the bus seats, so worn I can feel my arse-bone. My back stiff against the rest, a slightly wet sweaty patch in the centre making my T-shirt stick to my skin all chilly. It will dry off in the sun. My feet are firmly on the floor. I feel them solid, while knowing that unseen underneath is passing tarmac that would rip my skin from my bones if I were to grate off it at this speed. I am OK with this. This is a grounding exercise. It helps with the feelings of depersonalisation that I get with anxiety, the feeling that my body isn't mine, that I'm not in control. This exercise keeps my body, emotions and thoughts rooted in the present moment, and reminds me that only I am in control.

My breathing is slow and deep through my nose. For the first time in a year, I feel calm, confident and bloody happy. We move past Durty Nelly's pub in Bunratty. It's a gorgeous little thatched tavern, mainly used by American tourists, but it's not tacky. It's painted bright pink and has this cute river beside it, with jumping trout over a little weir. Dad used to take me there on Sundays for ice-creams in the car park. Behind Durty Nelly's I can see my destination, Bunratty Castle, towering above. The bus takes a right, and settles alongside the other coaches underneath the shade of some sycamore trees with fat June leaves. I get off, I feel resilient, I feel normal, my posture changes. I can't fucking believe that I've made it ten miles outside Limerick city, on my own. Just me. No help. I press my return ticket into my back pocket like an adult would do, taking note that I have five hours to explore the castle grounds. The weather is mighty, not a cloud in the sky, and that dry heat that bounces up off the tarmac and hits your chest. This is ice-cream weather for sure.

Bunratty Castle is one of the most well-preserved medieval structures in Ireland. It looms above me, with its ancient grey stone and yellow-white lichen growth that's probably older than my parents. Each stone hand-cut with the most basic of tools. I'm giving serious thought to focusing on the castle and surrounding cultures for my second-year dissertation, and I've come here to survey it myself, on my own. The castle as it is today dates to the 15th century, but there have been Viking settlements here as far back as the 10th century, which were raided by Brian Boru. It's thought that a wooden motte-and-bailey structure was built some time around 1250, when the Normans arrived. That's the shit that really excites me. To stand in an area with so much history and culture. To stand in a place that has been settled by so many different people, speaking in languages we wouldn't even understand today. Even when this castle was occupied by English-speakers in the 15th century, the English they spoke would be alien to our ears. The Gaelic spoken in the surrounding hills would be unrecognisable too. How would a 13th-century serf from Cratloe handle a panic attack? Did they even get anxiety, or depression? They had real reason to be afraid. They could be killed in their sleep by the O'Briens. Even a bout of food poisoning could end them in a weekend. They had real fear and danger in their daily lives. Did this give their life emotional sustenance? Or was being miserable just how life was then, and we are the lucky ones? It is this possibility of empathy across time that thrills me about history, that gives me a real feeling of meaning and purpose. I start to remember why I fell in love with it again.

I join a tour group. Our guide is Laura. She's about 26 and is so passionate, even though she probably does this tour about eight times a day. She leads us up the drawbridge to the castle gates and through the main entrance. As we enter, Laura points up at the murder-hole. This makes everyone quite uncomfortable.

'If you were a raiding party who had made it this far, you'd be dead by now. Above you is the murder-hole, through which boiling hot grease was poured on any intruders, who were trapped in this hallway with no escape. Any remaining survivors were stabbed, their heads impaled on poles at the gates as a warning to other intruders,' she says.

I know this of course, this is Junior Cert stuff, but Laura explains it with such passion that I may as well be hearing it for the first time. I fantasise about having her job, maybe next summer, getting the bus out every day, packing my own lunch, speaking to German tourists about history, slowly and in plain English, at their service, being a real adult. That thought makes me feel very happy.

We move forward into the main hall, which is the next section of the tour. The tall walls are whitewashed in lime, and the temperature instantly drops as we enter. The acoustics make the smallest whisper boom loudly in the space designed for harp players. Incredible to think that the builders had that in mind hundreds of years ago. A massive oak table stands against the east side. In the centre is a metal grated fire with magnificent cast-iron work that twists black. The smoke rises up to the ceiling and out a hole, which fills the room with the unforgettable aroma of burning turf. While Laura speaks about the antlers of an Irish elk that hang on the wall, I notice a second tour group, who are being spoken to in Italian. My attention drifts as I observe their enthralled faces. I wonder if the guide is telling the Italians the exact same stuff that Laura is telling us, or if their tour is slightly edited to suit cultural differences. The architecture of Italy in the medieval era was much more advanced. Ireland in the 1500s was nothing compared to Venice or Florence.

As I ponder this, I notice a familiar face. Standing amongst the humble group of Italian tourists is a late-middle-aged man. He is wearing tight cornflower-blue shorts above his knees and an orange T-shirt. On his feet are blue low-top Converse sneakers. His hair is dyed blonde and spiked up. As I look more intently, I realise that it is none other than Hollywood actor Sam Neill. Or at least an Italian man who looks exactly like him. My face must look ridiculous. I'm not shocked, more bemused. Either this is an old Italian dude dressed like Bart Simpson, or the famous actor Sam Neill is in Bunratty Castle dressed like Bart Simpson with a load of Italian people. I direct my attention back to Laura, who is speaking enthusiastically about a tapestry that was commissioned by the Lord of Thomond, Thomas de Clare, in 1278. It depicts eight greyhounds chasing a peasant, and each greyhound's tail is tucked between their legs. I try to admire the tapestry but I can't hold my focus.

I stare again at the Italian man. I walk closer to his group, feigning interest in some 14th-century ash-beams. From this distance, I begin to examine the lines on the man's face, his soft expression and the glint behind his eyes that frame a permanent smile. This is most definitely the man who played the role of Dr Alan Grant in *Jurassic Park*. As I make that realisation, he pipes up and with his unmistakeable New Zealand accent says, 'The greyhounds' tails look like their fucking cocks, hahaha,' while pointing at the De Clare Tapestry. The Italians are confused. My group shuffles, silent and uncomfortable. I laugh pretty loud. Everyone turns to look at me. Normally this would cause me to go very red and freak the hell out, but not today. Fucking Sam Neill is dressed like Bart Simpson in Bunratty Castle, what the actual fuck?

Laura beckons our group towards a tiny stone door that leads up a steep stone winding stair.

'Now I'll take you to the ornate bed chambers. It is very very important that you don't touch this exhibit,' she says.

I stall back, and walk over to the man.

'Sam,' I say.

'That's me, kiddo,' he replies.

I get fucking stupidly nervous and don't know what to say. 'Ah Jaysus man, I love *Jurassic Park*. Not just that, I know you've done more, but *Jurassic Park* was my favourite thing as a kid. *Peaky Blinders*, I saw you in an episode of that. You were a nordy Orangeman, your accent was spot-on. Cillian Murphy is such a ride too, my God.'

Sam stares in silence. I feel like a bit of a dickhead, I have this tendency to talk like a fucking bimbo to everyone, especially lads, and I hate it.

'Cillian Murphy is my enemy,' he retorts.

'Oh, sorry.'

Sam laughs loud and takes out a cigarette, which he then lights with a match. I don't know what to say. You most definitely are not supposed to smoke in here. Both tour groups have gone upstairs, it is just Sam and I in the medieval hall. He trounces around slowly and coolly like he owns the place, with the cigarette hanging from his lip. The rubber of his Converse pitter-patters on the stone floor, amplified by the magnificent acoustics of the space.

'Wanna see something cool, kid?'

When he asks this, I feel kind of uncomfortable, every bone in my body saying no. I can't tell if it is a rational fear, or just my regular chicken-shit inner voice that I am trying so hard to combat. But before I overthink it, I say, 'Yes, Sam. I'd like to see something cool.'

I think I say this out of anger, anger at myself, for never taking risks. Today I'm taking a risk and looking at the cool thing that Sam Neill has to show me. He stubs the cigarette out on the wall and says nothing as he walks towards the west wall. I follow him. By the door that two tour groups have taken is another smaller entrance that has a clear red-rope barrier – it is not for visitors, but employees. Sam lifts this rope and ushers me in. We climb a metal ladder that has been recently built, down a utility tunnel that leads to a corridor that has masoned arrow-slits.

'Look through there,' Sam says. It's the tour groups, in the next room, looking at a bedpost that belonged to the de Clare family. We can see them, they can't see us. Sam crouches beside me, with this look of passionate mischief in his eyes. He reaches deep into his mouth and pulls out a full set of false teeth that he displays in the palm of his left hand. I look at the teeth, pooled in saliva, then look up at Sam's gummy smile and mad eyes. He presses his palm hard against the limestone floor, cracking the teeth into their constituent parts. It sounds like Rice Krispies. About fourteen acrylic teeth lie on the ground shining like the pearls I stole from Eimear's bedroom. Sam Neill produces a wooden slingshot from his back pocket, just like Bart Simpson would have, and he hands it to me. He doesn't tell me what to do, because I know what he wants me to do. I pick up one of the iridescent teeth from the floor, place it in the leather sling receptacle and fire it through the arrow-slit, directly at the face of a fat Italian woman in the next room.

'Mamma mia,' she yelps, holding her face. Sam and I try hard not to be heard laughing.

'My turn,' he whispers. Two men have gathered around the Italian woman to see what her problem is. One places the tooth into his pocket, which is a bit of an odd thing to do with a worthless tooth.

Bam. Sam fires a lasher at one of the men's faces, hitting him just above the lip. I grab the sling and let fly another, real hard and close at an old Irish woman who is near the masoned slit. It bounces off her forehead and leaves a mark. There is panic in the room, and I feel alive. Now I am in control. I control their reactions, and they don't know what is happening. Their fear and confusion washes away my inner trepidation and my heart beats in a predatory way.

'Hurry, before someone narcs on us,' Sam says into my ear. We run out of the castle into the car park, giggling like fuck. Sam takes out a pen-knife, and I keep watch while he slashes the tires on the Italians' big fancy bus.

'I can do one better,' I roar at him, taking the pen-knife from him. I use the blunt end of the handle and smash one of the side windows on the coach. 'Boost me up, you auld prick,' I say to Sam.

'That's my girl,' he replies.

I climb on Sam Neill's shoulder and clamber in through the broken window. The glass sticks into my hands, but it's that type that's supposed to smash into little blunt bits so it's grand. I begin to rifle through all the Italian handbags, taking money and passports. Money goes in my pocket, and I pile all the passports up on the back seat. I flick through their faces and names. Mad names: Amatore Enzo, Amos Lallo, Urbano Cherico, Raffaele

Lanzone, Alessandro Corelli, Giocondo Passarelli. They sound like a menu.

'No looking, Sam.'

I take down my jeans, squat and piss all over the pile of Italian passports. The heat of the piss rises up and warms my arse. I feel very much alive, I feel like I have purpose, I am in control.

'Come on, you dork,' shouts Sam. We race each other to the side of Bunratty Castle and enter the folk park. It is a recreation of a medieval farm and village, with thatched cottages and the strong smell of turf-smoke. Sam throws a leg over a wattle-and-daub fence, into a muddy enclosure full of goats. The goats, used to tourists, are not startled.

'Give me that money you took from the purses, kid.'

I reach in to my left pocket and give him half, easily €500 in twenties and fifties. Sam grabs it all in one fist and attempts to mount a large billy goat with long grey fur and eyes like a snake. He is unsuccessful in staying upright and lays across the goat's back as it attempts to jock him off. The younger goats are disturbed and begin to make distressed barking noises. Sam stuffs the money into the goat's mouth, as it bites down on his fist, drawing blood.

'Look at me, woohoo, I'm Cillian Murphy, look at me,' Sam says.

A woman who works at the park sticks her head out of the gift shop to see what the commotion is. I tell her to fuck off, that this is serious business and she wouldn't understand. She goes back in like a turtle. I feel in control. I run to the next enclosure and begin bothering peacocks with a sweeping brush. All the tourists watch, in fucking disgust, staring at me, disapproving. I have flashbacks to the wall outside Boots when I nicked the deodorant, and I pick one woman. A middle-aged bint, who looks like that bitch who stared at me that day with the dyed-black hair. I march up to her, stare her right in the eye and slap her across the face as hard as I can, so hard she's knocked back and holds her mouth. I stand over her and scream. She looks terrified.

'They're gonna call the cops, kid,' says Sam. He's probably right. So we walk out of the folk park like roosters. Me and Sam Neill. But the police don't come.

We cross over across the car park to Durty Nelly's. I use the money I have left in my pocket to get us both giant 99 ice-creams and large glasses of straight vodka from the bar. Sam has no teeth, and he laughs loudly as he gums the 99 and downs his vodka.

'Why are you here, Sam? What are you doing in Bunratty? Why are you dressed like Bart Simpson?' I ask him.

'Because I live in the present moment, bucko. I picked this place at random, I just booked the tickets for the plane last night and arrived. I dress like the Simpson kid to feel young. You ask too many questions. What's your story?'

I tell him about my anxiety, my depression, I tell him about therapy, I tell him that I got on that bus and faced my fear, I tell him about my parents and my dead brother Gus. He tells me that heaven and hell are a choice. Hell is when your mind lives in yesterday or tomorrow. Heaven is when you live today in the now. He struggles to remove his tight T-shirt and without warning he bounds towards a picnic table of women enjoying the sun and jumps up, kicking their drinks all over the car park. He tumbles to the tarmac, quickly getting to his feet and runs out towards the busy motorway.

'You see this, kid?' he screams. 'If I take this traffic in the present moment, I'm invincible. If I think about what could happen, or what might have happened, I'm a dead man.'

With a steady pace, he runs freely across the motorway, back and forth, never stopping, never thinking. The cars, the buses, the motorbikes, the trucks, they all move around him, or run into the hard shoulder, but Sam never reacts. Sam just takes each step in the here and now as he races around the motorway. Sam controls danger, he controls risk. This is art. I join him. We both run around that motorway in an intense, meditative calm, as traffic dodges us. The drivers panic but we don't. We sit down by the hard shoulder, exhausted.

Sam takes a softer tone. He looks at me and says, 'You need to let go of your little brother, kid. You were too young to be around that grief. You're carrying a pain that's too hungry for your soul to feed.'

I feel the weakness come on. My power leaves, I am no longer in the present moment, and I cry really loud like a baby. I cry deep for Gus. I cry for my brother that I never knew. That tiny little toddler who drank poison. I imagine how happy he was to think he had found 7Up. I imagine his fear and pain as his throat burned. I cry for my dad who blamed himself, and my mum who tried to hold in her resentment for his carelessness while still loving him. Sam is reaching into a ditch and tugging at long strands of dry hay that he is forming into a crude shape. He hands it to me. It is a little straw man.

'This is your brother, Gus,' he says as he points at the stone bridge near Durty Nelly's. He doesn't tell me what to do because I know what he wants me to do.

I cradle Straw Gus in my arms, as I walk in a straight steady line towards the bridge. I gently toss him into the slow ebb of the river and let him go. I let him float, and watch him drift off. Gus and what happened to him is not in my control. I turn back to the motorway and Sam Neill is gone. The sky is getting pink. I reach in my arse pocket to feel my ticket and walk towards the car park to mount my bus back to Limerick, where the Italians are all huddled around their smashed-up coach looking upset and confused. I fumble at my collar to finger through Eimear's pearl necklace, but it must have fallen off in the castle.

VAL KILMER PLAYING JIM MORRISON

PlEASE REST IN PEACE JIM
DONT REST IN DEACE VAL

FATIMA BACKFLIP

Dingle afternoon in 1917

A She rattled down off the clouds up above in the ceiling and ran around the field after three Portuguese children with a pregnant schkelp of May nettles draping out of the ten fingers on each of her fists. Her pale blue finery followed behind her in pursuit of her hole, clumps of earth sticking to the soles of her feet with every thuggish gallop, her gown rippling like the sea on a soldier's postcard. She started swabbing the stingers off the backs of the children's legs and then shoving them in their mouths, accosting their jaws with nettles tops and young flowers. Nettles have flowers alright, small unassuming gentlemen that smell not too unlike an elderly gelding gander or a bottle of gammy vinegar that you'd let moisture get into, and the flowers, they look like bunches of green grapes, if the grapes were about four yards in the distance from your eye, about that size, and the leaves with the stingers bunch around that. I say stingers, but they're not really stingers either. If you look at a nettle up close with a jeweller's loop, you'll see that they are little hairs. Well, not hairs precisely, they're like glass pipes full of wet chemical, but they are so small to ourselves that you'd nearly call them hairs. But if you were an aphid or a bloodsucker sitting on the leaf of a nettle, then you'd call them big glass tubes full of chemical, if, that is, as a blood-sucker, you had a cognitive frame of reference for what a big glass tube was, which you probably wouldn't because only men in creameries make big glass tubes or acquaint themselves with big glass tubes, and a big glass tube to a man is probably like a Manhattan skyscraper to a bloodsucker or an aphid. But sure they've never heard of skyscrapers either, unless they've seen a soldier's postcard of Manhattan, which they haven't. That I can be sure of. Unless an awful quare soldier took it upon himself to broadcast his collection of postcards to a bloodsucker or an aphid, and if that happened, I'd buy a pint and a chaser for every man in this pub here with me now. The men who arrive back from France, who answered Redmond's call, they're all gone stone mad from swallowing mouthfuls of their friends' blood and brains whenever they opened their gobs for an ould scream in the trenches. But even that wouldn't drive you so mad that you'd take it upon yourself to show your postcards to a small bloodsucker – sure you wouldn't know where their eyes or their arses are, they're too small, it would be a pointless afternoon. Anyway, a nettle doesn't sting as such – the little hairs don't pierce into the recipient's hide, like the arse of a wasp would do. Instead what happens is that the minute glass tubes break, when you rub off them, they spill out a small drop of caustic juice, and you get a burn, not a sting. So the next time you get a sting from a nettle, don't be roaring about how you've been stung, roar about how you've been burnt, and then you'll be taken more seriously by your neighbours. Sure don't dock leaves cure it instantly? That's because it's a chemical burn, and when you squeeze dock-leaf juice on it, the chemicals in the dock leaf have an argument with the chemicals in the nettles, and the nettle burn gets driven off your hand in a type of pogrom. Not Hasidic Jews but acidic juice gets driven off your hand in the limey leaf pogrom. I wish I said that out loud, that's fair smart. Ned the Bend over by the Murphy's tap would have howled at that. I'll save it for later sure, when we talk about swimming. Well anyway, that's what Our Lady with her immaculate heart did to those three children up above below in Portugal, only a few weeks ago. Lucía, Jacinta and Francisco were their names, and their photos are in the paper, with suntans and sad eyes from the fear and the abuse. It's the talk of the parish – she appeared to children, stung them with nettles and warned them about the Great War. The poor craytors, what would they know about men in ten-foot trenches picking bits of their friends' skulls from out of their tongues? What would they know about drowning in a beige wind of mustard gas? Wasn't that awful selfish of Our Lady to burden three eight-year-olds with that? And there was no dock-leaf pogrom to be had for them that were full of the white bumps from the nettles' chemical burns. She ran around after them in a hot Portugal field, and gave them chemical burns all over their bodies. It was on everyone's lips in Dingle, and on all the gazettes, and there was an early novena with Father Ceannt who doesn't wash. Our Lady had appeared to the Portuguese children and flogged them, as an act of attrition for their sins, their original sin like, which wasn't theirs but ours, the sin that you're born with because your great-great-great-great-great-great-great-great-grandmother ate apples belonging to a long lizard. I'll have another Powers, please, Aeneas. I said that out loud. May the Blessed and Immaculate Virgin have mercy on our eternal souls. I said that out loud as well. Ned the Bend half-raises his drink and lobs an eye up from under his cap in my direction. And the Holy Mother appeared to these children last week in Portugal in Cova da Iria, and stung them with nettles, and told them secrets. And that's why I'm heading to Fatima, ya that's it, that's the plan. Glass put in front of me giving me a tingle just by the sound of it. The sound of a full glass of Powers landing on treated mahogany fills me with a little tingle every time, like the first tingle. I love the brazen thunder of the opening sip, hot molten leaba falling down my gullet, and I a reverse volcano that sucks it all back up and saves the people in the village from death before my boily red summit. I'll have a sharp suck of my pipe now. Nearly set the tweed of my breast on fire last Thursday. That's why I'm heading to Fatima next week. I'm going to make a ball of coins and drink port. There'll be want of rosary beads, and statues of the Holy Mother, and punnets of sacred water, and I'll pick nettles and sell them in parchment with bits of Gospels written on it. This won't be like the soldiers' postcards. That venture was a mistake. I misjudged that market. No one wants postcards in Kerry, sure who'd they send them to? I won't tell anyone about the dirty soldiers' postcards though. There was fine money in that. I'd cycle long hours under lateness to every bachelor's cottage in Munster with a false suitcase full of manky Parisian postcards. Two shillings a pop. They were smuggled into Bray by a Fenian getting ready for a war, who was raising money for

Michael Collins to rob all the barracks with hatchets and pistols. I'm getting out of here before the real war. Finbarr Gust and his soft brothers bought nine dirty postcards from me last February, and their mother found them and alerted a bishop who kept them for himself. But it killed my bones, all the cycling in the dark and wet, and the threat of being caught by the RIC caused me to wake up in the night with a beating heart. No more gutter postcards. But there'll be calls for ecclesiastical wares in Fatima, oh there will by Christ, and I'm the man to peddle them, I'm ahead of the trend. I'll stop in Lisbon first and purchase an ass. Have they any volcanoes in Portugal? A small sip of Powers makes the gulps of stout grow a halo around them. They dance with each other. Not like the nettles and the dock leaf. The Powers and the stout have a hearty conversation about building boats when they're down my throat. They laugh with each other. If you look into Ned the Bend's eyes for too long, he'll cry about his daughter who hung herself on a mountain. The poor man. Throw Ned a chaser of Powers please, Aeneas, I say out loud. Ned's face lights up until he sips it and then the wrinkles fall back into sadness. Poor Ned. I'll carve the children's eyes and mouths into bows of dried oak and take them to a monsignor to bless them and charge two shillings to women shaking and rattling with Jerusalem syndrome. Have they forests in Portugal? Or is it arid? I'm going to Portugal, on the back of an ass, and I'll leave all this behind. No more wax jackets, bony goats or cold shins. No more yellow fingers and green teeth looking back at me when I buy the coal. No more coal and bales of sticks. Only fields of purple flowers that smell like aniseed and wormwood, my pockets heavy with their lumpy foreign money. No more fat mauve clouds rolling over the sky like a wolfhound on a dead rat. And dragging its stinking back around with it, like clouds pull rain. No more wide rain, sideways rain, misty bastard rain, snakey cuckold rain, rain that jumps up from puddles and wets my feet, distant rain that hangs like bad curtains off the mountain. Because I'm going to Fatima to profit off the visions of those children. I'll take the last bag of soldiers' postcards and send them to everyone in Dingle who wouldn't buy one, and they'll see the front arriving in the letterbox, with images of beaches and lakes and horses, then they'll turn it around, and all they'll see is a drawing of myself lobbing back sherries and dressed like a landlord. I'll etch it in Indian ink. They eat salted fish and red spuds in Portugal, non-stop flaky salted cod. I suppose I'll miss fresh cod when I'm there, but the warm weather and the sherry and port will make up for it. You wouldn't dare ask for a port here, Ned the Bend would call me a Protestant, or try to sell me eels, but there's non-stop port in Portugal. The police refused to believe the Fatima children, even when they showed their nettle welts to them. They threatened to boil the children in hot oil if they didn't stop telling the villagers about Our Lady with her fist full of nettles and mouth full of secrets. Ye never met Our Lady, they said. Ye stayed out too long in the field, acting the bollocks with nettles, and made up a story so ye wouldn't get in trouble, they said. Someone put ye up to this to undermine our republic, they'd say. But the children swore by their story, and the villagers believed them. Now they're holding vigil in the field, waiting for Our Lady to reappear. Forcing the children to fast, forcing the children to strip down and flagellate their backs with nettles. Fierce cruelty. And that's why I'm going to Portugal on a leathery ass. To sell wares to those desperate eejits on their knees. I'll have one more porter, Aeneas, a half. Sure no, a full ta feck, and a Powers while you're at it. What about the secrets Our Lady told them? What were the secrets? Gack Tierney in the corner has a brother who's a Jesuit in Almada who said it's all a scam, that they leaked it to the papers a week in advance. You daren't say it out loud. But they told the papers to keep an eye on that field in Cova da Iria, that something big was going to happen. It's all a big Jesuit conspiracy, to stop the Bolshevik cancer, he said. The Jesuits are terrified of what's happening above in Russia. The revolts. The Portuguese had half a revolt seven years ago, and the Bolshevik one will come soon, then Spain. They think the poor tenant farmers will steal the Church lands and burn the priests in the fields in an orgy of Bolshevism. Secularism is the first step to Bolshevism, he said. What better way to get the poor and wretched to tolerate your boot than to get three innocent children to tell tales of Our Lady and her warnings of war? Dirty fuckers. I couldn't give a shite. Because next week, I'm heading to Portugal on a crippled ould ass and leaving Dingle behind.

- You cant do this
- why not?
- Because its plagiarism
- Plagiarising who?
- Roddy Doyle
- Roddy Doyle invented dialogue?
- Yes
- No he didn't
- He did, he invented dialogue
- Like, the first person to ever do it?
- Yes
- Ok I'll stop
- Thank you

HUGGED-UP STUDDED
BLOOD-PUPPET

He pinches his lip. Sloppy on his fifth can of Galahad. Sitting on a deckchair in front of the laptop in a mobile home with a neon blue glow spelling out his face in the dark. The haze of the wet can affronts the forward of his mind. The dribble off his chin stains his corduroys and vest. A lurcher mix is barking with a hoarse yelp outside.

He imagines cycling down by the pike canal, mouldy drunk, in search of 48 hours' worth of fags. The bike going sideways and him falling inside the hard shoulder of the motorway. The puddles on the road marauding his chest with cold and cheating his breath, shocking the body enough to immobilise him. A red bread van speeding frontways and rolling over his leg. His calf muscle exploding and spitting out brittle shin fragments. Glass bits of his own bone shards getting flung deep into his eyeballs and asking to be plucked out individually. Isolated on the road like a dead cat, hum of wet arse off the canal full of shopping trolleys and needles and razor cowries that washed in from the river.

Lad tugs his lip more, so that it was pursed between his fingers and looked like the orange beak of a mallard. Smoking Marlboro Gold. Starts rubbing his knees and face, which are clam and sweat, and his forehead feeling like it's tingling. He's after smoking too many Chinese weed. He's studying the front of the cardboard fag packet with the crinkly shiny mylar, the fags illuminated by the warm orange of a hot halogen lightbulb over by the kitchenette. The packet has government warnings on its facade: 'SMOKING CAUSES CANCER AND EARLY DEATH', says the fag box. A photograph of a concerned woman with pain in her gaze, draping her face on the chest of a pale man who has tubes hanging out of his nose like scaffolding, and a forlorn child banging her head on the shoulder of the woman.

Our lad feels his heart tremor all hot in his earlobes, he peruses the photo and knows it isn't real. They are cancer actors. Gowls who pretend to have cancer and agony as a pastiche, to get paid cash for appearing on the front of fag boxes. How the fuck can fags give you cancer if the pricks on the box are actors, our lad thinks. Why can't they use real cancer boys? If there's a load of real fag cancer boys, then surely they'd be first up to volunteer themselves for the front of the box as a warning?

'FUCK ARE YOU LOOKING AT, YOU GOWL-LIPPED SPASTIC?' says the fag box.

He leaps back from the chair and wonders if the fag box had really spoken to him, or if he'd imagined it. That's the way your head whinnies like bothered horses after a few lungs of bad boldy.

He spit-licks a Marlboro and spills out the baccy like the guts of a defeated foe onto a Rizla. Then backs it up with a fat bastard pinch of Chinese weed. That's what was causing the panic, and the mad notions of getting his shin burst open by a bread van on the canal. Irrational thoughts, fluttering like kites with slippy strings in a gale, uncontrollable and dragging him with them to the edge of heaven's bend. It's giving him a whitener, but he can't stop rolling it up into a joint. That Ennis weed, grown above the Golden Lotus takeaway. A grand takeaway, savage for a four-in-one or a chow mein, but everyone knew what was going on upstairs. On a warm day with wind, you'd smell it walking along a gust like nice silage. They're growing boldy upstairs, that sweet pineapple spicy bang that you can't ignore. Floating in the heat, warm hay, pine cones, black pudding, lime, the first sniff of an open beer bottle, that's that skunk stench of strong grass grown under hot mercury vapour lights, wafted through a cooker hood and pumped up with mad man's fertiliser. The takeaway tries to hide it with the odour of sesame oil and five-spice out the vents, but everyone knows the craic. They're growing weed upstairs, and the chips and curry are only a front for the weed-growing.

The triad gangs make them do it. The people watering the plants above the Chinese are illegals, the triads bring them to Ireland in those big innocent-looking containers that are piled on top of each other at the train yard. Tell them they'll get them enrolled in a business college, they'll learn English and economic commerce. But the triads lie. They rob their passports in Shanghai, shove them all in a tin for three weeks at sea. Herd them into blacked-out vans in Limerick docks and force the poor people to grow weed upstairs in Chinese takeaways up and down rural Ireland. They are slaves, hash-growing slaves with no identities, lost people. They have to pay off their debt for being smuggled into Ireland. Living like rats in rooms as bright as the sun and as hot as Corfu, never leaving the grow-house, food delivered through hatches.

It's happening all over Ireland since the recession. The owners of the takeaways are victims too. They don't want grow-houses above their businesses, hiking up the electricity bill, causing mould in the ceilings from leaky hydroponics. They just want to run a business. But if they refuse to allow the harvest, the triads will hurt their families back home in China. That's how the triads operate. They've been around for hundreds of years, fucking over their own communities the world over, like any country with a large and poor diaspora. The Sun Yee On triad run the weed in Ennis now the Limerick gangs have all been jailed and killed. They spray it with all sorts of fibreglass crystals and push out the local dealers. There's no Libyan hash around since the Ra decommissioned its bombs, only Chinese weed, sold by Polish lads and the odd Ennis head. The Irish are being pushed out of their own territory, silently and calmly. And the Chinese ganja, it drives you mad. They treat it with nonsense chemicals that jack up the THC to unreasonable levels. It makes you paranoid, and the hangover has other lads shouting inside your own head. Our lad had read about it in the *Ennis Tribune*: 'Triad gangs now control cannabis trade'. And when the gardaí raid the grow-houses, it's the poor slaves who get locked up, not the bowzies who pull the strings.

He crawls up from the deckchair and walks away from the laptop, with unreal munchie pangs and white fear. It's 11.23 p.m. on the phone, so the Golden Lotus is still open. His red eyes ogle the mobile home for the wallet. Delicious flavour-memories perambulate around his tongue as if they are real. Creamy peanut satay, the burny crunch of a salt-and-pepper piece of battered chicken thigh with spicy bell pepper, the scorched black taste of chow mein up your nose as you swallow, the salty mystery and soft mouthfeel of a bite of prawn curry and fried rice, green peas and onion crunching in the mouth with velvet brown curry sauce, crispy quick-fry chips, oily spring rolls, black-bean sauce. Mouth watering so much he's swallowing spit. He leaves the bike behind, lest he gets slaps off a bread van. Lad saunters on down yonder, out the shaky resin door, past the GAA pitch, through the main street, until he can smell the Golden Lotus takeaway. There's a hot July rain, the kind you didn't mind drenching you, hitting your skin at the same temperature as your body. It's the only type of acceptable Irish precipitation.

12.15 a.m. The pink-and-blue neon koi carp flickers above the false pagoda door arch of the Golden Lotus takeaway. Warm puddles emanate a wispy steam that you can only see when they catch the lavender rays of light from the koi carp fish. The interior is cramped with tea-stain wooden panelling up the walls. Soft midi piano plays through a ceiling speaker, parish community flyers hang in front of the cash register, beside which is a stout golden automaton cat that has a battery-operated waving paw.

Lien is positioned behind the counter, her soft friendly smile and clip-on bowtie are ready to take his order. She's seen our lad here before, several times a week for the past year. He orders the Singapore fried noodles, the sesame prawn toast and a tin of Club Orange, shyly avoiding Lien's eyes, the way he does when he meets women, then exits to the car park to rest the brown paper bag on a wheelie bin. Opening the aluminium container he is peacefully assaulted by oily fragrant steam. Clambering the plastic fork in his fist, gorging a mouthful of greasy rice noodles into his welcoming maw. Eyes closed and salivating, head back, the brackish mass of noodles satiates his munchies. Endorphins explode like fireworks in the brain, he feels it as a warm tingle on his forehead.

The neon lights of the flickering koi illuminate his flapping jowls against the honest backdrop of the black night. His large body feels at peace with itself, as waves of electrical jolts filter through his skin with that one sparkly gulp of his Club Orange tin. His whitener has subsided and he's back at a base level of stoned. He reaches for the half-burnt joint in his arse pocket and grooves on over to the alleyway behind the Golden Lotus to fire it up. He flicks the flint of a shitty pound-shop lighter and sparks the bifter. Leaning back agin the masonry wall, exhaling blue smoke up above his head and watching it puff up and dissipate like milk into a dirty lake. Thinking about herself, gone from him, above in Carlow with the mother in the wheelchair. Thinking about the night of the accident. If he'd have swerved the van, her mother would have been fine. It didn't work out like that. Now herself had changed her Facebook photo from a photo of him and her to a photo of James Connolly.

As he gapes up at that cool blue smoke, he spies the upper echelon of the talcy flumes getting disturbed to the left by the exhaling hot air of a grated vent. It's the vent from the upstairs weed grow-house. Up high on the wall, burping out that sweet shitty pineapple bang of happy grass, off above into the hills of Clare. His mind fizzles adrenal with all sorts of possibilities. Him bare-chested and steaming, climbing up the vent and squeezing through ducts. Landing in the middle of the illegal hash den like

Steven Seagal. A family of Chinese weed-slaves cowering in the corner, as he performs a roundhouse kick on the electrical ballast box from the grow-lights. Sparks flying high and bouncing off his veiny pumped arms. Kicking the door of the grow-house open and ushering the family to safety outside. Like a real white saviour. Police lights dancing outside, an applauding sergeant with a big smile awaits the hero. The attractive daughter of the Chinese slave family leaning in and shifting him on the mouth as the camera pans out and up, with the Golden Lotus in a blaze behind them. Fade to rolling credits, directed by John Woo with 'Gimme Shelter' by the Stones as the end track.

He's seen all the fucking Hong Kong gangster films, *Shinjuku Triad Society*, *Year of the Dragon*, *The Killer*, *Bullet in the Head* and *Hard Boiled*, watched them religiously. He knows how this would play out. He knows how the triads behave, there'd be ten of them upstairs in that grow-house, with meat cleavers and banana-clip black Uzis, with their tattoos and sweaty vests, but he doesn't care. He's had enough of them polluting Ennis with mad weed and turning innocents into slaves, and is ready to kick through the back door with fists presented, to protect the vulnerable inside and give them liberty. He will be their justice. If his end is to be at the hands of ten triad machetes hacking his neck, then he is ready to die.

His body rushes with the passion, and he fucks the bones of that joint onto the wet tarmac. Launches a shoulder at the side door of the Golden Lotus and dents it off its hinges. He kicks it and kicks it until he can't feel his shoe. The door batters sideways from its top hinge. He grabs the available side of the metal panel and bends it towards him, screaming and spitting and roaring. With door half-open, he squeezes his way through, as rough shards of the broken metal score bloody hashtags all over his right arm and chest, like Bruce Lee in the mirror scene of *Enter the Dragon*. Sad Chinese fiddle music plays in his head as he moves in slow motion, stomping up the concrete stairs to the blinding white and the ever-growing stench of strong skunk weed. He arrives at the top of the stairs. Through the mercury vapour lighting, with mouth open and fists out, he leaps towards a hazy figure. His leg snares a cable from a grow-light, and his body descends to the floor, dragging two light fixtures and a few hash plants with him as his skull cracks on the harsh grey mortar.

When he wakes up, it's black, real black. The ground underneath him heaves diagonally and he can't get his feet up from under his shins. The weight of the room pulls him to the ground. There's a large force at play. He crawls into a ball and is hurled towards a wall where he stays until the light returns. He can't tell how long he's been in the dark. Memories of shouts and screams, chains and whips, lights in the eyes and water down the mouth haunt his mind like the waking seconds of a hangover after a mad wedding. And the air smells salty, like the periwinkles they sell in Kilkee. He hears lads roaring Chinese or Cantonese, he can't differ. Metal corrugate slides with a harsh hiss and new light blinds him.

A hand grabs the scruff of his neck, while another set of hands wrap cable ties around his wrists. The light is giving him a fierce headache, the air is hot and damp, much hotter than Ennis outside the Golden Lotus. Waves crash around his ears, new accents chatter, distant traffic hums and honks, seagulls squawk and flap. He feels the imposing presence of gigantic towers leering down on him. Our lad soon realises he must be somewhere in China, kidnapped from Ennis. He's done two weeks drugged up on sleepers in a shipping container. When he knocked himself out in the grow-house, the triads must have used the slave Quaaludes to put him in a deep sleep. He landed into their hands, into the spider's nest. He feels a right fool. No doubt his wallet and any form of identity proof are gone too.

His head is pounding and his mouth is dry. Before his eyes accustom to the white of the gigantic megalopolis at the docks, he's fucked into the back of a Toyota Transit. Pitch dark again, battering around against aluminium panels, chickens clucking outside, roasting his bones inside, smell of foreign diesel up his nose from the loud engine. He can't think straight at all, two weeks of sleeping tablets and being fed vitamin-liquid through a water pistol will do that to you. But sure there's no one back in Ennis to notice he's gone anyway. Just the cats waiting outside the mobile home for a tin of mackerel. Herself with the crippled mother won't enquire.

The van stops, and it's clear that he's far from the tall buildings and the docks. It's evening now, and it's warehouses for miles, with dogs howling a few streets over. The distant city rumbles and hums the way Ennis doesn't. Strong-armed lads in Gola trackies and Adidas pants, big fuckers, take him from the van and into a warehouse where he's stripped down, untied and pointed towards an area that was once clearly a little warehouse side office with a shower and a jax. There's an open safe and a yellow calendar with photos of Kylie Minogue when she had curly hair. Whatever this warehouse once was, it hasn't been run as a business for donkey's years.

One of the big fuckers with the Adidas trackies lobs a bar of soap at him and roars a few bits of Chinese into his direction. Our lad showers. He's fucking stinking, the shower makes him feel like Christ climbing out of the tomb on Easter Sunday. Gorgeous warm water and lavender soap, washing off the journey, giving him back a bit of life, clearing up his head. He dries off with a towel and finds there's a nice soft dressing gown laid out for him. Lad sits down in an old armchair and a feed of noodles and dim sum is lobbed in front of him by one of the big fuckers. The shock and trauma was such that he hadn't even realised the hunger on him as he leaps into a soft pork dumpling. The big fuckers take out a pack of fags and offer one to himself. He relishes the drag. Things are chilling out a bit, he thinks. The two boys don't seem too bad, all things considered. He imagines that if they were back in Ennis, they'd nearly get a game of five-a-side going after a few jars in Halpin's Lounge. He can't understand a word they're saying, but they're grand ould lads, probably United fans, he'd say. He has a squint around the warehouse. Normally he'd be thinking of an escape, throwing a few flying kicks, rappelling through a window like Steven Seagal, but no, he was grand. Fuck it, he'd been kidnapped and taken to China, but sure there's bollock all back in Ennis. Free holiday, he says.

The two big fuckers get a bit jumpy after one of them points at the time on his phone. They take a military posture and start putting out the fags on the concrete. An orange light is flashing in the corner as the large roller-door of the warehouse opens up, pure like in the cinema. Blue steam from outside crawls in the door, lit up by headlights, followed by a black BMW 8 Series, a white Mercedes AMG R50, and another black 8 Series behind it. That's nearly a million quids' worth of cars, he can't fathom it. Judging by the servile posture on the two hard fuckers, our lad reckons their bosses are sauntering in. About eight lads in suits get out of the Beamers first, then a fucking suave-looking cunt jumps out of the Merc, flashy pants, silk shirt, aviator shades on his head, cool-looking prick. Lad knows from the John Woo films that these boys are a snakehead: the head cell of a triad gang, specialising in people-smuggling. These must be the cunts calling the shots over the grow-houses in Ennis above the Golden Lotus takeaway.

Flashy Boy walks over, not a word of English, but a gorgeous smile on him. He shakes our lad's hand in a most cordial fashion. One of the feens in the suits comes over with a very pricey-looking bottle of brandy, and glasses are presented. The brandy was unreal, like hot plums, he'd never tasted the likes of it. Flashy Boy is alright, he even takes out his phone and starts showing our lad photos of himself at home with his wife and two childer, cooking a barbecue, swimming, a family man. Not a hint of English though, but whatever he's saying sounds pure friendly. Our boy is starting to feel very comfortable. He knows he's been kidnapped, but all of these fellas are more or less treating him like a celebrity. He starts thinking that maybe they've heard about his action back in Ennis. Maybe they've found out about the hen party in the pool hall, where he took out Christy Bennis and Suntan Dundon with the Kerryman's end of a bike lock. Or the night he shattered Reptile Canavan's pelvis outside Supermac's in Kilrush. What if news travelled through the Golden Lotus all the way to China that he was out to get them? And that maybe they'd be better off with him on their side, as an enforcer rather than one of their enemies? He doesn't have all the facts at hand, but that's the game he's going to play along with. Because there's no fucking way he's siding with these evil pricks. They'd made a big mistake letting him into their lair.

The rest of that night is a blurred montage of fast cars, nightclubs, women and shots. Crowds parting when the gang walks into the parlour. Flashy Boy introduces himself as Shoushan and makes it very public by his proximity to him that our lad from Ennis is his new best friend. Shoushan Hueng is leader of the Sun Yee On triad snakehead, wanted the world over for people-smuggling, organ-smuggling, weapon-smuggling, the grow-houses back in Ennis, the lot. He's far too high up to be prosecuted, he has dirt on every member of government in Beijing. His only danger is the rival 14K triad, but even they wouldn't risk war by taking him out. He hasn't touched anything directly contraband in years – his day-to-day work involves producing action films and blackmailing wealthy businessmen.

The night ends as the rubbish trucks and road-sweepers groom the city. Shoushan accompanies our lad to a tower on the docks and upstairs to a fuck-off apartment and leaves him the keys. Our lad can't believe it: white marble floors, full kitchen, giant LCDs on the wall, a bathroom bigger than the mobile-home in Ennis and a fifteen-foot window overlooking the Hong Kong harbour below. He reaches into the pocket of the Estée Lauder suit they'd decked him up in and pulls out a crumpled packet of Chunghwa-brand fags. He examines the bright red box, no photographs of cancer actors pretending to die, just an inviting yellow building with a pagoda roof. He sparks up and cheers like a sliotar just crossed the bar at a final, jumping up and down on his voluminous magnolia leather couch, with the fag pursed between his lips, ashes flaking all over the gaff. With an introspective solemnity, he stares out over the Hong Kong skyline onto the docks. Millions of flickering lights rise up and poison the clouds with a pale green that you'd normally see on the torso of a sick toddler. Miles Davis-style jazz brass plays in his head as he scans the skyline. Innumerable lives beneath him, behind little windows, the quality of those lives rising with the size of the windows and how high up they are in the towers. And he's at the top.

His gaze switches from the city to the reflection of his apartment's interior on the window-pane. He sees a white envelope on the glass coffee table. He opens it, it's written in English. The letterhead reads, 'Hueng Films, Great Eagle Centre, Fleming Road, Hong Kong'.

He reads the note:

> *Dear Sir,*
>
> *We were highly impressed with your attempts to infiltrate our operation in Ennis. I oversee a film production company. We specialise in action movies. We believe you have the potential to become a great leading hero in Hong Kong action movies.*
>
> *Please enjoy your apartment. For your safety and convenience, we have placed personal security outside your door, who will also tend to your needs.*
>
> *We will be in contact.*
>
> *Yours sincerely,*
>
> *Shoushan Hueng*

Fuck me, he thinks. These lads have reckoned him to be a new Steven Seagal, he wasn't expecting that. But he can definitely see their angle. On the walls hang posters in glass frames of Hong Kong films produced by Hueng's company: *Bullet Cops*, *Tradewind Dragon Boys*, *Hero Fight*, *Dog Eagles*, *Triad Banquet*, *Lucky Dagger*, each looking more class than the next, with explosions and beures and guns and lads with machetes.

These bowzies are the real deal. Our boy's moral position begins to shift – ya, they're the same lads who traffic those poor slaves to Ennis and force them to grow crazy weed. But this action film arm that they have going seems fairly harmless. Maybe they'd even do a film about him in Ennis rescuing the weed-slaves and it could raise awareness for the hundreds of innocent Chinese migrants who get jailed every year back in Ireland. Maybe herself and the mother in the wheelchair would see it. Fuck it, if that happened, he could still maintain a sound moral position, but also get to be a big massive movie hero too. Win–win. That night as he sleeps on his gigantic waterbed in silk sheets, he finally feels a sense of purpose and meaning that is alien to him, but comfortable.

The next morning, the Hong Kong sun creeps through the room, its warmth across his chest wakes him up. He reaches out with both arms, as if to hug the rays of light on the sheet like they're God's flashlight finally finding him in the abyss and picking him out for salvation. The door of the apartment is opened by security and a team of caterers rush in with a selection of pastries, followed by some very trendy-looking lads with spiky hair-dos. They sit him down, start cutting his hair, measuring up his body for some tailored suits, washing his teeth, taking his photograph from every angle and shaving his face. He could get used to this.

They leave another note:

> *Dear Sir,*
> *I hope you enjoyed the services provided by Hueng Film's team of personal stylists.*
> *Before we find you a leading role and begin filming, it is important that you look appropriate for the big screen. We advise some work to be done on your teeth, and some minor alterations made to your physique.*

This has all been taken care of and we will be in contact with details soon.

Yours sincerely,

Shoushan Hueng

He isn't insulted by the note. Sure, he was 38 in October and action movies are a young man's game. An ould tummy tuck would be no harm, and in fairness his teeth look like they'd been shot into his mouth with a musket from forty yards.

Across the harbour in Fa Yuen, near the Mong Kok markets where you buy the fake handbags and electric-eel wallets that fuck up your credit cards, Shoushan Hueng is screaming and roaring in a back office. He's owed several million in bitcoin from a director of the Sumitomo Mitsui Bank, Japanese lad by the name of Masatoshi Busujima. Mr Busujima has been ignoring demands for the money for yonks. Filthy dirty lad, into all sorts of sordid depravity, he has everything and anything trafficked into Japan for his increasingly bizarre sexual urges. One of these creeps who's so rich that every conventional desire a person could have is at his fingertips, so he must continually test his own boundaries to get the horn and feel alive. Hueng is his procurer: whatever Busujima wants, Hueng sources. It started off with Estonian amputees; moved on to famine victims with inflated stomachs from South Sudan; by last March it was disabled children who had wealthy western parents. Hueng wouldn't ask questions, he'd sort it out, for the right price. But Mr Busujima is rich and powerful enough to tell the Sun Yee On triad to get fucked and not pay his bills. He's too high-profile to be threatened by any sort of violence. But what Mr Busujima is unaware of is that the triad has purposefully purchased enough shares in Sumitomo Mitsui Bank that they are entitled to attend Friday's annual general meeting, which is to be a very big international affair. The triads have a taste for revenge, and Mr Busujima has just sent detailed photoshops and instructions to Hueng of his next sexual request. It's to be delivered via a deep-web livestream tomorrow night.

Back in the massive apartment, our lad from Ennis is drinking a Heineken on the couch in his Estée Lauder suit. He's flicking through two potential scripts for upcoming films that he could be the lead in. One is about a jazz trombone-playing New York cop, dispatched to Singapore to take out the 14K triad heroin ring, who ends up addicted to heroin himself. Another is about a simple Irishman called Blobby Sands, who sets up a potato shop in Shanghai and finds himself fighting the local 14K triad as they try to extort his spud shop. The hero character's specialities are making car bombs, being drunk, singing songs about Englishmen and fighting with a shillelagh. The character wears a potato sack and a famine-type hat from the 1840s, but also has platform shoes and flares from the 1970s, topped off with an Aran jumper. He wasn't too keen on that script. He felt the Asian writer, though well-intentioned, had a very limited knowledge of Irish culture and had penned a story that relied upon tired, stereotyped tropes that represent only the negative aspects of Irishness as portrayed through the colonial lens of media and film. Swirling the final sups of Heineken around the bottom of the emerald bottle, he's troubled over which role would be the best to start his career. He has a very strong preference for *Singapore Junkie Cop* rather than *Black '47 Triad Paddy*. They're both something he'd stream online if he came across them, subtitles or no subtitles.

There's a sharp rap on the door, and he's ushered down to a car that is taking him for his cosmetic surgery in a private hospital. The journey is pleasant, and the limousine has sparkling water and Pringles. No queues or nothing at the hospital, he doesn't even have to sign in at reception, he's brought directly to the operating theatre like Mariah Carey off for a tit job. Gowned out and ready to go under anaesthetic, he lies on the table with lights above him and the smell of antiseptic up his nostrils, thinking about the hunk he'd meet at the other side of the surgery. The doctors are incredibly friendly and he's receiving high-quality medical attention. Our lad is scared of needles so they give him the gas, and as he goes under, the room wobbles and ripples like he's peacefully descending beneath the surface of a swimming pool and looking up at the ceiling.

He comes around from the anaesthetic in agonising pain, the darkened room is surrounded by computer monitors. The surgery feels extensive around his frame. His mouth moves like it's full of cotton and nettles, and when he asks for water, his own voice sounds unfamiliar and high-pitched, which very much frightens him. He senses confusion, like when he first woke up in the shipping container. As he looks down at his body, he notices that his shins have been entirely removed and his feet are now attached to his thighs. Same with his arms: his hands are now where his elbows were. He tries to shout out, to tell someone that a mistake has been made. Again, no words come from his throat, only high-pitched warbles like those of a child. On his chest are several moving tentacles that have been fused with his skin. An injured heart kicks shock to his head, which becomes light. He moves an eye left and is confronted with his full reflection in the screen of a darkened computer monitor. The entire back rib-cage has been removed and is hooked up to a large mechanical apparatus that pumps his blood from wrist valves into large canisters, which is fed back into his limbs with tubes.

To his right, he peruses some badly photoshopped blueprints on the wall. Sketches with Japanese, Chinese and English lettering depicting the rough predictions of what he now appears to be. One drawing he can read, as it's labelled 'Western Octopus Sex Child Man'. Standing beside the sketches is Shoushan Hueng, whose usually cordial disposition is now a nonchalant blank stare smoking a fag. Our lad is livid with betrayal, anger and disappointment. If he could speak or move his body, he'd lob a headbutt straight at Hueng's nose. He realises that the triads have double-crossed him, in the name of some sick prank. The promise of a career in action movies was a ruse to get him to agree to surgery and be transformed into a Western Octopus Sex Child Man. Hueng ignores the emotions in our lad's eyes and gives a thumbs-up to his cronies in the background by quipping something in Cantonese. The computer monitors are turned on, in the centre is a webcam that has a red LED, which switches to green.

On the central monitor, Mr Busujima sits naked. Our lad stares at the nude middle-aged Japanese man on the screen in bemused terror. He watches his washed-out stomach, flashing blue and shadowed by pasty bitch tits, his receding hair and shiny scalp, his savage jowls. Busujima's voice distorts over the tiny speaker as he howls repeatedly, 'Watashi wa sekushī ni kanjiru. Anata wa sekushī ni mieru.' The triads in the room all laugh when they hear this. Lad's stomach rumbles with nerves when the loud machinery revs up, and blood is pumped as his skin flushes from pink to pale with every circulatory transfusion from his body to the machine. Hueng orchestrates a control panel on an iPad. The tubes and wires in the back of our lad from Ennis tense up, which is excruciatingly painful to the fresh stitches all over his skin. His body begins to jerk autonomously. He has no command over his limbs. Hueng controls him via the hydraulic blood-pumps bluetoothed to the iPad. Our lad, now four foot tall and howling high-pitched like a boy, performs involuntary sexual manoeuvres on his body using his octopus tentacles. Mr Busujima screams, 'Sekushī, sekushī, sekushī', and masturbates on the other connection of the livestream.

What Mr Busujima doesn't know is that Hueng is video-recording the whole session. Tomorrow night at the Sumitomo Mitsui Bank AGM in Tokyo, Hueng will broadcast the video of Mr Busujima masturbating to the four-foot remote-controlled octopus child man to all the other shareholders. By that evening it will be international news. Our lad from Ennis will be a world-famous Hong Kong film star alright, just not the type that he had imagined.

MY HAND

THIS IS MY HAND.
I PROMISE I WILL ONIY USE IT
AS AN INSTRUMENT OF LOVE
I WILL NEVER USE MY HAND
FOR DOING ACTS OF HATE

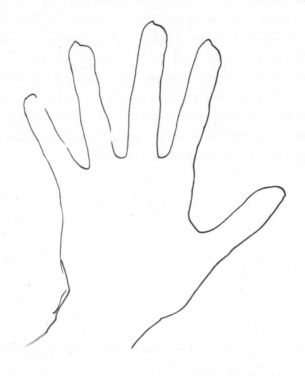

THE BATTER

'm currently eating chorizo from Listowel and Gubbeen cheese on rye in my new gaff on Sitric Road. Lol.'

That was my Twitter status, but it's true, it's what I'm doing right now. I moved in three weeks ago. The landlord is my dad's best friend so I got a serious rate. Whole place to myself. Theo and Ocras came over last week and did the space up with deadly graff, not the stupid cliché tagging shit for thirteen-year- olds – next-level graffiti, loads of hentai-type stuff, with a Die Antwoord vibe, and up on the back wall over the plasma a whopper throw of Kurt Cobain getting sick into a toilet except emojis are coming out of his mouth. We live-streamed the whole thing and Harbo even shared it on *Lovin Dublin*. Ocras nearly decked a lad for trying to Insta the Cobain piece with a filter on it, fuck off. I had a pizza oven set up, I got it off Amazon for 300 yoyos, and I just started banging out free slices of pizzer to anyone who walked in. Spanish Martá made a tomato sauce based on a family recipe from Seville, and we put gouda and Centra ham on it. Fucking mentaller I am, Italian pizzer base, Dutch cheese, shitty rubber Centra ham, wood-fired but with a Spanish marinara. What are we like? Aoife came over with a set of Technics and we had chewins. Before long someone had hashtagged it #BANTERGAFF and even Kav mentioned it on his Snapchat story the next day and he wasn't even there, deadly. The guy who runs Body & Soul festival saw the live-feed and now we'll be curating a pizzer and grazzer space there in June. Ocras graffing up plywood with insane shit and me pumping out pizzer slizzers from the oven like a food DJ, hahaha. Cans of Dutch and loads of K, lol. If you're from Tipperary or somewhere, you need to know that Body & Soul is only the coolest boutique festival in Ireland. My mate's dad is a big music promoter and reckons he can get Syd from Odd Future to drop by our space to hang out.

Because of the housewarming going crazy viral, I'm now known as the lad in Stoneybatter who owns the pizzer oven in his gaff, and everyone started dropping in after the sesh. Buzzing. After only three weeks of being here, I can say that this neighbourhood utterly destroys Wicklow, it's ten times infinitely better, and the 'rents are happy too. They can head over to the Palermo house as much as they like now that I'm standing on my own two feet. Myself and Ocras were totally ripping each other last Tuesday. Ocras said that as soon as *Joe.ie* mention the oven, we're throwing it in a skip up by Smithfield and the junkies can have it, hahaha. But even if that did happen and the pizzer oven became old news, I'd switch it up for Body & Soul and do a big giant paella pan instead, get Spanish Martá involved. Make the space a genderqueer friendly zone too, it's very important to create genderqueer spaces and not label people with the pronouns they were assigned at birth by society. That's what Sorcha told me and she goes to NCAD.

Things have pretty much been that insane for the past three weeks, non-stop knocks on the door, everyone dropping over, tweeting about it, snapchatting the oven and the deadly graff. I gave one of the Ukrainian bouncers from the Grand Social a bag of green and he looked after the door to keep the dickheads from DIT from ruining it, like that group of engineering students selfieing themselves dabbing in front of the Cobain mural like it was 2016. Dorks. Le Galaxie played a secret gig one Wednesday, the bald guy on the synth and the other just banging pots and pans with a wooden spoon. It was so creative. They did Fleetwood Mac covers and made it sound fresh and uncringey. It was all so whopper.

It's kind of slowed down a little now though. I blame Síofra Condon with the bull-ring in her nose. She's in the middle of her Masters in Trinity. She did a Facebook post about why my #BANTERGAFF supported patriarchy, because I'm a man and my pizzer oven was a symbolic representation of a woman's reproductive organs, and by giving out free pizzer I was reinforcing men's control over and entitlement to women's bodies, and my pizzer gaff graff parties were a brothel that condoned rape. It got like a thousand shares, and my phone almost crashed from all the DMs calling me a pig. So I responded by apologising on Tumblr, and also by giving Spanish Martá control of the oven and charging money for the pizzer, and anyone buying pizzer had to ask the oven for consent. Nobody showed up anymore after that, and Evan Fallon called me literally Hitler for being a capitalist. Evan is a Trotskyist and listens to *Bad Brains* on tape, on a Walkman – he's really creative – so that hurt bad.

I'm not feeling too good right now, so after I finish tweeting about the chorizo and Gubbeen I take one of the Xanax that my step-mum Caroline gave me. Xanax is so mellow and cute. Even though I can't stop thinking about the fact that I'm now abso the biggest loser in the Batter, I can't feel what I'm thinking, if you get me. Does that make sense? Like, if I was watching cats having sex out on the road from my room? But I've got really good double-glazed windows, so I can't hear them screaming, but I can see them? Coz it's always the sound that's the most annoying part. That's what Xanax is like. It turns down the haters.

Ocras totes ignored three texts and a FaceTime request. There's definitely lots of talk going on behind my back. So I leave the house, wearing my REPEAL jumper with three-stripe Adidas trackie-bots and Docs. Now that everyone thinks I run a rape brothel and am literally Hitler, I have to show face, raise myself up the flagpole and see who salutes. There's this really quirky pub called J. Morrison & Sons, it used to be a Supervalu. It's totally like a culchie pub from down the country, but don't be fooled, it's really unique and creative. The menu is teeming with outside-the-box ingredients, mixed in with regular Dublin pub food. There's even some old locals that go there, from back when Stoneybatter was just plain rough. The barman gives them free pints so they don't leave, coz they couldn't afford it on the dole anyway, hahaha.

I walk in the door, and it's so dark. The bar has loads of rare cask whiskeys for the new cocktail menu. Guff the mixologist was washing a glass and talking to the old locals. He's got this tiny leather book in his breast pocket from America in the '30s that cost a bomb. It's all about bartending and he reads it when he's not serving. His new sleeve of ink is rocking, I better tell him it's dope, and then maybe show him my back tatt of the triangle. But when Guff looks my way, he defo snubs me. Oh no, he's turning his back and pressing the volume up on the system. 'Shame on a Nigga' by Wu Tang btw, classic old school. I decide to sit down somewhere abso obvious, beside the fire, hoping that if Guff makes eye contact again I can do that Wu Tang W sign with both hands, so he knows I'm down with Shaolin. The fire has actual lumps of feckin turf burning in. Lol, they look like square hairy poos. I mean, where do they even get those up here? So cool. It smells so fragrant and smoky in the pub. Guff told me once that the smell of turf in the pub opens up the palate and complements the notes on the menu. Guff used to slum as a voluntary homeless person in East London before hipsters ruined it and once got into a knife fight with an African guy at a bar in Dalston. He's, like, thirty. He knows Disclosure from before they were famous, he used to serve them when they were underage because they'd heard of Frankie Knuckles and that meant they were men and not boys.

Guff comes over and says, 'What will yizzer have?' He's not even from Dublin, he's from, like, Kildare, but he says 'yizzer' because he's friends with the old Dublin characters at the bar. The moleskin notepad is out to take my order and I kind of freak out a little. Guff always sits beside you at the table when you order, like, always. Even if he doesn't know you, he sits right beside you and says, 'What will yizzer have?' That's what Guff does, he invented the sitting beside you to order thing. They even copy him out in like GBK in Swords Pavilion, yuck. But he's not sitting beside me today, he's just standing there with his pencil, looking pissed off.

My fucking nerves made me blurt out, 'The cheese toastie with house-made jalapeno mayo.' Yikes, total cringe. What a basic thing to order. I sooo should have gone for the Northside coddle with tripe sausage and Croatian truffle oil. That's what people who like their palates challenged eat, and I just ordered the cheese toastie like I wandered in from Finglas.

Guff writes it down. 'Drink?' he says next.

My face is so warm, which means it's red, and I hope Guff blames it on me sitting beside his deadly fireplace. My thoughts are all over the shop. I have to redeem myself. I could go for one of the saltwater IPAs, weissbier or a cacao stout? But even tourists drink those now. Guff just sighed impatiently, oh no. I look up at the bar, at the old Dublin characters with their Guinness and Heinekens, and then I take a big risk. I look at Guff and say, 'I'll have a Harp.'

Guff pauses, and says, 'Niiice.' Success. Only a select few know that even though it's mass-produced, Harp is actually a really balanced lager with a traditional craft recipe that's often overlooked.

He puts his fist out and we bump. Then he looks at my pro-abortion jumper and says, 'Repeal, ya?' and I say, 'You know it, bredren,' and then he says really loudly, 'Dude, yes, do it for the sisters, show them respect. We got their backs man,' and walks backwards to the bar with his hand clenched in the air like that black lad on the podium at the Olympics in the '60s from history documentaries, #blacklivesmatter.

After about five minutes – masso speedy service, I know – he returns with the toastie, which is amazing, by the way. The bread is plain Brennan's sliced, toasted golden, but the cheese is really creamy manchego made with ewe's milk from La Mancha, melted perfectly. It washes down well with the Harp, which totally sets off the jalapeno mayo. The old Dublin characters are at the bar shouting and burping about the Luas workers' strikes.

Guff tells them that his grand-uncle taught James Connolly how to play hurling in Edinburgh, wow, and that when Guff was younger, he thought about joining the INLA but was talked out of it by a Catalan anarchist. Double wow. Then he pours the old Dublin characters another round of free pints.

I'm feeling pretty good, all things considered, the Xanax has even worn off, giving serious thought to planting myself up at the bar, getting Rothmans or John Player from the fag machine, and chatting with Guff and the characters for the day. Imagine the stories they'd have? Maybe later they'd invite me back to one of their flats, and their wrinkly wives would feed me stew or Crispy Pancakes or something. Then the fucking unthinkable happens. I get an email on the iPhone from Body & Soul saying they're cancelling my pizzer and graffiti space because it would make patrons feel unsafe. That they'd read Síofra Condon's post about my 'patriarchal pizzer oven'. My throat drops. I feel stunned, and my face is freezing and wet. I'm having a full-blown panicker. Sitting here on the stool with my half-drank Harp.

Oh fuck, now Guff is calling me up to the bar with the old Dublin characters. I cannot let him know that I get anxiety attacks. The song 'Inside My Love' by Minnie Ripperton comes on over the system, vintage '70s soul/funk, but I prefer the original by Leon Ware. I get up off the stool and walk sideways towards the door like that crab I saw when I was eight, on the rocks in Portrane Beach with Uncle George. I pinch the chest of my REPEAL jumper with both hands and pull the fabric out like tits, because Minnie Ripperton died of tit cancer and I abso have to let Guff know that I'm familiar with her music. He looks at me with a bit of a confused look as I leave, but I'm sure later he'll understand what I meant.

I run out the door of the fucking pub. Oh shit, there's Conor on the unicycle who got an interview for an acting job in the Abbey. I hide behind a delivery van. My chest is pumping. I legger down Sigurd Road, noticing noise from Dúsallaigh Ó Ceallaigh's open window. I look up. My God, he's playing Limp Bizkit really loudly, they are due to be cool right about now. Go Dúsallaigh, ironic as fuck, dude. I scarper down an alley and curl into the shape of crumpled paper, where I can have my panicker in private. I feel myself up, looking for one of Caroline's Xanax. I find it, it's beside my condom in the pocket of the trackie-bots. It's raining hard. I cup a hand of rainwater from a puddle and slurp it down with the pill and wait for it to stop the shame. Ya, I know I'm fucking drinking out of a puddle like a crow, but it doesn't matter once the xanny kicks in.

It kicks in. I am level. The cats are screwing but I can't hear their screams, lol. I sit down on a bench and watch the sheeple on the Luas with their normal uncreative boring jobs. The concrete has that oil smell that rises when it rains for the first time in weeks. They look so upset and pale, huddled together, scowling at each other like they all just want to vomit into the air. Stuffed on the tram, each person is the other's ugly reflection, and they hate the guy across from them and themselves. Forced to stare ahead in a wet moving bin full of mutual failure. Gross.

I'm devo about my Body & Soul space getting cancelled. Dad told me last month that I'd have to get a job in Dublin, that he'd ring one of his ad agency buddies because they always need highly creative people like me. I asked him to chill the beans a bit, because I had something big planned for the festival that was probably going to make me famous like Andy Warhol. So he agreed to keep topping up my account with a few grand every month until I had that sorted. He was already impressed with #BANTERGAFF and how I'd proven my ability to curate a space. He bragged about it to all his friends in Palermo, especially Aidan Holmes the economist from Foxrock whose son Zach got addicted to coke and now has a colostomy bag and can't even go to college.

I'm defo fucked. There has to be a solution. I gotta think of something so big that Body & Soul simply cannot ignore it, and has to reconsider giving me a space to curate. I need something huge that will go sooooo viral, something on trend, but risky, and not like other stuff that content-creators in the Batter go for. Something that *Huff Post* or *Broadly* would pick up. Maybe I could, like, do video profiles of all those old Dublin characters up at the bar in J. Morrison & Sons? Like, follow them around for the day and profile their lives. Give them GoPros and they can vlog. Follow them with a drone. I bet they were all molested by Christian Brothers or GAA coaches when they were kids, and they don't even know it. Like, I could interview them, about their gritty lives drinking Heineken, watching soccer and smoking Rothmans, and get them to start crying on camera and talking about when a priest had sex with them when they were five, or how their dads used to beat their mothers in front of them or something. I'd use Freudian stuff to get them to remember all the ugly incidents that happened to them. Do it in black and white and show their little flats in Smithfield with Thin Lizzy and Aslan music playing over it, but then switch it up and add like Burial or Autechre tracks too. That could be fucking huge. Like *La Haine*, but with ould lads. It would be such engaging content and really heartfelt, and I'd be like a new Ken Loach but better. Then maybe Ocras could, like, sketch their faces up like anime characters and we could graff those on the window-display of Brown Thomas, and I'd hand out free paella. Caroline is a manager there, she could swing it. Body & Soul could not walk away from that. It's subversive community-based art and branding in one, so creative.

But what if it's dangerous? What if I got one of the old lads to confess that he'd been molested on camera, but then his son didn't understand art and came to try and kill me for putting family secrets on videos? Threw me into the boot of a stolen car and burnt it out in Darndale? The boot would be like an oven, it would probably be the hottest part of the car, so it would turn me to ash, vaporise me. I heard on *Breaking Bad* that when it's that hot your teeth explode like popcorn and you can't be identified. There'd be nothing left of me, I'd actually totally disappear and never be found. Oh my God, what if that happened and then everyone thought I'd committed suicide? Like, jumped in the canal and that's why my body wasn't found? How morto would that be? People thinking I'd topped myself and then anytime my name would be mentioned at a party, you'd have to go quiet and change the subject. Oh no, Ocras would totally do a suicide awareness video about me if that happened, he'd defo do that, the snake, and that's all anyone would remember me for. I'd be remembered as a loser.

I take a third Xanax. I chew this one, it tastes like hairspray. But I absolutely can't do the video with the old Dublin lads just in case, bullet dodged. My brain is overloading with creativity, so I take out my iPhone and open Facebook, which I hardly ever do because it's just for dads these days. My young cousin Conlaoch had been online. He plays Xbox for days on end, and his profile photo is that meme of Pepe the Frog wearing a red Trump hat. He's a self-confessed alt-right shitlord, a total racist sexist little dick, but he's a good kid at heart and mostly does it for fun. He'd been sharing conspiracy theory videos that he makes on his timeline. It's just him shouting into a camera, while gaming with his headset on, then lots of loud noises and memes. One was called 'SHILLARY CLINTON TO REDUCE EUROPEAN POPULATION THROUGH AIDS CARRYING RAPEFUGEES', self-explanatory. Another was about lizards building the pyramids and using them as broadcast towers to control radios inside our heads. It was called 'LIZARD BRAIN RADIO CUCK PROOF. EYE OF HORUS. CHILD DIES ON CAMERA AT THE END'. He has tonnes of these conspiracy videos, crazy stuff. But holy shit, he's getting, like, 80,000 likes a post. I click on the Hillary Clinton video, and wait a bit for the YouTube app to open, not long though, 4G around here is super-fast. Suffering shitballs, it has 15 million views and comments are streaming in. That is totes insane. How is Conlaoch getting all these views? Some of these comments are from, like, South Africa and America. I DM Conlaoch immediately.

Me: Hey cuz, watsup dude, how you get so many views. Rad stuff. *smiley emoji* *black clapping-hand emoji*

Conlaoch: Reeee. I hear you're Lord Cuckington in Dublin? Seen those feminazis shut you down. Should have doxxed them IRL. *laughing-crying-face emoji*

Me: I know dude, total buzzkill sluts. Lol. I fucked most of them anyway, don't worry. How you get views? *100 emoji*

Conlaoch: I search the most googled words that week for males aged 10 to 25 then use those words in the YouTube titles. That's it. *laughing-crying-face emoji*

I start devouring Wikipedia articles on conspiracy theories.

I could totally bring something new to this genre, something quirky and outside the box. There's lots to take in: 9/11 conspiracies, Saddam Hussein owning a Stargate in the dessert, Obama controlling weather to invent climate change, the Hollow Earth theory, celebrity Illuminati puppets. But this is all basic shit. But seriously though, 'Yo, what would I do if I was early '90s RZA from Wu Tang Clan and I was about to make a dope beat that changed hip-hop production forever?' I wouldn't copy trends, I'd sample classic soul, stuff that's still there in musical consciousness but hasn't been touched yet by hip-hop, then mix that up with some contemporary gangster shit to keep it relevant and gritty. YESSSSSS, that's it. The fucking 'moon landing was fake' theory. The Robert Johnson of all conspiracy theories, the originator. No one talks about it anymore, no one thinks about it. That's what I need to do.

The theory goes that the moon landing was faked by the US to put the shits up Russia. That it was filmed by Stanley Kubrick in a Hollywood back-lot, and the sheeple ate it up because it was on TV. What if I proved the moon landing was fake, but not faked because of the Cold War, faked to distract us from Islam taking over Europe? Yes. It was fabricated, and Islam was invented in the '60s, under our noses, but we were too busy looking up at the moon to notice it happening. The CIA, KGB, Mossad and M15 rewrote all the history books and invented this big religion, to enslave us and keep us in fear, all because in the '60s we got too woke from taking acid and listening to Hendrix. Shit, maybe they killed Hendrix because of that? Jim Morrison and Marley too. Mainstream media has fed us this myth, this fake religion that was made up while we were obsessed with exploring planets and building rockets. You put a dude on the moon, it's so mind-blowing, you can feed the world any bullshit lie. Why not?

What else happened in the 1960s? The first mass immigration of Islamic Algerians happened in France (hired actors). Israel started throwing its weight around (anything with Jews is great). Peak oil from Saudi Arabia (follow the money). The roots of the EU were sown (one-world government). Think about it. Those countries were just Arabs before the '60s, like Aladdin and stuff. They went around rubbing lamps on camels. Look at the film *Casablanca* from the '40s, it's in Morocco, you see any Muslims in that? No, just Arabs rubbing lamps and wearing turbans and smoking hash. No Allah, no burkas, no jihad, no sharia. Now all we care about today is Islam this, Islam that. They tell us that Islam is a threat, and what do we do? We shit our pants and obey whatever the one-world government wants us to obey, like good sheeple. It's made up. It all ties in. This is all an easy sell. I'd believe it. It's perfect. That's that gangster shit, that Wu Tang shit. The moon landing is the obscure soul sample, the Islam stuff is ODB's gritty lyrics about selling crack. Damn, this is so creative. This will get eaten up. If I just throw the right soundtrack on it, maybe Erykah Badu or Death Grips, I can get *Huff Post* sharing it, *BuzzFeed*, *Lovin Dublin*, fucking *Vice* would share it. They don't care what they share so long as it gets views and has the appearance of being woke.

Those alt-right edgelords who normally make conspiracy or Islam stuff are just computer dorks. They get the branding wrong every time, using basic system typefaces, bad editing, awful soundtracks. I'm the Marshall Jefferson to their Kraftwerk. Those pricks at Body & Soul will beg me to curate a space, and I'll show everyone. Ocras, Aoife, Guff, Síofra Condon, the total cunt. I heard she sucked off a guy at Irish college and isn't even a real lesbian, she just pretends so people don't call her privileged. My hands have that twitch they get when they want to shake with excitement but can't because I took three Xanax today, lol.

As I slump on that shit bench by Smithfield Luas, the Dublin clouds over the Liffey look like black tyre smoke, blocking the faggot sun that whimpers out a mushroom colour. The sun is such a dry shite loser. I could even stare at it directly because it couldn't penetrate the cloud. It looks like a crap Penney's lampshade behind a curtain in a student flat. The sun over Dublin is a pathetic weak asshole, too scared to express its true potential. Always asking permission from the rain to shine, letting the stupid drizzle get its way every time. Puffing out passive-aggressive UV rays through the mist that would give you freckles on your nose and you'd never even know what caused it. Not like the one on the continent, or in Croatia or something. It's probably the reason everyone around here are such buzzkills. They catch loser off the sun. I should move to Croatia after the moon-landing video.

I fix the brim of my paddycap and make my way back to the gaff, with the sun tapping me on the back like an old woman telling me I've too many items in my basket for the queue I'm in. What are the logistics of getting this video made? I'll need to borrow Dad's 4x4 Land Rover and round up my film equipment. Two Canon D7 cameras, zoom mics, tripods and maybe a few strong lights on stilts. All sorted, only Dad's in Palermo and has the keys to the Rover.

The next morning, I'm forced to book a bus ticket on Bus Éireann, which is the worst service known to man. The drivers are ungrateful and smell like dried-in sweat, the floors on their buses are filthy, and I know someone who got tetanus from sitting on a fingernail that was jutting out of a seat. All the camera gear packed up in two big rucksacks. Feeling a bit shit because I took two more Xanax before bed so I could get to sleep. I had to take one when I woke up too, to stop feeling like shit. The bus is leaving at 11 a.m. So I get an Uber down to Busáras near the Liffey. I'm going to west Clare by the way, to this place called the Burren. There used to be this fridge magnet in Mum's kitchen, on the fridge obviously. I always hated her shitty apartment. She lived there after her and Dad split but it was only bought so Dad could rent it out to Polish people. So I despised it when she had to move in. I was like eleven, she'd just stay up in her room, whimpering and drinking. It was the first time I ever got depressed or scared. I used to stare at the fridge magnet of the Burren, to try and pretend I couldn't hear her cry-drinking in the next room. This little photo of a pale stony desert, I couldn't believe it was in Ireland. It was just grey rock, for miles and miles. I was the one who found her body. I thought she was just having a lie-in, but when I walked into the bedroom, her skin was violet and she had puke all over her face. She was naked too, which was even worse. I stared at that fridge magnet of the Burren while I waited for the ambulance to arrive, and it's the last thing I remember from the apartment before I left to live with Dad and Caroline in Wicklow. The Burren looked like a different planet. It looked like outer space. I couldn't think of a more perfect place to nail this moon-landing video.

I'm halfway through this bus journey and need to piss furiously. It's one of those regional services that takes about a bajillion stops in the most isolated areas. It's basically just going left from Dublin and stopping in every sparsely populated ditch that has people with green teeth, hurling jerseys and that muck-savage look of confusion that conveys a fear the British will be back at any moment to steal their spuds. Actual human cows who have sex and fight at the same time to a Kings of Leon soundtrack. I never even knew Ireland could get this rural.

The bus climbed shitty purple mountains for, like, a half-hour, those mountains that don't even have grass, just short brown stumps that are always wet. Like in the film *Braveheart* where Mel Gibson is dressed as a smurf. This whole place is a Jameson advert for thick Yanks. The driver goes up these mountains, only to pause at a fucking pole in the middle of nowhere and not one person gets off. The bus stops themselves haven't even been changed since the '70s, they still have the old logo of the red setter. This is why these Bus Éireann pricks need to be privatised and replaced with actual hard workers who want to get up early. They're wasting everyone's time, going to bus stops that no one is getting off at. The way down the mountain tickles my bladder, which swells to a whopper aching sting as the bus descends more. When you need to piss this bad, you get an intense pain on top of your dick and then think about dying. I take three Xanax there and then. There's no way I'm getting him to stop this bus, just so I can piss, and then everyone can look out the window at me pissing and I become the guy who pissed in the grass for the rest of the journey. The other passengers would probably film me pissing against a rock on their bogger Nokias and put it up on Bebo or whatever they use, and then everyone up in the Batter would see it, and they'd call me piss tourist. I'm not being the guy who pisses on the floor of this bus either. I'm just going to have to pretend that the next stop is my stop, and then wait for the next bus.

It's at least another twenty minutes of tiny isolated road before the driver stops and shouts, 'Polagoona, anyone for Polagoona?'

There's two elderly women and a man with Down Syndrome left in the cabin. I get up off my seat with the utmost care, and grab my sack full of gear. I'm tip-toeing down the aisle with scrunched knees, my stomach pushing my belt because it's so full of piss. The engine vibrations cause the piss inside to swirl around but the three Xanax make it feel tolerable.

'This is my stop,' I say. The driver doesn't give a fuck and he smells like dried-in sweat.

On the roadside, I wait for him to drive away, then watch until the back of the bus is far off on the road. I pull my pants down around my ankles and try to push out a piss. I've been holding it for so long that it shocked my bladder or something, because it's not coming. No matter how hard I try, I can't piss. I try thinking of a river, I try squatting, I even drink some of my water. No piss. I can't fucking believe this, so I take one more Xanax. If I can relax a bit more, the piss will just exit naturally.

I'm staring at the yellow-with-condensation times on the bus stop, there's no second bus coming after the one I'd just gotten on. Typical. I'm stranded in some gaff called Polagoona, in what I can only assume is either Galway or Clare. It's starting to get dark and a bit cold. There's a cluster of lights a few miles away in the distance that defo has to be a village. I've got my credit cards. If I can just get as far as there, I can get a hotel or something, relax, maybe have a pint. It's going to be fine. Everything will be OK. I'll be laughing about this later in bed. I'll head to the Burren tomorrow and shoot the moon-landing video then. This whole situation makes for a pretty masso tweet anyway – people will think I'm fucking loopers, down here in boggerland.

'Lost up a mountain, in a secret location, working on an exciting new project,' I type. No fucking reception on the phone though, literally not one bar, so it doesn't send.

I look up from my phone and it's gotten darker still. The road that leads down the mountain to the lights is snakey and convoluted, with no streetlights. This is scary. Well, like, it should be scary, but not really because I'm very dozy from all the Xanax. It's going to be a pretty long journey down that road, and it'll get darker with every step. I'll probably be hit and killed by some in-bred culchie driver who's after drinking paraffin out of a tractor engine.

Those lights in the distance aren't going anywhere though. It's probably shorter to literally go straight for them across the field. Like, a beeline. Just walk straight at the lights, across that big field. It looks pretty flat and uncomplicated as fields go. No big hedges or anything. My stomach is still so inflated with piss that I have to completely open my jeans. But that kind of hurts when I walk so I'll just take the jeans off. Better take my underpants off too to be safe. This is the biggest erection I've ever had. When you need to piss this bad, your bladder expands and stimulates your prostate, and that gives you a piss horn. I'd read that on Google on the bus. We must have been in, like, Kildare when I looked that up because that's the last time I had 4G internet on the iPhone.

I'm determined to get to those lights. I don't care that I'm walking through a field with no pants and on a boner. There's no one around anyway. This ground underneath is pretty mushy. My leg got stuck a few yards back so I pulled it out with my arms. Got mucky hands. Good job I'm not wearing pants because it would make this way more difficult. There's this odd smell the deeper I walk. I've definitely smelled it before. It's kind of cheesy and earthy and eggy. Where do I know this from? This is worse than trying to name a song, why can't there be a Shazam app for smells? OMG, that's so creative, I better patent that when I get back. What the fuck is that smell? Oh shit, I know. Guff's fireplace, in J. Morrison & Sons pub. The turf. The ground smells like the bucket of turf beside Guff's fire. I must be walking across a peat bog. Mum used to tell me stories about these when I was a kid. She was a blow-in from Clare, but she went to college and met my dad in Dublin and never went back. She used to tell me about cutting turf in the summer with her dad.

It's too dark now but I'd love to see what this bog looks like. Maybe I could get some turf for Guff and bring it back. I'll take out the iPhone for the torch and point it at the ground. It's all brown and wet, but crazy spongy, like a bouncy castle. I'll walk around another bit, look for a good patch with the light, and then rest the phone on my bag. Fuck it, I'm here anyway, why not? I'll dig a bit of turf for Guff and bring it back in the rucksack. Might as well. How cool would that be? Who the fuck up in Stoneybatter would just wander into a pub with their own turf that they cut, lol? I can get one of the tripods from the sack and use it like a kind of shovel to dig bits up. It's really cool, the stuff gets spongier and less like earth the deeper I go, the eggy smell is way stronger when I dig. I'll keep digging for a bit. Shit, I think I hit something?

With the iPhone light shining I'm seeing what's like this strand of dark leather. I pulled loads of muck and turf away, and I can make out a long thin shape. Call me nuts, but this looks like a weird skinny leathery black leg. Oh fuck, no way. It's a fucking bog body. Oh shit. They've only ever found like six of these in

Ireland. I can't believe this. We studied these in Leaving Cert, they even took us into the National Museum to see them. Irish mummies, my teacher called them. So basically, these dudes, like, kings or something, would, like, get murdered or die thousands of years ago, and then they'd get buried in a bog and their bodies would preserve perfectly, until they get found by legends like me. This is such a me thing to do. If ever there was proof of what a total ledgebag I am, I fucking step foot into a bog for the first time in my life and find a fucking bog body. Ocras is going to hate me.

I reach into my rucksack to take out the 7D camera. I have to start vlogging this discovery immediately. Fuck the moon-landing video, this is history. I just discovered history. Holy shit ... what if I claim the body as my own? I should do that. Fuck giving it to a museum, he's mine. I could like take the bog body back to Stoneybatter and put a cool hat on him. Maybe take him to Body & Soul and put him behind a set of decks, call him DJ Bogger. Fuck ya. A bog-body DJ? That's next-level. Daft Punk can shove their robot helmets up their hoops. DJ Bogger is what's happening this summer.

I don't fucking believe this, where is my 7D camera gone? I think I placed all the cameras in the other rucksack, I must have left it on the bus because I was so distracted by needing to piss. For the love of Jah. OK, one more Xanax before I flip out. I still need to piss. Do not even tell me I'm not getting this act of ultimate ledgebaggery on camera, and my phone battery has just about enough to use the torch a bit more. If I even chance the iPhone camera, the battery will go, and then I've no light. FML. Maybe it's for the best. I'd have to vlog with no pants on a piss horn, that would take hours of keying a blur in on Premiere.

It doesn't matter. I'm already planning on digging this ancient fucker up, throwing him on my back, and making it down to those lights. I can ring the bus company and get the cameras back in the morning, although what if that Down Syndrome lad stole them? No time to think like that.

I get down on my knees and start pulling the turf away from around the body while I still have light from the phone. I can make out little details the more I pull. The legs are real skinny and mashed together with rope around the feet. This rope looks like it would fall apart if I touched it. His dick is tiny. As I scrape away more turf, I can see that his stomach is, like, ripped open and even his gut casings are intact, all black and leathery. This is fucking incredible, dude is perfectly preserved, except for his nipples that have been cut off. He defo had a gruesome end. Someone really hated this guy, he must have been a total asshole.

As I dig further up, where his neck should be, my hand slips and I fall forward on my stomach, on top of the body. I reach with my fingers and realise that I've obviously been lying just at the edge of a ledge. I grab the phone to shine some light ahead of me. There's a big sinkhole and I'd almost fallen in, close call, but now I'm lying on the rim of it, on top of this bog body. Couldn't see it in the dark obviously. The rest of the bog body is protruding from the wall of this sinkhole. It must have been recently sunk, and that's what budged him to the surface.

My chest is on his, as I poke my face over the ledge and shine the light. Looking down, I can see his head sticking out from the wall of the sinkhole. He's got a big mouth full of teeth grinning up at me and this baldy head with one tuft of red hair. He would look so cool DJing at Body & Soul, my God. I'd put a tank-top on him, with an LGBT rainbow. There's easily a ten-foot drop underneath his head, with water at the bottom. I could pull his legs, that might drag him from the hole's wall, but his head would probably come off if I applied any pressure. He's no good to me without a head. I'm defo going to have to climb down that hole and clear the mud around him that way. Shit, this will be difficult, but not impossible. I place the phone on the ledge, so that the light points into the hole, and I climb over and kick my feet into the soft wall to get some footing. Good thinking, very Bear Grylls, so creative. If I can just dig the mud out from around his head, I can take the whole body and then bring him down to the village.

I'm making good progress, but it's starting to rain, which is when my leg fucking slips so I grab onto the head and hang off it. I clamber with my other hand to reach the ledge, but it's too fucking wet and the rain is getting heavier and washing all the mud down into the sinkhole. I can feel the bog body starting to loosely slip towards me and out of the wall, with me on the end. It's stretchy and leathery, like a dog's chew toy, but it can defo hold my weight. I have him headlocked, but he's just pushing out of the wall of that sinkhole like a difficult shit exiting a rectum. The rain looks fat in the blue light of the iPhone on the ledge. This is so slippy. He comes free and we both splash ten feet below. Thank fuck this water is only reaching as far as my knees, but the hole is filling up with rain and mud pretty quickly. I try to think of how I can get back up to the surface, but then the light on the phone that's illuminating us goes and I'm standing in pitch black, down a hole, holding this bog body, with nothing but the sound of rising mud around me. I hadn't told anyone back in the Batter that I was going to Clare. No one knows I'm here. My only hope is that someone will find me in the morning, someone walking up from that village in the distance.

I remember Mum's stories about the bogs. About lights known as will o' the wisps that flicker over turf when gas is released. How these lights lead people off their paths. There is no fucking village. There are no people. This is the middle of nowhere. Just me down a hole, with a bog body, getting ready to drown in muddy turf and be dug up in another ten thousand years. Cradling this cunt who died a millennium or so before me and I've no pants on. I want more than anything to feel fear, regret, doom, panic, I want to fight for my life, to feel anything at all. But I'm too numb from Xanax. I feel nothing, I can't feel my last moment. But at least I can finally take a piss.

VIRAL INTERNET DOG

ARSE CHILDREN

Eamon de Valera bent his weak chest out over the alabaster windowsill of the Mansion House and cast an anxious eye across the crawling November fog on Dawson Street, which had sauntered up the Liffey from the fat smog flumes of the Guinness Brewery with that dog-food smell. It was close to 11 p.m., and he awaited the glimmerman, who would extinguish the gaslights and drown the cobbles in a covert darkness. A slight man, with ticking veins that cut like canals on a map up to his eyelids, de Valera had the appearance of a sun-bleached stork corpse who'd been tailored in a Saville Row suit. On his long nose rested circular-framed brass glasses with thick lenses that magnified his pupils comedically. Young children would single him out as he walked down Sackville Street and make jovial quips about his gigantic magnified eyeballs. This hurt him deeply, and the pain would often resurface when he scolded his subordinates rather brutally with a thin length of copper wrapped in damp Hessian.

A great trouble was coming to Dublin city. Éamon's chattering teeth exhaled pops of tepid breath that became visible in the frigid air of night and spelled out doom as they laddered up towards the sky like demons escaping hell. Éamon de Valera, President of Dáil Éireann, had been waging a successful war on the occupying British Crown forces in his country. But the British had had enough, and Prime Minister Lloyd George himself had dispatched a specialist group of undercover intelligence agents to crush the aspiring Irish Republic. The IRA were cornered in a Turkish bath-house of their own creation.

Éamon de Valera was wearing neither britches nor underpants as he ogled Dawson Street in anticipation of the glimmerman, but had opted to keep his shiny brown brogues and black socks on. Behind Éamon stood a large man, a younger man, in suspenders and slacks. His proud torso and stocky arms imposed a presence on the empty boardroom of the first Dáil. This man was General Michael Collins. Normally resolute, confident and stubborn, tonight Collins had the look of an abandoned child. His sweat rose from his pits and had that faint tang of black-currant jam a man gets when he's stressed. This honk congested the boardroom.

He approached Dev and rested his chin on his shoulder, with one hand on the cord of the venetian blinds. Not a word was spoken between them as they waited pensively for the glimmerman to extinguish the Dawson Street gaslights. The gloomy boardroom was irradiated tangy by the citrus green haze that penetrated the window through the slots on the open blind, casting the exploded projection of the two men against the palisade, which was a hurried omelette of papers and different coloured strings of twine pinned down where relevant. Photos and documents smuggled out from the intelligence catacombs of Dublin Castle were sliced up with horizontal lines of shadow that sang a slow song to the Cairo gang. Under each photo was listed the name and address of each of the IRA's potential judge, jury and executioner, dangerous men who served their time dismantling revolutions in the most exotic stretches of the British Empire:

Lieutenant Henry Angliss, 22 Lower Mount Street
Lieutenant Peter Ashmun Ames, 38 Upper Mount Street
Captain Geoffrey Thomas Baggallay, 119 Baggot Street
Captain George Bennet, 38 Upper Mount Street
Major Charles Milne Cholmeley Dowling, 28 Pembroke Street Upper
Sergeant John J. Fitzgerald, 28 Earlsfort Terrace
Lieutenant Donald Lewis MacClean, 117 Morehampton Road
Captain William Frederick Newberry, 92 Lower Baggot Street
Captain Leonard Price, 28 Pembroke Street Upper
Names like vandalised gravestones on the wall.

Dev jolted as a flicker hit the inside of his glasses. The glimmerman had arrived. Dressed in a waxed trench-coat and well over six feet tall, he extended his wooden pole up and down the footpaths and attended to the Georgian lamp-posts. They were always tall men. He opened the little glass door, fifteen feet in the sky, with the hook on his pole, and duly turned the switch that extinguished the flow of gas. Michael Collins watched as his ulcer played up, and was reminded of his time working in the Welsh mines as a gas-boy holding a canary. The gas-light flames looked like little yellow canaries in cages getting dowsed to death in black paint, heralded aloft Dawson Street like puck-fair goats. Glimmermen did this all over Dublin city, and by the time they were finished, it would be morning and they'd have to turn them back on again. Glimmermen didn't sleep.

Soon Dawson Street was in complete darkness, a dark so dark that your ears take over from your eyes and turn up the volume of distant horses trotting and the hollers from late pubs a few blocks over. Dev and Collins stepped back from the window.

Dev: What are we going to do?

Collins: We're going to take the fuckers out. I have my best men, ready to go. They know their faces, they know their names. We have the pistols you got from the Yanks. I'm on it, Dev.

Dev: Your men? Ha, your men? The twelve apostles, is it? What could they do to anyone? Half of them Connolly's ex-lackies, the other half with the smell of cow shit on their collars.

Collins: Ah Jaysus, Dev. What am I supposed to do?

Dev: The fucking squad, Michael? Get real. The Cairo gang have faced worse than the squad. They've taken down Moors in Algeria who wouldn't think twice to strapping dynamite to themselves.

De Valera removed his shoes and socks. Michael Collins dissolved into a leather swivel-chair as Dev crept across the room towards a mini-bar, completely naked from the waist down.

Dev: Caipirinha, Michael?

Collins: Go on so.

De Valera began to crush fresh limes in a rocks glass with the end of a bar spoon. He sprinkled sticky brown demerara sugar on to the pulpy, zesty juice. He reached into a bucket to retrieve ice cubes, which he bashed with his fist and danced into the glass with long fingers, upon which he poured 80-proof Brazilian cachaça, a white rum variant made from sugarcane juice. He shook the glass gently and while maintaining eye contact with Collins, stirred the drink with a steak knife, which he pushed then deep into the back of his throat and pulled slowly out, savouring the limey, sugary, rummy concoction that finished on his lips. He handed Collins his caipirinha.

Dev: Before you take the swally of that caipirinha, remind yourself that Cromwell sold your ancestors to Barbados.

Collins: Your point?

Dev: He sold them as slaves, treated worse than the African, on the sugarcane plantations, up and down South America. That caipirinha you drink is an Irishman's drink.

Collins: Alright Dev, I will.

Dev: I've a better plan to take out the Cairo gang. No need for the squad.

Michael Collins's face juddered with sheer bemusement at de Valera's assertion. What did he mean? What plan could be better than getting the squad to take out the Cairo gang? What plan could be better than the blood-anger of Joe Leonard, Paddy Griffin or Frank Bolster, the greatest guns in the IRA? Collins had already given commands for the assassinations to take place in a week, to coincide with the All-Ireland Final and provide some civilian cover. That shit really confused the Brit soldiers – they broke down when a load of Tipp lads arrived on donkeys. The wheels were already in motion and he didn't want to risk counter-manding his orders, lest a dispatch be intercepted by the G-men.

Collins: What do you mean, Dev?

Dev: Fine notes of coconut on this cachaça. An oak barrel they had it in, I'd say. Maybe even ash, judging by the nose. Have you ever had reason to acquaint yourself with a cooper, Michael?

Collins: Dev, the squad! Tell me what you meant.

Dev: There's things I haven't told you, Michael ... I have powers.

Collins: The whiskey?

Dev: No, powers, catechistic powers, dark knowledge that I attained from my time with the Carmelite Order. They ushered the compassionate heart of Our Holy Mother under the auspices of Saint Berthold to grant special abilities on my body in the name of Ireland and her noble destiny.

Collins: Fuck you on about, Dev? You haven't gone Boland's Mill on me, have you?

Dev: I've been granted a womb, Michael, in my body.

Collins: ...

The general crossed his legs with an uncomfortable disbelief and a desire to leave the room. However, despite his frustration with de Valera's loose grasp on reality and increasing inebriation, Collins was a resolute professional, in full awareness that his president was addressing him in the offices of Dáil Éireann. He took in a large portion of air and remained calm while de Valera explained further.

Dev: The Carmelite Order asked Our Lady to grant me the ability to give birth, and she answered this plea.

Collins: But ... you have male equipment dangling off you, Dev, I'm looking at it now before you.

Dev: No, Michael, in my bowels. Our Lady grew a womb just underneath my large intestine. It allows me to give birth to two-foot-tall warriors from my hole. Several in one go, if I wish. For a time, like now, when Ireland needs it most. However, I need darkness to do this. That's why we waited for the glimmerman.

Collins: Is that why you took your pants off?

Dev: It is, Michael. These arse children, I can birth them. Do you know the way I've been asking the volunteers to skin dogs on the northside because they might be Protestant?

Collins: Of course.

Dev: Well, I've been hoarding their pelts. For a day like today. I'm going to birth my Carmelite arse children. We'll dress them as dogs, put guns in their hands. And they will assassinate the Cairo gang. We can't do it with the squad. It's too hot out there. Every G-man from Dublin Castle is watching us, watching our volunteers. We need to do something that's never been done. This is the plan that's going to unfold. It's the only plan.

Collins: I don't know what to say to this, Dev. This is a lot to take in.

Dev: It's perfect, Michael. You tell the squad to hold back, they can stay in their beds. The arse children will take out the spies. Then when the right time comes, we'll credit the assassinations to your squad, every paper will believe it. The men will be heroes for centuries. The truth would be too much for Ireland. The squad will be shot if they go out next week. Please trust me, Michael.

Collins: Dev, we've been through a lot together and as mad as this sounds, I'm listening.

Dev: Thank you, Michael. But the birth of these arse children isn't easy. I will need your assistance.

Collins: Whatever you require, Dev, I'll be here. I'm your servant. We'll do it for Mother Ireland and for the men who died in '16.

Dev: No ... Michael. I need your assistance. I can only carry these arse children and expel them from my rectum, but they require a father, a father who is a warrior, a warrior that can trace his blood back to the ancient high kings of Éireann. You must father these children, Mick. I have a short gestation period, approximately six to eight days. We need to get working immediately so that our arse children can perform the assassinations next week. Any longer and it'll be too late. The Cairo gang will have gotten all they need to take us out by then.

De Valera's mercurial eyes said it all. Michael Collins was faced with a dilemma. The only way to save Ireland was for him to have anal sex with de Valera. He had had a quare feeling all night. As soon as the Dáil adjourned, de Valera had removed some clothing for no apparent reason. Collins found this ritual peculiar. However, Dev was a strange fish and had spent his time in Boland's Mill during the Easter Rising wearing only pyjama bottoms. Collins was always very sensitive of Dev's rattly disposition. But this time it was different. The conviction in Dev's face when he spoke about the arse children was otherworldly in its intensity. This didn't appear to be a stunt, nor a cry for help under intense duress. This was real, it was happening, and Collins knew he'd have to discard any personal heterosexual inhibitions to secure the freedom of Ireland and the safety of his men. With the broad awkwardness of a forty-year-old man at a Debs, he offered his services.

Collins: Well ... how are we going to go about it then?

Dev: Will you have a lemon daiquiri, Michael?

Collins: I will.

Dev advanced to the mini-bar and procured a shaker, into which he placed two fists of ice cubes. Expertly, he poured nine parts white Cuban rum, five parts of fresh lemon juice, three parts sugar syrup, a dash of angostura bitters and flaringly performed a theatrical shake before decanting the bitter amalgam into two cocktail glasses and garnishing with lemon zest and a maraschino cherry from a jar belonging to Erskine Childers.

Collins: Ah Dev, we'll never hear the fucking end of it if you go taking Erskine's cherries.

Dev: Tonight is an exception, Michael.

Collins: Well, then put my one back in the jar. I'll just have the lemon for garnish, no need for the cherry.

Dev: More for me.

De Valera greedily placed two maraschino cherries on the side of his daiquiri, with a flagrant disregard for Erskine's ration.

Dev: The daiquiri is a special drink, Michael. It comes from your ancestors who fought for the Mexicans against the Yanks in the 1840s.

Collins: Ah Dev, come on.

Dev: Hear me out, Michael. The sweet daiquiri was the only thing that cooled their lips in the hot adobe cottages of Santiago as Yankee cannonballs whirled overhead. Men with names like McCarthy and Scanlon. Meditate on that when you take the first swally of daiquiri.

Collins: I will, Dev.

Dev: And they were called gringos, the Irish soldiers who fought with the Mexicans. Do you know why they called them gringos?

Collins: Can we move on to the issue at hand please, Éamon?

De Valera stumbled forward and whispered the next phrase into Collins's tired face.

Dev: Because they were always singing, Mick. Singing 'Green Grow the Lilacs' when they were fighting that war. Fighting in white alkali desert flats scattered with beige cacti, and not a blade of grass to be seen for years. That song was their sad cry for Éireann. The Mexicans misheard it and thought they were saying 'griiingooos'. Ever since, it means foreigner over there. Say it with me, Michael.

Collins: Griiingooos.

Dev: Now have a drop.

Collins: Dev, can we get down to business please? Get your hands off my collar. We need a very serious discussion about how the mechanics of this operation will work, and I'll be honest, I'm very uncomfortable and a bit frightened. Fucking sit down opposite me there, and we'll plan this out.

Dev: Will I make a pair of dry martinis?

Collins: Nooo. Sit down ta fuck!

Dev fell back. Collins heard the familiar squelch of bare arse on leather and got a shudder of reality. As far as he knew, he was fully heterosexual and resolutely devoted to his girlfriend Kitty Kiernan. He'd had his knee-tremblers in Soho during his stint as a postal clerk, but other than that was quite inexperienced. He was also a Catholic, more out of duty than faith, but a follower of Rome nonetheless. He knew that relations between two men was a mortal sin, punishable by hell fire. But the occupation of Ireland by the Brits was a sin too. Who was he to measure up sins? Dev, on the other hand, was staunchly Catholic, at one point even considering the priesthood. Collins anxiously pondered how this situation was to sit in de Valera's moral lunchbox.

Collins: Coitus between two men is a sin, Dev.

Dev: Is killing not a sin, Michael? Have you not tugged the trigger on your Luger at many a Sassenach?

Collins: This is war, Dev. There's no sin in war.

Dev: Exactly, Michael. And you'll be fathering these children for the efforts of the war. They'll be more useful than ten thousand rifles, or a hundred bombs, or a thousand dead British soldiers.

Collins: Then I suppose, shouldn't we kiss first or do some goose-petting?

Michael Collins grappled the milky-white daiquiri in his paws and necked it back his craw. Aching for a vessel of more significant purchase, he sequestered the bottle of white rum and took a brutal command of several inordinate gulps to the disdain of de Valera, who urged him to at least take a squeeze of some class of citrus zest, out of respect for the candour of the neat spirit.

'Take off your top, Dev, for fuck sake,' ushered Michael, who had internally resolved the materiality of ensuing copulation by appropriating the hawkish zeal of a team captain at a county final. 'Tog off ta feck.'

Collins clapped his sweaty hands and paced aggressively, pausing at intervals to hop up and down on the spot as he removed his clothing and yelped. Then de Valera unbuttoned his white cotton band-collared shirt with his bony hands jittery from the drink. The room smelled like men. Azure moonlight trailed in to reveal a torso like a splatter of dog's vomit that a child had flicked old ha'pennies in, a pale sunken chest darted with malignant black moles and the occasional jutting rib.

Collins spat on the rug and eyed Dev up as he would the crossbar of a stolen bike. He launched forward and shouldered Dev as if they were competing for a high ball. Dev's much smaller frame battered off the wall behind him, the force of which disturbed a mounted portrait of Thomas MacDonagh. Grounded and staggery from daiquiris, Dev attempted to rappel himself up by the cord of the venetian blind. He swung pendulous like a frantic cat for a short moment, then tugged the blind loose from its fixture, down on top of him in a fierce loud crash of thin aluminium corrugates.

'Jaysus Christ, Dev, you'll alert a bailiff or a sergeant with the noise. Do you not know the G-men are always posted near?'

'Gin,' said de Valera, as he splayed on the floor naked in a metal venetian gown. Collins dutifully swiped a bottle of Cork Dry Gin, took a few gulps himself and poured a skinful down into de Valera's open mouth, which splashed off his protruding teeth. 'Waterboard me with gin, Michael,' pleaded Dev.

'I can't have you passing out either, Dev,' warned Collins. 'Turn over.'

De Valera rolled over so that he was belly-down on the corrugated aluminium blinds. Collins shook off his own slacks and removed his long johns. He dropped down over de Valera as if he was to perform one hundred press ups, his flaccid penis dangling like a greyhound's tail grazing up and down the crack of Dev's arse.

'Well, what now? Are you ready for it? You're the president,' said Michael.

'You'll have to kiss my neck or I won't be able to receive you,' said Dev.

Collins lowered his chest so that it was pressed against Dev's back. He obediently protruded the tip of his tongue and darted it all along the inside of de Valera's ear and hairline. Dev could smell the vinegar tang of his saliva and was becoming uncomfortable with the venetian blind sticking into his ribs. Collins, too, was deflated by the oily fortnight of human hair grease banging up his nostrils.

'Get up, this way isn't working for me,' said Dev.

Collins leapt to his feet and pulled Dev up by the hand. 'Well, it's not great for me either, Dev, to be honest, and plus, whatever about you getting relaxed, I'll need to get excited. So what are your thoughts there?'

'I'll have to take your prick in the gob. That's the most judicious approach. That might calm me down too, and we'll be off then,' said Éamon de Valera.

'Plan B so,' said Collins.

The two men moved the procedure to a sturdy writing desk situated near the mini-bar. Dev retrieved a small brown apothecary bottle of bergamot oil that he had been using to add body to single-malt whiskies and bourbons.

'Right, I'll commence a gobble. When you feel that you can keep your prick up, you rub a fist of this bergamot oil all over it, and then go straight up my hole when I turn around. Is the consecution of those constituents clear, Michael?'

''Tis, Dev.'

De Valera dropped to his knees, and took Michael Collins's floppy dick into his mouth. It was dry, warm and had a rubbery degree of stretch to it. He began rolling his tongue around the foreskin, which ushered into existence a slight promise of tumescence. Collins, with eyes closed, tried to imagine his days back in Soho, when he would get a two-bob gobble from East End girls behind the theatre with the smell of perfume and talcum rising up to meet his nose as their heads bobbed him to climax. His mind drifted, until he heard a muffled 'You're ready now' from Dev. Collins pulled out, and drenched his hands and penis in slick bergamot oil. The room began to smell very strongly of Earl Grey tea. De Valera stood up and climbed on the low writing desk, prone on all fours, with the cheeks of his arse spread as wide as possible.

'Now, get in now. Grab my lad while you ease in. Tug it like you're ringing the bell to stop the tram, about that speed. To dilate my hole.'

Collins obeyed instruction. Like stone penetrating cold wax, he forced his dick into Dev's arsehole.

'Aaargh, go handy, go handy!' screamed Dev.

'You'll have to just take it whatever way it comes, Éamon, I'm concentrating on staying hard,' said Mick.

'Throw the rest of the bergamot oil on it, loosen it up.'

Collins poured oil on the slow thrusting penis and his pelvis slapped against Dev's hoop like an open hand on the hide of a cow at mart.

Collins: Tell me I'm George V, Dev.

Dev: Wha?

Collins: Tell me I'm George V. And you're Her Highness Mary of Teck and you want me to fuck you. I'll lose my fucking horn if you don't, come on.

Dev: You're George V. Fuck me, Your Highness.

Collins: Tell me you're Mary of Teck.

Dev: I'm your devoted wife, Mary of Teck. Make shite of me.

Collins: I will. Tell me what you want me to do to Ireland. Tell me!

Dev: I want you to crush them, my powerful king. Crush the ungrateful Irish swine, Your Highness.

Collins: More.

Dev: Starve the people of Ireland, let their children die. Send in the soldiers to kill their leaders.

Collins: Who?

Dev: Michael Collins, George. Send the finest soldiers in the Empire to murder Michael Collins and drag his mutilated corpse through Sackville Street on horses, as a message to the Hindu and the Arab who'd dare to follow in his example.

Collins: Aaaaaaaaaaaaaaaaaaaarrrghhhh!

A dark presence descended upon the room, which seemed to strip it of air or smell or time. De Valera's rectum rejected Collins's penis as it began to close over completely. A deafening roar like a distant bell shook the parlour, and knocked all photographs of the Cairo gang off the wall where they were stuck. De Valera's torso lit up with an intense glow, as if he had swallowed the bulb off a lighthouse.

Dev: It's happening.

Collins: Is it working?

Dev: It's happening, Mick. It's the hand of Saint Berthold acting in vicarage of Our Lady's Immaculate Heart. The conception of my womb has begun. My arse-child pregnancy has started.

The room returned to normality. Both men sat sweaty and naked in the dark, with the overpowering stench of bergamot oil in the hot clammy sex air.

'I'll open the window,' said Collins, who lit up a Sweet Afton cigarette while looking out over a darkened Dawson Street with mixed emotions. He felt comfortable with having had sex with his good friend and president. It was a new experience, and had opened sexual horizons for him. However, his mind poked at the open sore that was his climactic vision of being King George V, raining down a fist of steel on the poor Irish people who Collins had worked so hard to liberate. Why did such a contradictory window of voyeuristic power excite him sexually in that way? Why had this part of him lain dormant for so long before emerging tonight? Why did he associate colonial brutality with heightened sexual arousal? He began to feel an empty loneliness, for having the burden of such internal revelation and also for being unable to express it to another soul, not even a priest in confession. He felt embarrassed for having discovered this fantasy in the presence of his comrade de Valera.

Dev: It's kicking already, Mick.

De Valera sat on the edge of the writing desk, wearing a shirt and holding his back.

Dev: Mick, I can feel it in my back. They've started to grow already. Make me a mai-tai.

Collins: What? Are you serious? Already?

Dev: It's a speedy womb I have, Mick. I'll be showing in the morning. With the help of God, I'll have a litter of about sixteen. That gives us a clear error of margin if one of the assassinations goes awry. Mai tais please, Michael, we need to celebrate.

Collins opened up the mini-bar. 'Dev, you're the man for the drinks. Can you not make it yourself?'

'I'm pregnant in a bad way, Mick. I'll tell you the recipe. Reach up there to the cupboard and fetch those two tiki glasses, they're the brown ceramic ones with the design,' said Dev.

Collins fetched both vessels, which had a type of Polynesian or Maori design on them, almost like the sculptures of the giant heads on Easter Island.

'We'll do a poor man's version, Mick, you wouldn't have the skill for the shaker. Half the juice of a lime into each glass. Teaspoon of the almond orgeat syrup, then two shots of the white rum.' Collins followed Dev's instructions to a tee. 'Now, this bit is important. Lob in a teaspoon of the demerara sugar into each glass, give a small stir and fill up three quarters ways with the crushed ice.'

'Alright, is that looking OK?' said Collins.

''Tis. Now, last bit. A dash of the blue curaçao, it's the orange-smelling stuff. And on top of all that, a nice generous slurp of that dark Jamaican rum. A straw in each, a slice of pineapple, and a few of Erskine's cherries,' Dev said with a cheeky wink.

'Ah Jaysus, Dev, not Erskine's cherries again. He'll box you into the face,' Michael scolded at his president.

'He wouldn't hit a pregnant man, Mick. Not even Childers would chance that.' Both men laughed and sipped their mai tais.

Collins: So, how is this going to pan out, Dev?

Dev: Over the next few days, I'll grow bigger and bigger as the arse children develop. I'll start to grow a bump on my back and will only be able to situate myself on all fours. As you saw, my anus has closed up completely. It will remain like that for the next week, so a liquid diet is essential. I suggest daiquiris, White Russians, negronis and the odd old-fashioned to balance it out.'

Collins: I'm not complaining Dev, but that's a full-on job. Could we not get a few of the men to chip in?

Dev: No, Michael. The men must never ever find out. This is an immaculate conception. It's like quantum mechanics. Have you heard of that? It means the incubation can only exist when it's not being observed by an unfaithful party. It is imperative that only you and I stay in this room for the week. No one must find out about any of this.

Collins: What will I tell the men?

Dev: I'll instruct the Dáil to take a week off. You'll tell the squad to prepare for assassinations as normal. They'll all just think the two of us are preparing to take out the Cairo gang and sorting logistics. It will be grand. I'll need you here, Mick. We can communicate to the outside world with the telegraph. This is our bunker for the coming days.

Collins raised his palm towards his face and moved it in a wiping motion from his nose to his chin repeatedly in internal disquiet. He was impressed with the level of foresight and planning that Dev had envisaged for the birth of the arse children, but sure then again he'd been preparing for this day for many years.

Dev: What is it, Michael? You're looking a bit shook.

Collins: I said some stuff, Dev, while we were conceiving. I said some stuff about King George V, about wanting to be him and to crush our countrymen.

Dev: And I played along, and pretended I was the queen. So what?

Collins: It frightened me. It frightened me to have gotten such sexual pleasure off that roleplay. It frightened me that I had that inside myself.

Dev: Have you ever heard of a man called Freud, Michael?

Collins: I haven't made his acquaintance, no.

Dev: He's an Austrian man. A psychologist, no less. I've read his work in journals. He has very interesting things to say about sex. He says we all have these deep dark urges for murder and riding, and that we keep them locked down, because they are too frightening for us to think about. That, if we could think about them, we'd go stone mad, so they find other avenues to express themselves that are more acceptable to us.

Collins: How does that explain my urges though, Éamon?

Dev: Well, Mr Freud reckons that the desire to kill and the desire to have sex are very closely linked in our minds. It wouldn't surprise me at all that a great leader and patriot such as yourself would get sexually aroused by the potential for absolute power. There's an eroticism to the control one would have in that situation.

Collins: But I wanted to destroy my own people, Dev. I wanted to be an arrogant bastard of a king.

Dev: Mick, I would imagine that your repressed desire to murder your countrymen has sublimated itself into an organised passion for destroying the colonial powers of the British Empire, as a defence mechanism. That would be my verdict on the issue, based on the work of Mr Freud.

Collins: But does that make it right?

Dev: When Ireland is a free country, then it will be right. And damn any man who says otherwise.

Collins: Sure fuck it, Dev. Here's me thinking I'm a freak and you sitting there with arse children growing out of a womb in your bowels. You're correct as usual.

Dev: Get up the yard ta feck.

That night the two men fell asleep in the offices of Dáil Éireann in the Mansion House of Dawson Street. Collins experienced very intense and strange dreams as a result of uncovering hidden and threatening material from his sexually repressed unconscious mind. He awoke with a splitting cocktail headache and the morning sun stinging his eyes. In his ear he heard very heavy breathing. As he looked up, de Valera was laying on his side with a tumour of roughly two metres protruding from his lower back, which was veiny and translucent. As he inspected closer, he could make out tiny shapes like pupae, their little veins and beating hearts. These were the arse children. De Valera's face was strained and red as he attempted to puff out words.

Dev: Vermouth.

Collins: Hold on.

Dev: Vermouth.

Collins fixed a glass of French vermouth, which he poured into Dev's mouth. Dev's back pulsated ecstatically as the alcohol flowed around the spine-sack and into the arse children.

There was a knock on the door. It was Cathal Brugha. 'I've a dispatch for you, General Collins.'

'Not now, Cathal, myself and Dev have important business here. Go home for the day,' said General Collins.

'But Mick, it's about the movements of the Cairo gang,' Brugha exclaimed.

'Go home for fuck sake, and await our next orders, Cathal. We have it under control in here. Tell the squad to stay away from Dáil Éireann unless there's news of a raid by Dublin Castle.'

'Will do, Mick,' said Brugha as he descended the staircase and left through the front door.

Collins: Dev, if your back is the size of a sow after one night, what will you be like after a week?

Dev: Brandy or port please, Mick.

As the week passed, the pregnant tumour on Dev's back grew to be several metres long. By day five, it was the length of three men, and two metres wide. De Valera's fragile body was merely a brittle appendage on one end of a bulbous translucent sausage-like mass. The arse children began to take shape, and had little scrunched faces and black eyes as they kicked and grabbed at the skin of their gigantic womb. When one moved, the rest would follow and the whole addendum would undulate like a sick lung. This would cause de Valera to groan in intense agony, and acidic green bile would trail out his mouth as his internal organs pressed against his rib-cage. It was upsetting for Michael to watch this happen to his dear friend. Collins began to cover the appendage in warm wet cotton towels, as this kept the arse children docile.

As acting Minister for Finance as well as General of the IRA, Collins was growing concerned with the amount of Ireland's petty cash that he was spending on liquor and cocktail ingredients, which were delivered every evening by van. New bottles of spirits arrived in crates at the back door of the Mansion House, where the previous night's empty bottles were left for collection. The arse children had inherited de Valera's appetite for tiki cocktails. Collins had developed significant skill in churning out several mai tais and Singapore slings at a time. Éamon's face was frozen in petrified misery as Collins poured drink after drink of sweet alcoholic mixtures into his mouth to satiate the pangs of the shit litter. The room also smelled very strongly of faeces. Dev's rectum had closed up at conception and would not open again until the moment of birth, resulting in a backlog of excrement that acted as an amniotic fluid. It did, however, leak into de Valera's bloodstream, where it was expelled as breath and sweat that smelled like an open sewer.

By day seven of gestation, what was left of Éamon de Valera was merely a solitary face protruding from a pulsating mass of thin flesh that had taken up 80% of the boardroom. Collins had come to realise that the pregnancy was going to most definitely kill Dev if it was allowed to go on one more day. He recognised that these arse children were a parasite, who would likely feed upon de Valera when born, like the offspring of spiders. He searched the mass of skin for his friend's face, which was now just an unfamiliar arrangement of mouth and pupils in a wall of flesh.

Collins: I can't watch you like this, Dev. This is killing you.

Dev: *muffled wheezing groans*

Collins: I'm cutting them out to save you, Dev. I don't give a feck. It's you or those children. And I'm choosing you, if giving birth to them means you dying.

Dev: Nooo.

Collins: I'm doing it, Dev, I'll take a blade to them.

Dev: No ... you ... must never abort ... Ireland will not succeed without these children. Let me die.

Collins: I can't, Dev, I'm cutting them out.

Dev: If you cut them out prematurely, they will die, Michael, and all is for nothing. I must die for them to be born. I kept this from you, as I knew you would not cooperate. Let me go, for Ireland.

Collins burst into uncontrollable tears at the agony his companion was experiencing.

Dev: Do not cry. Michael ... these children will save our nation. Let me go.

Collins raised his hand to his forehead and saluted his president for the last time as life slipped from de Valera's open eyes. The twiggy remnants of his hands and legs went limp and floundered. At that, the appendage thrashed and bounced as the rectum at the end burst open with a flurry of slurry that spilled on to the carpet. Collins pulled the sleeves of his shirt up to his elbows and proceeded to deliver the arse children at the request of his dearly departed friend and ally. One by one they burst forth, and started to gorge on the shit and skin of de Valera's fifteen-metre stretched body. Each arse child was roughly two foot in height. They were round, like Gaelic footballs, with skin like dry cured pork. They had tiny legs no bigger than carrot stumps and full-sized human hands. Their scrunchy faces bore an uncanny likeness to both Collins and de Valera. They waddled around the room, not forming words or even vowels but bleating melodic noises that sounded like West Cork accents as heard through a locked door. There were twelve in total, slightly less than Dev had hoped for, one to perform the duties of every member of the squad.

That night, as Collins fed them all drink, he showed them the addresses and photographs of the members of the Cairo gang. They seemed to have a sense of deep understanding and determination about these instructions, and were quite clearly natural-born killers in every sense of the phrase. They swarmed around the room in geometric formations, and communicated positions and instructions to each other. Only a few hours old, they were behaving like commandos who were highly experienced in all areas of military and counter-insurgency tactics. Collins began to feel less heartbroken about de Valera's death, as he realised that it was steeped in purpose and meaning. He was sure that the arse children would complete their mission with brutal efficiency. Collins issued dispatches to every member of his squad, which detailed the cancellation of the following day's planned assassinations of the Cairo gang. The squad were to remain in allocated safe houses, with nobody, not even their wives or families, to know of their whereabouts.

The next morning at 6.30 a.m., the arse children were fitted out in the dog pelts that Dev had prepared, tailored and left in the attic of the Dáil. Colt M1903 hammerless pistols were placed in each of their hands and hidden under their pelts. What looked like a pack of wild terriers left the door of Dawson Street to let a river of blood flow through the cobbles of Dublin city on the morning of 21 November 1920. Michael paced around the empty boardroom, and retrieved de Valera's flattened and rubber-like face that he had saved from the hungry mouths of the arse children. He took his old friend's remains to the back garden of the Mansion House, wrapped them in de Valera's Carmelite robes and said a short prayer to Saint Berthold before issuing an unmarked burial.

As afternoon commenced, the news of the assassinations travelled quickly around the Empire. They had shaken the Brits to their very core. The British were unable to fathom how the IRA had not only identified their crack team of Cairo gang members, but killed every one of them in their homes in the space of one morning. In an act of cowardly brutality, the British took their revenge out on civilians. At 3.15 p.m., Dublin and Tipperary were due to commence the All-Ireland Gaelic football final in Croke Park before an audience of 5,000 spectators. A convoy of armoured Black and Tans entered the pitch and murdered fourteen civilians and injured 70.

In the pubs of Dublin, whispers celebrated the brave men of Michael Collins's squad who had taken out the Cairo gang as glasses were raised. Men like Charlie Dalton, Sean Healy, James Conroy and Stephen Behan were toasted as heroes. Songs were sung for the twelve apostles. Collins later told the squad that the real assassins had been a team of American Fenians sourced during de Valera's last US fundraising tour, men well accustomed to the bloodshed of New York gang life. The squad were to keep this information private in exchange for handsome pensions and secure civil service jobs upon the establishment of the Irish Republic.

The arse children returned to Collins that night, their eyes blood-mad from the English lives they had taken. Collins, extremely wary that their existence would be too strange a burden for Ireland and even the world to accept, made a swift decision. After they'd handed back their weaponry and drank celebratory rounds of mojitos, he personally shot each and every one of them. He burned their little rotund bodies to ashes in the back of the Mansion House, where no one would ever discover the dark cosmic secret that he and de Valera had shared. Except for one man.

Steven Fagan was a tall and skinny character from the Liberties, a quiet and insignificant volunteer who bore an uncanny resemblance to Éamon de Valera. Collins approached Fagan due to his appearance and informed him that Dev had accidentally shot himself with a pistol, but that his death could not be revealed as it would be too damaging for IRA morale. Collins offered Fagan a deal. Collins would hide the death of the real Éamon de Valera, while Fagan would attend O'Leary's pub on Abbey Street that night, and inform all friends and family that he was leaving for Australia the next morning to pursue a vocation in haberdashery. He would then assume the identity, accent and mannerisms of Éamon de Valera, with which would come an everlasting power over Ireland.

Fagan and Collins started off to a strained relationship, as Fagan did not possess any of the welcoming traits of de Valera. Collins, in a state of mourning for his friend, would often attempt to prepare mai tais and caipirinhas for Fagan, who would rudely decline as he was a staunch tee-totaller and control freak. Fagan was of little use as a leader or president and took a puppet role, with Collins controlling almost entirely the orchestration of the ongoing war against the British. They grew further apart, with Fagan becoming quite comfortable in the role of Éamon de Valera and the trappings of power that attached the role. He had, to all purposes, become Dev in his head too, often walking past the old streets of the Liberties where he had been born with no sense of familiarity or recollection of his childhood or family. He had repressed the identity of Steven Fagan to his unconscious mind and completely forgotten that he was anyone other than Éamon de Valera, born George de Valero to Catherine Coll of Limerick in New Jersey, 1882, a phrase Fagan would replay in his mind perpetually. This was who he was now. However, this unconscious repression self-sublimated its energy into an irrational and bitter hatred for Michael Collins. Fagan was unaware that this loathing was because Collins was the only man who knew his true identity; it simply presented itself as an intense anger whenever Collins was present or even mentioned in conversation. Fagan began to plot and connive the demise of Collins.

The weeks passed and in July of 1921, eight months after Fagan became de Valera, a truce was agreed between the Irish Government and the forces of the British Crown. Collins knew that this transpired because of the assassinations of the Cairo gang at the hands of his and Éamon's arse children. He pined for his friend, imagining his joyous reaction to the news of the war's end. But Fagan had other plans. In October 1921, British Prime Minister Lloyd George called for the negotiation of a treaty between Ireland and Britain. Fagan, having listened to the members of Dáil Éireann, knew this treaty was a poisoned chalice because the British had recently partitioned the uppermost region of the country into Northern Ireland. A united independent Ireland was not going to be negotiable. 'De Valera' was invited to attend the treaty negotiation in London, but instead chose to send Michael Collins as his representative.

Collins returned to Dublin having agreed to the establishment of the Irish Free State, an independent dominion under Britain with the king as its head. Worse, Collins, as predicted by Fagan, had failed to secure the freedom of the north of the country, which would remain under full British control. This caused uproar around Ireland. Collins was demonised by half his men in the IRA. Fagan as de Valera took the opportunity to break with the treaty, and a bloody civil war began, pitting brother against brother, Fagan against Collins. The civil conflict ravaged Ireland for several months.

On 22 August 1922, Michael Collins was visiting his home county of West Cork to inspect recently conquered territory. He believed himself to be off-limits for assassination in his homeland. It would have been unthinkably disrespectful to bring harm to him in Cork, even for an anti-treaty enemy. He was still the great Michael Collins who brought the British to their knees. 'De Valera' had found his moment, having heard unconfirmed rumours that men close to Collins were referring to him as Fagan the Changeling. Michael Collins was shot in an ambush on the orders of Fagan that day, and Ireland's heart dropped into its mouth.

The sad and brutal death of Collins brought a swift end to the civil war. Fagan did not care for Free State or Republic, and his secret had died with Michael Collins. He was now free to spend the rest of his life as Éamon de Valera. He founded the Fianna Fáil political party, and spent long hours poring over the personal diaries of the real de Valera, which had been kept in a safe in the attic of the Mansion House. These diaries contained musings on Dev's political leanings, his plans for a republic and his opinions on the Catholic faith in accordance with his time at the Carmelite Order. One such diary was dedicated solely to very specific instructions around pregnancy, birth and abortion.

It outlined the miracle of conception as the personal cosmic intervention of Our Lady. It outlined explicitly that abortion was to never be carried out, even if the life of the mother was at risk, that the survival of the child was to be the only factor to consider. What Fagan did not realise was that he was reading coded instructions for the birth of the immaculate arse children. De Valera had prepared these instructions for Collins, in the event that the arse pregnancy had rendered him completely unable to speak. 'De Valera' went on to write the Constitution of the Irish Republic in 1937.

*

This body of text was published on a Facebook page named *Hidden Irish History* on 5 May 2018. There were no other posts on the page, no link to a website or even a contact email, only this single piece, which claimed to be based on leaked documents retrieved from under the floorboards of a house on Merrion Square during its conversion into a mobile phone shop. A user called Gerry Parch, with no profile photo, began to link said article into the comments sections of many popular Facebook pages in Ireland, such as *The Irish Times*, the *Irish Independent*, *TheJournal.ie*, *Joe.ie*, as well as the official pages of the major political parties in the country, Fine Gael, Fianna Fáil and Sinn Féin. It slowly began to gain traction as it was spread around Irish social media.

The comments under the article were a plethora of the type of blind fury commonly associated with online discourse. Facebook user Enda Gibson, whose profile photo was of two Alsatians lying in the garden of a bungalow, wrote, 'Utter Disgrace, Taking the names of Michael Collins and Eamon Devalera like dat. What sicko wrote dis filth? Utter Disgrace. Collins is the greatest man that Ireland ever saw, he was not a FAGGOT. Digrace. What braindad moron wroye dis? They need to be shot.' This comment received 278 likes from people who staunchly agreed with its sentiment, with many responding to Enda's comment with 'Well said *clapping emoji*', while some tagged friends and family.

Other comments included a contribution from a Mary Berkerey, mid-fifties with a profile photo depicting her enjoying wine on a recent trip to Greece: 'Disrespectful. Disgrace. Show your face whoever wrote this. Cowards.' 60 likes.

Síofra Condon, 21, with a Repeal the Eighth logo on her profile, wrote, 'Shocking portrayal of LGBQT sexual relationships. THIS IS NOT OK. Please delete this hate speech. I am reporting this trash, it needs to be removed from Facebook. This is an ignorant and harmful portrayal of queer relationships, and trivialises issues facing Irish women. It reduces both queer sexual politics and women's bodies down to a servile anecdote. This is HARMFUL.' 176 likes.

An account named ShitLord Uprising with a profile photo of Pepe the Frog wearing a red 'Make America Great Again' cap retorted underneath Síofra's comment with 'STFU you fucking Feminazi baby killer slut'. 96 likes.

Guff Sweeney wrote: 'Dudes, I'm a pro mixologist. This is fake AF. No one drank mai tais in the 1920s, those drinks come from Tiki culture, which was a pretty cool movement in mixology that happened in the States post WW2. US soldiers (rather racially and colonially, I might add) used to long for the drinks they tasted during their time posted in Polynesia, so Tiki culture was born in the form of mai tais, and hula skirts etc. Alongside some pretty rad Afro Cuban jazz by Martin Denny and Arthur Lyman.' 0 likes. One user wrote 'Pretentious cunt, and your tattoos are shit' under this comment.

Peter Clarke, 28, UCC graduate, wrote: 'How grown up. Nice try at being edgy. Whatever apeshit wrote this hasn't a fucking clue about Irish history either and clearly took their only inspiration from the film *Michael Collins*, which is itself rife with inaccuracies. Also, Glimmermen were NOT a thing in 1920. Read a fucking book for Christ sake.' 228 likes.

A contribution that received 56 likes under Peter's comment came from a Fiona Ward, who stated, 'I agree Peter. Shocking recollection of history on display here, clearly the work of a troll who's looking for attention. I'd nearly give them points for imagination if it wasn't for the colossal inaccuracies. In particular the conversation between de Valera and Collins about the caipirinha re slavery. The Irish were never slaves in the Barbados. It is true that many Irish were sent to plantations by Cromwell in the 1600s alongside African slaves. However, the Irish were indentured servants, not chattel slaves. The Irish could work for their freedom and be free, the African chattel slave could not. This "essay" perpetuates that shitty myth and is pretty irresponsible.'

Peter replied 'I know Fiona. WTF? And the bit about gringos? I've never even heard that, think he made it up lol. Btw you interested in seventeenth-century history of the Irish diaspora? Had a look at your profile and it said you did History in Maynooth? I bet you know my friend Gav. Will you add me for DM? ;)' Fiona did not respond to this.

Bernard Dundon wrote, 'Why are we calling this an essay? It's clearly written like fiction? If I was handed this by a student as an essay, I'd ask for a rewrite. Can we call it what is please?' 34 likes.

Other comments simply expressed that the piece of writing was hugely offensive, and had gone too far, in particular the manner in which it portrayed the Irish heroes de Valera and Collins having sex with each other. A number were similarly offended on religious grounds, and the manner in which it detailed immaculate conception, a common response being 'Let's see you write this about Islam. No didn't think so. Fucking coward.'

Some comments were in support. Sennan Fogarty wrote, 'Guys, clearly satire relax' (57 likes), and Jordan Dunleavey wrote, 'Wow, maybe this is fucking real? I don't know about you sheeple, but I'm keeping an open mind. Read up on the Rothschilds and the shit they get up to. Looks like de Valera and Collins were into some serious Satanic shit, and this here is the proof staring us in the eyes' (275 likes).

The text became known by the abbreviation *HIH*, and the intense Facebook arguments around it eventually found their way into the headlines of clickbait sites and the Sunday tabloid newspapers. 'This Facebook post is dividing Ireland – you won't believe what it says,' wrote *Joe.ie* who chose to have this particular article sponsored by Wilkinson Sword razors. '50 SHADES OF DEV. DISGRACEFUL COLLINS PORN ANGERS IRELAND', read the front page of *The Sun* newspaper. 'Ireland needs to lighten up about *HIH*,' wrote Oliver Callan in the *Irish Independent*. 'Unpacking the problematic nature of *HIH*' was the headline that was chosen for Aoife McGarry's opinion piece in *The Irish Times*. 'Casement was gay – why can't Collins be?' exclaimed an article on *TheJournal.ie* that received several shares; however, this particular article managed to offend some Facebook users who pointed out that the relations between de Valera and Collins in the story were more a portrayal of sexual fluidity rather than homosexuality.

The bottom line of the scandal was that the vast majority of Irish people were not at all comfortable with the masculine founding fathers of their republic being portrayed as anything other than straight, powerful, Catholic men who did not even engage in sex, let alone have same-sex relations. Soon the zeitgeist in Irish public life demanded that the author of the controversial post identify themselves and come forward. The Catholic lobbying group The Knights of St Vitus in the Immaculate Partition were the first to call for this, and began to enquire as to the legal possibilities of prosecuting the author under Ireland's blasphemy law, which Éamon de Valera himself had written into Ireland's constitution in 1937, an anomaly by western democratic standards. The law states that a person can be guilty of blasphemy if an action they take is deemed to be offensive to the core teachings of a religion and causes offence among a significant amount of people in that religion. The *Hidden Irish History* article most certainly fell into this category, for its description of Carmelite black magic and the immaculate conception of de Valera's womb via Holy Mary. The blasphemy law, however, is not applicable to works of art or fiction, but the author who wrote *HIH* presented it as an actual historical account by posting it under the title *Hidden Irish History* and giving the back-story of its discovery. Its explicit intention was to exist as a historical document. Darren Quinlavan and the The Knights of St Vitus in the Immaculate Partition lawyers complained to the gardaí, who obtained a warrant for the author's arrest. He was now wanted by the gardaí. TKOSVITIP had achieved support from the Irish public in this venture, which shocked the unpopular organisation, as Ireland, a modern liberal country, had grown to distance itself from Catholicism due to historical clerical sex abuse.

Users of the forum Reddit volunteered their services in unearthing the identity of the *HIH* author. They did this by discovering that the email address cuntypops654@gmail.com was used to register the Gerry Parch Facebook account that originally shared the *Hidden Irish History* page. One Reddit user who worked in Amazon.com anonymously broke protocol by searching for this email in the customer database and found the email had been used to order a lava lamp to an address in Ranelagh in the south of Dublin city. Soon the address was posted on Reddit. Within hours users had identified a man living at the address as a Donal Prendergast and had obtained photographs of the man from his LinkedIn page.

Donal Prendergast, 24, skinny with a short red beard, paced around the cramped granny-flat in the bottom floor of his parents' house in Charleston Road, Ranelagh. He had been awarded a UCD arts degree the previous June, and was struggling to find direction in his life. His parents urged him to pursue a postgrad qualification so that he could become a primary school teacher. Donal was confident that this option would constitute a personal failure. He wanted desperately to become a writer. Donal's father, Brendan, was a retired barrister who had recently been diagnosed with multiple sclerosis. His mother had been smoking since she was twelve. Donal sometimes fantasised about his mother dying and he becoming his father's full-time carer, with the family home over his head and claiming a carer's allowance as his income. Such thoughts occasioned him to feel anxiety and shame, which culminated in bouts of depression, soon followed by enthusiastic periods of mania where he would engage in risky and unmeasured behaviour. His counsellor was unsure if he was suffering from bipolar disorder or struggling from mental health problems brought on by existential crisis.

Having sent the manuscript for his first novel to several publishing houses, he was devastated when it was outright rejected by all. Donal was unwilling to self-publish online as he considered this option the avenue of losers. *Puddle Dungeon* was an 80,000-word thriller about a dystopian future where a lake in Drogheda becomes sentient and sits the Leaving Cert. Angered by the rejection of *Puddle Dungeon*, Donal was thrown into a dark depression, and he pursued an unsuccessful attempt at ending his life. The failure of this attempt lead to a period of mania, during which he wrote the *Hidden Irish History* piece as a deliberate anonymous viral stunt. He had hoped this work of historical fiction would bring his work to the attention of the Irish public and subsequently get him a book deal as a result of the controversy. However, he did not expect the story to offend as many people as it did. He fully intended for it to be controversial, but failed to predict that it would illicit such fury, especially in light of the 2015 marriage equality referendum. The Irish public's acceptance of queer relationships did not extend as far as its founding fathers.

At first he enjoyed the rush of watching his art anger the people who read it. But when this anger called for his painful and slow death, he became reluctant to reveal his identity to the public. On the walls of Donal's apartment hung many detailed and expertly drawn illustrations of Michael Collins and de Valera having sex, alongside other inflammatory scenarios concerning figures from Irish Republicanism and religious deities. He was a talented draughtsman and illustrator. It was his intention to upload these drawings to the *Hidden Irish History* Facebook page, as a means of drip-feeding that the story was a hoax, a plan he had now abandoned. He sat upright and attentive in his swivel-chair, iPad in hand, while his heart thumped out red blood and adrenaline around his limbs and his stomach knotted to a tight ball of queasiness. He watched as the Reddit forum revealed his identity, his personal details and the location of his house. As he froze, silent and numb, his phone started to vibrate incessantly as hundreds of numbers began to text threatening messages to him. Before he could reach his phone to inspect, the onslaught caused the device to freeze completely. Donal bolted up the stairs to the kitchen where his elderly parents were listening to the radio.

'Get out, please go out. I've done something really stupid and I need you to leave.'

His tired parents, familiar with his manic behaviour but unaware of his previous suicide attempt, obliged and took the car out to Dalkey for an evening walk. Frantic and anxious, Donal knew he wasn't safe. His thoughts raced with possible shameful scenarios where he would be exposed or publicly humiliated. He saw his face on the front page of newspapers, he saw his old school-friends reading the front page of those newspapers and calling him a freak or a failure. This flurry of anxiety coupled with his otherwise manic behaviour led him to conclude that he must end his life as soon as possible.

News of Donal's identity soon spread from Reddit to Facebook, with many taking it upon themselves to express the intention of venturing to his house in Ranelagh to enact vigilante justice. An Garda Síochána urged people to stay away from the Ranelagh house, as an arrest was imminent. Conservative Darren Quinlavan, leader of The Knights of St Vitus in the Immaculate Partition, quickly organised a procession of Our Lady to attend this arrest. Liberal, feminist, LGBQT journalist Aoife McGarry of *The Irish Times* privately expressed her intention to travel to Ranelagh to observe the arrest, to ensure that the issue wasn't hijacked by the Catholic lobbyists and to act as a watchdog over any potential Garda violence. Sinn Féin leader Garry Fallon, deeply offended as an Irish republican by the portrayal of Collins and de Valera, expressed his intention on Twitter to attend the arrest, to ensure it was dealt with 'legally and in a civil fashion', but mainly as an act of political point-scoring and to lead by example in an issue that angered but united many Republicans.

By 8.24 p.m., what should have been a minor arrest involving one squad car had become a large operation involving over fifty members of An Garda Síochána, primarily to manage the massive crowd that had descended upon Ranelagh to catch a glimpse of the *Hidden Irish History* writer. Any attempt at a barricade was unsuccessful and by 8.30 p.m., Charleston Road was a mass of people, flashing blue lights, rainbow flags, Irish flags and an effigy of Our Lady with candles carried aloft by single middle-aged men and followed by elderly women clutching rosary beads. Donal's house was number 46, three storeys high, with magnificent red brick and Georgian windows. The extensive driveway was covered in small pebbles that scrunched audibly under the feet of the chattering masses. Leading up to the great red door with an ornate brass knocker was a flight of concrete stairs. Situated at the top was Sergeant Ambrose Houlihan, six foot three, with the build of an ex-hurler, his fluorescent jacket creating strobing issues on the camera screens of the hundreds who held their phones up to record and livestream the arrest of Donal Prendergast.

'Ye're to stand back, and let the members of the force handle this. Any fuck-acting and ye'll be dealt with,' he shouted at the crowd.

ARSE CHILDREN

'I'm knocking the little prick out,' burped a man from the back, which received a cheer.

'He insulted Our Lady, he's the divil. He should be dragged out here and gutted like a lamb and offered to the Immaculate Heart,' screamed an elderly lady with a Kerry accent. This exclamation received a combination of support and jeers.

'He's a disgrace, Collins would have him shot if he was still alive,' said a strong Dublin accent. This received the loudest cheer.

The situation was beginning to get out of hand and the gardaí feared that they would be unable to prevent any potential violence. Sinn Féin leader Garry Fallon pushed through the crowd, to the foot of the steps. Phones recorded as Fallon whispered into the ear of a deputy, who passed his message to Sergeant Houlihan. Soon Fallon joined Houlihan on the top step.

'I'm appealing for calm,' said Fallon in a thick Belfast accent, which garnered a cheer from republican elements present.

Aoife McGarry soon repeated Fallon's actions, and joined him on the steps, gaining support from the LGBQT and liberal members of the mob. Finally, Darren Quinlavan, feeling left out, joined all three on the top step of 46 Charleston Road, which garnered a hushed mumble from the Catholics present.

Sergeant Houlihan boomed out, 'I can appreciate that everyone here is feeling quite emotional, but Mr Fallon, Ms McGarry and Mr Quinlavan have offered their support in ensuring the gardaí can carry out the arrest properly. All four of us will enter the premises and conduct the detainment.'

This was met with a sobering lull of rational support from the crowd, motivated by an unconscious collective relief. Despite the anger, no one in the mob was truly prepared to act violently towards the young man behind the red door; it was mostly just emotional posturing.

Donal cowered in a small space underneath the staircase of the large hallway. His face was bright red and puffy as he listened to everything that was going on outside his house. The chants of 'Get him out, get him out, get him out,' were his mother's loud pounding heart in the minutes before the dreadful hysteria of birth. His mind drifted back to childhood, when his parents would take him for walks out in Wicklow and to the intense comfort and safety he would feel when his ma would press his forehead into her stomach and he would feel the warmth of her body and smell the washing detergent of her jacket, while his dad took photos of flowers and trees close by. He wanted to be back there. As he hugged his knees to his chest, he murmured, 'Mummy, help, please,' through gasps of agitated tears. He looked up at the noose he had prepared for himself with electrical cord that dangled from the rafter. He got up, and placed his head in it. His thoughts became regretful. He wished it hadn't come to this. His mind said, 'I would have copped on, I would have applied for that postgrad in teacher training, and now it's all going to be gone.' He swung forward from the pile of magazines he stood on as the electrical cord strangled his neck.

At that moment, Sergeant Houlihan kicked the door in, followed by Fallon, McGarry and Quinlavan. Houlihan, an experienced guard, had anticipated that the culprit might attempt to take his life and immediately spotted the open door of understair space in the hallway. Reacting autonomously, he bounded for the alcove, and wrapped his arms around young Donal's swinging body to relieve pressure on the neck.

'Help,' the sergeant yelped, as Aoife McGarry began to detach the electrical cord from around the rafters. Donal, whose face was now blue, opened his eyes to the silhouettes of four figures looming above him. Four figures who had saved his life. Fallon and Quinlavan felt a wave of compassion flow over their bodies, as they looked down at the young 24-year-old man who had just attempted to end his life due to his fear of their fury. So did Sergeant Houlihan and McGarry.

'You're some fucking eejit, youngfella,' said the sergeant, as he reached to his side to retrieve his handcuffs.

'Wait,' said McGarry. 'The poor man can barely breathe, Sergeant. Can we not hold off on this shit and make sure he's safe first?' The sergeant, looking embarrassed, put his handcuffs back into his pocket.

'I'll go and throw on a kettle,' said Quinlavan, gesturing towards the kitchen.

'I'll help with that,' said Fallon.

The sergeant spoke into the radio that was on his collar. 'Pádraig, we have the suspect apprehended. We'll need an ambulance, I'd say. Give us about fifteen minutes in here and calm down the crowd, over.'

Every member of the party sat down at the kitchen table, where Fallon and Quinlavan had prepared a pot of tea and Mikado biscuits.

Sergeant Houlihan: You've upset a lot of people, lad. You've caused a lot of hurt.

Aoife McGarry: But it's just a stupid blasphemy law. Your parents look like the type that could afford to pay it. That's no reason to end it, dude. Just give a public apology, it will blow over.

Garry Fallon: Aye, Aoife's correct. I know some people who can give you help too. Good counsellors. I'll see to it myself.

Darren Quinlavan: You're a young man. You have a full life ahead of you. I'll even make a case for you, for our followers to forgive you. But you must take the hit on the blasphemy law. And as Aoife said, it's just a fine, and no judge would prosecute anyway, they'll throw it out.

Garry Fallon: I think I speak for all of us when I say that we overreacted. You attacked ideas. History is only an idea, you're entitled to artistic freedom.

Sergeant Houlihan: We'll have to head outside now, there's an ambulance waiting, nice and close to the door. I'll give you my jacket to put over your head, and keep you safe, lad, no one will see you.

Donal was in intense shock and stared blank with a tired white face. He was incredibly shaken by the events, and just wanted to rest. Behind the shock was a distant wave of relief. A relief that he would see his parents again, a relief that he could have a think about where to go with his life when this was all over. Sergeant Houlihan conducted a brisk inspection of the kitchen and hallway. He was sensitive to Donal's current mental state and did not want to bring him through the hallway, feeling that seeing the area under the stairs where he'd attempted to end his life would be too traumatic. The sergeant noticed a door at the back of the kitchen beside the Aga cooker that led down to the granny-flat below. He ushered everyone to exit through this door and leave the house via the downstairs side entrance. All five descended the narrow stairs as they entered the small granny-flat where Donal spent most of his time.

As they walked through, the procession stopped abruptly.

'What the fuck?' said Garry Fallon.

Donal stared at the ground, as the rest slowly performed 360-degree turns while gazing open-mouthed at the drawings on the wall. What they saw were the blueprints for what was to be further instalments in the *Hidden Irish History* saga. There was a detailed line-drawing of Éamon de Valera doing cocaine from Michael Collins's face while an erect James Connolly inserted the greased-up end of an Armalite rifle down his urethra. Another image portrayed Holy Mary draped in a British flag shouting 'fuck Spaniards', and in the distance was John the Baptist, crying while receiving a Chinese burn from Wolfe Tone, with 'IRA' carved into his chest and bullet-holes in his knees. The largest image was an expansive projection of the GPO during the 1916 Rising, with hundreds of bare-chested volunteers showering in fluid from a gigantic penis that hung from the clouds, beside which was written 'Gods stupid dick lol' with an arrow pointing at it.

The sergeant, McGarry, Fallon and Quinlavan all searched each other's expressions with the same look of intense and furious shock. They turned to Donal, who kept his eyes focused on the ground as he very quietly said, 'At least I didn't draw anything about blacks or Islam.'

They could hear the baying crowds chant, a beat with a terrifying muffled rhythm: 'Get him out'. The passion of their offence and the energy of the outside mob took command of their hot foreheads. Simultaneously, the four grasped at Donal's body with all their strength and began tearing at his clothes and flesh, ripping pieces off as blood flowed. Uncertain of the reasons for their actions, each was unified in the druggy inebriation of a rage so intense it transcended their humanity and opposing systems of belief. They were now a blood family.

They had become the flesh-eating arse children that enraged them so much. Aoife McGarry pulled off a golf-ball-sized piece of Donal's thigh, which she calmly studied as it wobbled and dripped in her hand. She stared at the pink muscle, soaked in burgundy, flanked in hairy skin with a protruding blue vein. She made direct eye contact with Darren Quinlavan and inserted the bloody piece of raw flesh into her mouth. Quinlavan answered this behaviour by biting directly into Donal's shin, who at that moment passed out from the agony and ecstasy. The mood was one of turn-based call and response. Garry Fallon used the heel of his left shoe to disembowel Donal, and gorged on the contents of his stomach as his famous Republican beard became caked in thick dark mucosal gore. The sergeant bent down, and passionately placed his teeth on Donal's tongue, which he pulled from his mouth and swallowed whole. All four rested silently, dressed in raw human offal. Thinking about what they'd tell the crowd outside.

A POEM

IM A BIRD FROM THE BOOK OF KELLS
CAN I SLEEP ON YOUR COUCH?
CAN I EAT FROM YOUR FRIDGE?
WIII YOU ACCEPT ME AND LOVE ME?
OR WILL YOU TURN ME AWAY?

MALAGA

o you ever look off into the distance at the trail left by a jumbo jet? When they're really high up? They look like they're crashing downwards in a furious droop. Like they're careering towards the ground, somewhere far off, where you wouldn't be at risk of the wreckage. My da used to tell me that's how we know for sure that the world was round. That the plane, from where it's flying, is actually going in a straight line, but gravity curves around the earth like the fuzz on a tennis ball, so the plane is really bending with the earth. That's why, from the ground, where we see it, it looks like it's dropping hard. Perspective, he called it. He said perspective is what we gain in life, and my lack of it was why I wasn't old enough to take a shit on Daniel O'Connell's head.

I was born up in Gardiner Street, behind the flats. My da had shat on Daniel O'Connell's head, my ma did it, my uncles, my brothers, everyone did it. It's a rite of passage. You do that, you can get a partner, get your hole. That's the rule. We spent our childhoods practising outside the GPO on Jim Larkin. You'd hop onto a stop sign. Poise yourself on the edge. Eye up Jim with his brown arms wide open, pounce down, and leave a trail of shite that he'd catch in his massive hands. If you weren't cautious, you'd get a slap of the number 30 bus to Finglas. A fair few of the lads went to early graves that way. My da would laugh and say they deserved it, it was never meant for them to progress on to O'Connell. On Saturdays, we'd head up Westmoreland Street past Trinity College and Dawson Street. Settle down in Merrion Square and take extravagant shits all over Oscar Wilde's chest. That wasn't even difficult, he was secluded in a quare corner behind hedges and protected by a railing. The park was quiet too, usually full of civil servants eating sandwiches. Hot glints of sun snaking through the leaves and warming our backs. We'd just sit on his head, and all of us would take turns on his chest and lap. Extra points if you got the book of poems in his hand. Up to Grafton Street then, at around 7 o'clock. The shops'd be closed and the crowds not out for pints yet. We'd go mental and get a fine feed out of the Burger King bins. Back up to the top of Gardiner Street then, before it got dark, to give each other hugs under the bridge.

Tonight is my last night as a young lad, because tomorrow I'm due to take my first scutter on O'Connell's head. The uncles, the aunts, they were all talking about their first time doing it. My family were the only ones to chance it in the middle of the 1916 Rising, no other family this side of the river went near the place during that week. But we did, my ancestors braving the bullets and bombs, the smoke, the fire. Straight down from Nelson's Pillar and then let fly, cascades of bright shit all over

O'Connell's shoulders. I stay quiet while my mother tells me about her first time, during a harsh fall of sleet. Everyone under the bridge listens to her, pure solemn and reverent. It will break her heart if she discovers that I have no intention whatsoever of taking a shit on Daniel O'Connell tomorrow, that I never want to do it, that I want to get the fuck away from this. I want to be like the jumbo jet, I want to fly so high that people think I'm falling to my death, but I'm not, I'm flying straight and they're just watching me ride the earth's curve. I want them to think my windows are stars.

My best friend Dara is a wren from Mountjoy Square, tiny hazelnut lad with a big chest. There's no more wrens apart from him left in Mountjoy due to all the hipsters keeping stoats. He's the last wren. His parents never came back one day so he climbed out of the nest and walked the whole way down to the bottom of Gardiner Street. He was tiny when he did that, not much bigger than those lumps of chewing gum you pick off when looking up the underside of a bench. The tourists are always taking photos of Dara when they see him, throwing us bits of Romanian pizza from Talbot Street, laughing at the sight of a little wren hanging around with pigeons. Neither me nor Dara fit in around here. That's why we're best pals, and if anyone ever touched Dara, I'd peck that fucker up and down Dublin. That's why tomorrow, we're both leaving together, getting the fuck out.

When my family and cousins under the bridge aren't talking out their holes about shitting on statues, they love filling us young ones with fears. People say chickens are always frightened, but fuck that, it's us pigeons, we're the chickens. Under the bridge it's non-stop talking about our weak wings: 'Only fly in short bursts. Never go so high that you can't still smell the Liffey. When the air has no smell, you've gone too high. A pigeon's brain conks out when you get the air up there. The wind up there will buckle your tail, and you'll bomb to the ground in a spin.' All that shite. That if you fly too far from the city, you'll starve. That there's no food in the country. That there's foxes that will cut you down when you rest. Blah blah. Non-stop terror and rules and limitations. We never leave; we just stay until we die. I'm not having it. I've flown high with sparrows over the tall chimneys off Clontarf Bay. I'd watch the way they pull their wings back, make them flat behind their necks in a V, shoulders up, head down, tail straight, and soar, then bob, then soar, then bob, none of this fluttering shit like a moth. I've done it, I've trained.

It's morning. We leave. Still dark but with a beige promise peeking over the east horizon. Fat, dry, smoky cold that makes your eyes blink. Us flying among the taxi drivers that leave half-eaten breakfast rolls on the Talbot slabs, no cars around to stop you munching them. The family are still tucked up in the rafters under the Butt Bridge, pure asleep, puffed up and huddled, with the odd little coo from my aunt Brigid when the Dart rumbles above. An ould red battered chimney with chalk hanging off it is where myself and Dara meet, up above below on Belvedere Road. He'd been training with me, training with the Clontarf sparrows. Tough bastard. If you think pigeons aren't the best at flying, wrens have it worse, but Dara was having none of that either.

We look at each other and say, 'Fuck Daniel O'Connell and his big brass balls'. We jump with vigour, whipping our wings so fast that you'd hear the cracks from Parnell Street. Our feathers shaking the dawn like distant gunfire, each thrust pushing us up. We keep an eye on each other, we had words about it. Crack as hard as you can until the air has no smell. That's the difficult bit, the climb. I gape down and watch it all disappear beneath me. Daniel O'Connell is a nare, a small dot, and from here I can see that he's only a pisser's distance from Gardiner Street. I can see it all, all of Dublin below. I can see the peaks of Wicklow. The city is tiny from up here.

When I was very young, there was this ould man outside a café on Abbey Street, eating brown bread. I was only small and I perched on the table next to him, pure giving him a side-eye. He put the brown bread in his mouth. I love brown bread, it's gorgeous. I hopped up closer to him, then on to his shoulder, and he let me eat the bread out of his teeth. When I'd picked most of it away, he opened his jaws wide and put my entire head inside his mouth. I started flapping my wings hard, scratching his cheek with my feet. I could feel the pressure of him biting down on my neck. I hit his face with my wings, then he let go, and I flew off. I never told no one, because I felt fear and shame that he'd done that. I couldn't understand why it had happened, why a human would do that. When my head was in his mouth, I could see his teeth, all cracked and lined up in a row, a mixture of white, with black, grey and brown stains, uneven and jagged. That's what Dublin looks like from up here, that's what the buildings below look like, the inside of that man's mouth.

We climb as high as the clean air, heading north, myself and Dara starting to sparrow-bob like we'd practised – soar, bob, soar, bob. It's not even that hard up here. There's no wind in the way, you cut through the air like weapons. Dara looks like a king, his little fat proud chest out, wings back in a V, the soft feathers on his face fluffing up with the speed, a determination too, gaze fixed north. A rare joy behind his eyes. He's been through so much. No wren has flown this high. Legend. This is fucking difficult, don't get me wrong, and it's terrifying too. My belly isn't settled at all, I feel like puking, but anger has a way of keeping all that down.

We've flown beyond East Wall, over Artane. It's getting greener below. Dara is struggling, so I slow a bit. His wings are tiny, we'd anticipated this. If he gets tired, we have our plan. I lower myself underneath him, and he takes a hold of the back of my neck with his beak. Then he rests on me as we fly. I feel his breath move across my ears, he's panting hard, the poor fucker.

'Have an ould rest for a bit, Dara, we'll be grand. We're halfway there, and we'll fly down and chill out in a hedge if we have to,' I tell him.

I use the coast to gauge an idea of where we're at. We're at about Portrane or Malahide at this stage I'd say – I can tell by the size of the beach. Once I reach Donabate, I'm pulling sharp lefts. The city is gone, we're out above the countryside, very odd to see all this grass and trees. And then, there in the distance it is, a little grey oasis. Dublin airport with the jumbo jets. That's when I grab the hard left, and Dara gets his second wings.

'The finish line is in sight,' I howl.

I take formation ahead of Dara so that he can ride in my slipstream and keep up. We're going faster than either of us have ever been, the wind with us too. Propping us up. Two legends we are. I cast looks on my grey-blue destination and hear a most unmerciful wallop beyond my rear flank. I lob back the eye, Dara is gone. I panic and lose my sparrow-bob, start fluttering again. This throws me off and I lose a lot of altitude. Below me I can see a little dark dot spinning down. It's Dara, fuck, and he's being chased by a massive buzzard. I thought those lads were gone forever, but I heard a rumour that they'd been deliberately reintroduced to north county Dublin. Nasty fuckers, big, fast, strong bastards, a bit like eagles, who want the likes of me and Dara for dinner.

I drop down, to get to Dara. The buzzard batters into him again. I see feathers flying off Dara, but he isn't giving up. The buzzard is coming for him for a final slap, and Dara, instead of flying away, turns and goes straight for him. Mad bastard. I watch the huge buzzard and this tiny dot collide with force, then both of them locked together and falling. Dara is wrapped inside his talons and tearing chunks out of his face with the small beak on him, g'wan Dara. Get the cunt. By the time I reach the ground, the buzzard has Dara's guts ripped out all over a meadow, with his foot down on Dara's head. His little back wing is still twitching with nerves, and his tongue is out. The buzzard has that dickhead stare that they have, with their snake eyes, and Dara's blood all over his beak. I flip, I lose all control or sense. The look on that prick's face when he sees a pigeon coming for him. I draw down hard on his back and bate my wing off his head, knock him over and jump on his chest. Up close, standing over him, he's twice my size. I see the little face wounds that Dara had given him, they're hardly worth talking about. The poor lad, he fighting for his life with everything he had, and he'd barely injured this buzzard. I fuck my beak straight into that buzzard's eye and rip it out, bite down on it, scream into his face. I've poor Dara's guts all over my feet. The buzzard throws me off, wailing with his lost eye.

I leg it. I fly as hard and as fast as I can – not like a sparrow, like a pigeon. I make good ground, I've crossed that Dublin Airport fence and am flying low above the tarmac. Buzzard catches up, he's not letting me away with taking his eye, this is me done for. Ahead of me is a jumbo jet, just after landing, driving along the runway. It looks unreal, this big giant white bird. I can't believe I'm seeing it up close. If I'm dying by that buzzard then let that mighty plane be the last thing I see.

I fly straight for the aircraft. I hear the screams of that buzzard behind me, baying for my blood, getting closer. I'm twenty feet from the plane. I fly for the space under the wing, I go underneath and then: Brrrzzzzzzzzzzzzzzzzzzzzzzzz. No more screams. The buzzard had gotten sucked into the engine, with a mighty noise, the engine spitting out blood and feathers at the back.

I can't believe my luck. I fly straight down into an open luggage compartment of a Ryanair airbus that's getting ready to leave for Malaga. Settle myself on a nice soft suitcase at the rear, and just flop. Everything has been taken out of me. I can't even hold myself up.

Across the tarmac, I watch the fire engines inspecting the jumbo to see what caused the left engine to stop. Hosing the buzzard off the runway they were. As the door of the luggage compartment closes, I puff up my feathers and think about Dara, and how I wish he was coming with me to Malaga.

BEST FILM EVER   ITS AGAINST CAPITALISM

                  SO GOOD
REAL MEN   ID JOIN A FIGHT CLUB
          LETS START ONE IN MALLOW   OK

RÍTHE CHORCAÍ

We were both staring in the window of the jeweller's, looking at the class feather earring. We tossed for it; I won. I bought the feather earring. My ear wasn't pierced so Ciarán did it for me with a Stanley knife and a lighter. We both had our savage denim jackets on. Fuck the world, we looked like Rod Stewart. Rory Gallagher was gigging in a week, and we had something big planned. We were going to poison him, skin him and then both of us were going to wear his skin on stage. We'd be legends in Cork. We couldn't wait to do it boy.

He was playing in the Cork Opera House for the big homecoming gig. Rory is some man. We listened to the albums non-stop, *Calling Card*, *Tattoo*, *Stage Struck*, *Top Priority*, the lot. We worshipped him. We made our own Rory Gallagher patches out of curtain and sewed them into the back of our denim jackets with wire. I'd one I drew myself onto a bit of beige fabric: I drew him with a marker, he'd a fine grin on his face and he was playing a guitar but instead of strings, it was a few big lovely fannies and he was fingering them and they were making musical notes. It was on my shoulder. It got me kicked out of the English Market.

We had it all planned. Ciarán has an uncle from Ballincollig who's a vet, so he robbed some ferret poison pellets off him. We'd our seats bought and all, up on the balcony. Like royalty, up on the balcony, letting the hair down and headbanging over the edge. The plan was that we'd use a slingshot and fire the ferret poison into Rory's drink during the first song. Then he'd take a sip of that and start to get pure poisoned. We were roaring our plan at each other non-stop, out in public and all. We had a drink we made that was a mix of turpentine and cider, we called it cocka walla after white dog-shit. We'd drink cocka walla and shout into each other's ears down an alley off Panna.

'I'm skinning Rory Gallagher, Ciarán,' and then he'd grab me by the cuff of my jacket and scream into my face, 'I'm poisoning Rory Gallagher with ferret's poison, Philip.' Then the two of us, 'And we're wearing him and playing his guitar.' Fucking Philip and Ciarán, boy, the two maddest fuckers in Cork city. As soon as Rory played 'Sinner Boy', which was about quarter way through the set, everyone would go to the bar. You'd need a pint after that solo: 'weeeowww, wah weeeowww wah wah woooo'. Rory would go off stage to tune up his Dobro: he'd always do the first half electric, then the second half acoustic, and then back out with the electric guitar again then at the end. Anyway, after 'Sinner Boy', we'd rush past security. He'd be feeling the effects of the ferret poison at that point. Ciarán would have a hammer with him, and he'd bate that off the faces of the security lads. I'd have Rory in a headlock, then I'd take out the Stanley and make long cuts from the side of his head all the way down each side of him. I'd have a pound of salt with me. You rub the salt in under the skin and it pulls away from the flesh. We'd practised it on goats and horses up in Blackpool. One night we both skinned a goat, then drank a load of cocka walla and fucking terrorised everyone up in Patrick Street, dressed as a goat. Running up off a fat woman from Montanotte, shoving our goat horns into her arse and making her scream, up and down Panna. I was at the front of the goat and Ciarán was at the back. We were drinking cocka walla under the goat skin. We fucking destroyed Patrick Street, boy. People were climbing up stop-signs, scared for their lives, thinking that there was a mad goat who smelled like cider and turpentine trying to kill them on Panna. A guard came down to try and bate the goat with a truncheon, but then he looked and saw that the goat was wearing four Doc Martens and not the regular goat shoes that they have – hooves, boy. The guard got pure wide to us when he saw that it was two lads dressed as a goat. So we ran off, jumped into the Lee and we swam for it. And all the blood from the goat skin washed off our denim. Fucking mad langers. We always wore full denim, head to toe, both of us, identical denim.

So anyway, after I'd have Rory skinned, I'd peel off the skin. And then we'd both climb inside it. The whole thing would take ten minutes. No one out in the audience would be wise. So we'd both step out on the stage of the auditorium and start playing the Dobro inside Rory Gallagher. Everyone cheering, clapping and headbanging. I'd control the neck of the guitar and Ciarán would handle the strumming. We did it before with a horse. We skinned a horse in a garage in MacCurtain Street. And then we both climbed inside the skin and marched down to Panna again, inside a horse, and we both playing blues on one guitar. Everyone on Panna had their jaws around the floor. Looking at a horse trotting down the road playing Blind Boy Fuller's blues on a guitar. Someone spotted that the horse was wearing Doc Martens again though, they got wide, and we were attacked by boys from Togher. We pushed the horse skin off and I fought the boys with the guitar, and Ciarán had a varnished pine cone that he threw at a fella and it stuck in his eye. We ran off, bawling Rory Gallagher songs and went up the side of a house after drinking cocka walla. I climbed on Ciarán's shoulder and I started banging on the first-storey window of the house. There was a businessman in bed, in the nip. And I banged on his window and shouted, 'He's going to poison Rory Gallagher, and I'm going to skin him, and we're going to wear him.' The man started crying.

Most nights we'd get mad on cocka walla, and if we hadn't skinned something, we'd jump on each other's backs, and joyride around the roads. Taking turns joyriding each other. The guards left us alone, they were scared of us. We were the Kings of Cork, boy. Then we'd find man-holes and jump up and down on them, make loads of noise banging our shoes off of every manhole in Cork city. We'd climb down chimneys as well. We'd climb down chimneys, and get our denim covered in soot. And then we'd go into the living rooms of houses when people were all asleep, and we'd roll around together on the couches and get black soot all over the couches. And we'd whisper, not so much that it would wake anyone up, we'd whisper at each other, 'We're going to poison Rory Gallagher, and we're going to skin him and wear his skin at his gig.' We'd exit through front windows and leave fingerprints everywhere because the sergeant wouldn't dare knock on our door about it.

We were best friends. We'd go to a café and get a pot of tea, and pour boiling hot tea into our mouths, and spit it at each other too. Boiling hot pots of tea, boy. And no one would touch us, because they knew well that we were the Kings of Cork, and any night we could come back to the café as a horse with a guitar and it would stay with them forever in their dreams, haunting them. When you're drinking cocka walla, you've to keep it down, enough for the cider and the turpentine to hop off each other so you get a mad buzz. But if you keep it down too long, the turpentine would kill you, so we'd drink warm grease, boy. We'd turn up at the chipper and the queue would part. They'd see the two of us in our denim and everyone in the chipper would back away out of respect. Gorgeous chipper, fine fluorescent lights and marble draped on the floors. Posh-looking. Then we'd slam our fists on the counter and do out a drum beat, and Enzo Schillaci who runs the chipper would give us a tin punnet of warm fat with a ladle. And we'd drink from it. The grease would make you puke out the turpentine. So we'd run out into the road, and we'd both bend over a bin, enough distance so we didn't get any grease-sick on our denim. And then we'd puke our rings up. We'd roar, boy. We'd howl and roar like bulls when the puke flew out. It would rise up from our bellies and we'd roar as loud as we could as it came out, and then go jump on man-holes with our Doc Martens. Mad off the cocka walla, Kings of Cork.

A girl tried to break Ciarán's heart once, so he shaved his head and buried the hair on Clonakilty Beach. And we fucking hugged each other and said we'd never let a woman in between the middle of us again.

The night we headed to Rory's gig, we were fierce excited, the type of excitement where you'd want to spill all the blood out of your body just to drain it into a pail and look at it. Swirl it around and get hypnotised staring into a bucket of your own blood and shove it back into your body before you faint. Fucking queues, boy, up Lavvitt's Quay and down Emmett Place. Rockers in their leather and patches and their plaid shirts and denims with the long curls falling off their skulls. Crowds parting when they saw us. A crisp night, the type of night you'd drink out of a pint glass. Cool and dry, where'd you'd see your breath getting lit up by the lamp lights.

I'd to tie the laces on the Docs, so Ciarán went ahead. As I was looking up, I could see him getting hassle off the bouncers. I fucking pounded up, slamming my Docs down on the tarmac, screaming, making as much noise as possible.

'Do you know who he is, you fool? He's one of the Kings of Cork,' I said to the bouncer.

'Do you know who I am?' said Ciarán. 'I'm one of the Kings of Cork.'

The bouncer replied in a jackeen Dublin accent. 'I don't give a fuck who yiz are, he's trying to get in here with a hammer. Ye're barred.'

We started howling, beating our feet on the ground, spitting up at the sky. 'We'll come up to Dublin as a horse, boy. We'll run to Dublin wearing a horse and you'll regret the day you turned us away.' That line would usually put any bouncer in his place, but Rory was obviously bringing his own security with him, foreign lads, and they'd never heard of us.

It didn't matter anyway, because there's a cellar at the back of the opera house and we could go in through there. So we walked away like cool fuckers and went around the side to Half Moon Street and kicked in the window of the cellar. We both crawled in.

Pitch dark, boy, with a tangy smell of sour porter. Ciarán found the light-switch, it didn't work though. Sure we'd feel our way around the walls with our hands until we get a door, no harm.

I noticed something on my foot and went quiet. I reached down and grabbed a mouse or a rat or something. It was squirming in my fist, so I let go. Jaysus, there was fucking loads of them running around the floor, I could hear them scuttling.

'There's mice in here, Ciarán. Pull your socks up over your denims.'

Ciarán started panicking, he's terrified of mice.

'Calm down and pull up your socks,' I said.

'I've 'em pulled up … Oh Christ, oh Christ, oh Christ,' he started. 'I can't handle this, boy. I'm not right with this, Philip.'

'Give it another few minutes until we find the door,' I said. 'Calm down.'

'I can't,' he said.

I heard little patters on the ground. Ciarán was throwing the ferret poison pellets on the floor to try kill the mice.

'You stupid fucker, how are we supposed to shoot them into Rory Gallagher's drink? You've given them all to the mice.'

'I'm sorry, Philip, I can't handle this.'

I was fucking furious with the cunt. The bouncer had already confiscated the hammer and now this meant I'd have to skin Rory while he was able-bodied, and he's a big fucker. I hadn't planned for a struggle. I was pure annoyed. I reached down with my hand, I searched for Ciarán's ankle and gave it a pinch so he'd think it was a mouse. He let out a mighty yelp. In the meantime, I'd found the door and let light in. Ciarán was on the floor with blood pouring out of his gob and his snozz. He'd gotten such a fright from the pinch that his knee came up and met his face, and he busted his own nose wide open. I started laughing like a lunatic, I couldn't stop, I'd never seen anything funnier in my life. If there's one thing that Ciarán hates more than mice, it's being laughed at, so he rose up and grabbed my denim collar. He launched his teeth into my nose, started biting down and pulling as hard as he could boy.

That's the reason I have the hole in my face sure, I knew you'd be wondering. Myself and Ciarán haven't spoken in over thirty years since that night. Tell me about yourself anyway. How are you finding Cork? Have ye heard of Rory Gallagher in the Philippines? You're a fine-looking woman for your age. Is this your first night at speed-dating?

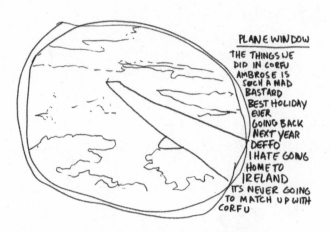

PLANE WINDOW

THE THINGS WE
DID IN CORFU
AMBROSE IS
SUCH A MAD
BASTARD
BEST HOLIDAY
EVER
GOING BACK
NEXT YEAR
DEFFO
I HATE GOING
HOME TO
IRELAND
IT'S NEVER GOING
TO MATCH UP WITH
CORFU

SHOVEL DUDS

'll be honest. I'm telling you this now from the interrogation room, and I'm in a fair amount of hassle. Be careful who you confide in online, because they will rat you out.

This is the craic. I can't stop looking at the videos. I watch them on the bus on the way into work, underneath my jacket so no one else sees. I watch them on my little cousin's Asus tablet when I'm over in Aunt Maeve's for Sunday dinner. I tell the family I'm going for a big long shit, and then I take Jack's tablet and watch them in the bathroom on earphones. I never logged out the last time, and Jack couldn't sleep right for months after I handed his tablet back. Aunt Maeve knew it was me, but never said nothing.

I watch them on LiveLeak, like. Sometimes you'll get the really new ones on Twitter before the accounts get deleted. It looks so fake when you watch it. It looks like *Terminator* or *Alien*, but the thing is, I know it's real. I'm looking at a photograph right now. I saved it, because they get deleted pure quick. Yellow desert sand, the same colour as the shit part of a sponge cake. And this lad in a blue shirt lying on his back, wearing this normal blue shirt like my da would wear, like the ones the boys from Scoil Íde wear under their jumpers. He's got one hand on his stomach, the hand kind of twisted into this claw shape and looking stiff. His foot is resting on another lad's head. The other lad is dead too. Around his body is this dark black pattern that fades into red. The spill of blood. When I see them on my screen, they don't look like pools of gore. They look like the outlines of countries that haven't been discovered yet, that's what they're the bulb off. This lad here on my phone lying in the sand in his blue shirt, not sure if he's in Syria, could be a Coptic Christian from Egypt too, he has that big forehead, but he's surrounded by an irregular blood pattern, darkening as it soaks deeper. It's so red you could paint a door with it, and not a soul would notice.

You know the videos are real when the lad's head peels. In the cinema, when someone is shot, they crack their head, like an egg. If you watch it, the bullet goes in the front, makes a little hole, and then the back cracks open and squirts the blood on a wall behind them, like water pistols. But in real life, on the internet, when a person is shot, their head peels open, like the skin of an orange opening up or a fist turning to a palm. When lads get shot in the face on the internet, with a big gun, like an AK, their face opens up into this rose blossoming in fast-forward. These lads are fucking deadly. They truly don't give a fuck. I watch all their videos.

Most days in work it's quiet. I burn off the hairs with a torch, but after ten months I'm ready for cutting throats. Hair-burning is no craic, their hair fat and bristly like strands of bail twine. It melts down to the skin, like the fuse on a firework, then lots of little strands of the acrid bone-smoke flake up my nostrils and my eyes go dry. Pádraig lances throats. He feeked Eileen McQuinlan on lunch-break and got me to smell his finger. It smelled like the bottle-cap of a BPM energy drink or a comfy bra after wearing it three days straight, pure grapefruit. Not sure I'd be too happy if some lad went around getting his friends to smell his fingers after me. But that's the game here. Pádraig thinks I'm some sort of eejit coz I'm a girl, reckons I wouldn't have it in me to cut the throats, thinks he can shock me by making me smell his fingers. If he only knew how much I wanted to slit the throats.

We work in an old hangar that used to be for small aircraft. But Mr Bradley converted it into an abattoir. Bradley's alright, one of those ex-Brit hippies, small bit soft from acid, but old money. Now he runs an organic miniature beef farm. Royal beef, fancy beef, tiny beef. Free to roam 23 acres of alfalfa and vetch, loaded with 'assorted victuals to game the meat', Bradley says. There's short black-and-white Belted Galloways, who only dine on acorns and hazelnuts for six months of the year. Their shit smells like Nutella. They get cured into beef ibérico. We've Zebu lads from Zimbabwe, who are gorged on apples and corn for sausage meat. Pear-sucking Dexters, with long ears like old man's balls and double-chin goitres. Holsteins on molasses and buckwheat, with a type of malted weak beer for their sups. The lot. Bradley has the best organic bull meat in Ireland. I burn their hairs and Pádraig slits their throats. Bradley does the butchering by his own blade. Traditional slaughtering too, not the machinated way. We kill by hand, to protect the meat, make sure it's bled and hung right. Any machinery we do have is hand-operated. Cast-iron crank elevating hoist mounted on a trolley for transport to the bleeding zone. Rolling hooks that clank on the wire. Induction-hardened pneumatic working platform for eviscerating, with a small conveyor for red and white offal. Brisket saw. Hot skinning knife with galvanised edge. Two-hand splitting saw. Hot galvanised steel non-mechanised tubular rails with detachable chassis. And a ten-foot blood-bath. We're well equipped, boy. I wash it all down every evening when the two gombeens go off to tea.

The bones of my day is on the hanging floor. It's down at the end, behind the partition. Pádraig kills, I burn, Bradley cuts, in that order. When I hear the screams next door, I actually shiver, like I'm on the bottom end of a rollercoaster going down. It does this thing, this vibration thing in my head that travels all down to my limbs and flutters my tummy, like shrinking white suds in a sink of dishes, and it's the most real feeling. Say that out loud and they'd think I'm a looper. The calves scream because they know what's happening next. Dangling upside-down with the hook through their hooves. That's the scream that gives me the tingle. If Bradley or Pádraig knew, they'd go apeshit, but sometimes I frighten the bullocks before they get cut. I go to the pen, and bang their cage with my house-keys. Once I flashed the flame of the torch at them, enough to burn their arses. When they get excited like that, their heart beats heavy. Then when Pádraig slits the throat, the blood gushes out with the pump, splashes out over the bleeding tray, onto the floor and through the partition. Where I watch it rolling in burgundy, boy. Pádraig gets the raw blood pumped into his mouth and has to gawk like a baba. Tastes like bad coins, he says. The terror leaping out of a cow's jaws to me is like a feed of Ben & Jerry's to someone else, how it changes in tone and pitch when the blade goes into the windpipe. It's my one criticism of the ISIS boys. They gag the lads during beheadings. You need to hear how the scream changes from high to low to gurgly. That's the master stroke.

I saw a video last week, I watched it in the bathroom of Hook & Ladder in Limerick. Aoife's boyfriend was being difficult, and I'd to listen to her shite on about him choosing five-a-side over her. Anyway, I sat down in the cubicle and opened up LiveLeak with the headphones on. It was this lad in a cage, like in the zoo, like where you'd have an aardvark or something, that sized cage. Miles out in the desert. He was Arab-looking, and they had him wearing a bright orange play-suit. He must have done something horrifying coz the ISIS boys were having none of him. But he was wearing this suit like a big orange pyjamas. And at the start of the video, he was telling some story to the camera, and then they had squiggly writing on the screen and it cut to shots of green fields with loads of bombs going off in the mountains. And bodies, bodies, bodies. A montage of bodies lying on the ground. I'm telling you. When it's real bodies, they always look fake. I can't explain it proper. Then a hospital with children wearing masks. Then a beardy lad with a beard talking to the camera, he was holding a big gun and had on a green military-looking vest.

I fast-forwarded most of the shite talk, to get to the end. So beard lad was roaring to the camera, and then yurt, that's when it cut back to the orange play-suit man in the cage. They dragged the chains, pure fucking with him. The camera looked like the films, slow motion, like *The Fast and the Furious*. Unbelievable detail. You could make out the hairs on his nose, like. They obviously had the jumpsuit doused in petrol anyway. Because Beardy lit the chain, and yellow flames trailed up the lad's back.

And they hugged him, I swear, the flames came over his back like he grew them as wings and they hugged his chest. His eyes had a quare expression. He looked more irritated than anything else, but his hands seized with the agony of the fire. Couldn't bat it away. Closest thing I could compare him to is when you're sleeping, and you wake up frozen, and you want to move and scream, but you can't, coz you're stiff. I think that's what a person being burnt alive must feel. After a while, lad was charred. Then the sick cunt on the camera zoomed into his burnt black face, coz his tongue was sticking out and bubbling. The air and fluid in his lungs and body were boiling, and escaping all bubbly out the mouth. I felt empty and helpless, like nothing is real. Then my mouth started to water when his tongue bubbled, and I said to myself, 'Ciara, you're one fucked-up bitch.'

I knew then I'd have to head to Syria. That's the only place for me. It's not that I want to hurt anyone, I'm not angry. But the vulnerability of any creature when it knows it's going to die is fucking beautiful. That look they give you. Where they are gone beyond fighting, and just have this stare of handing all their power to you. It's the same look a baby gives the first set of eyes it sees when it comes out. That's how it was when my cousin Jack was born, and he looked at Aunt Maeve. It's the look the frogs gave me when I'd chop them up with the sharp knives when I was nine. But by Christ, I need to see that look in an adult man. I want that powerless look behind the eyes of something that's capable of complex emotions. That's my buzz. Fuck slitting bullocks. I'm not thick either, so I'm hardly chancing that shit in Nenagh, I'd get caught rotten. And also their families would miss them, and I wouldn't like to be disturbing the town like that. I'm not an asshole. But I need to get as far as Syria, and have ISIS take me in and let me cut lads up and set them on fire. That's my vocation.

I've been chatting to a feen who's calling himself Malik on WhatsApp for three weeks. Found him through one of the Twitter accounts that uploads the videos. WhatsApp is safe enough because it's encrypted. But Jaysus, Malik doesn't trust me at all. He thinks I'm a police who's pretending to be a girl from Tipp. And when he does infer that I might be legit, he asks if I've a brother who'd be interested instead. I've made it fair clear that I've no interest in religion at all. I haven't the first clue about their religion, or what they believe, that's their business. I skip past all that in the videos, and they're in fucking Arabic anyway. I can't even be arsed checking Wikipedia, reading isn't my thing at all at all. Malik says that bit is grand, they don't care what my beliefs are. I reckon those ISIS lads don't believe anything either. Deep down, they're into feeling that power of killing, same as myself. They have that addiction too. Abu says I'd have to leg it to Jordan or Turkey, and snake across into Syria, and that I wouldn't have a hope of making it as an unattended woman. Fucking gobshite. Freckly red-haired girl from Tipp offering to join them, and he trying to talk me out of it? I'll cut my hair and pretend I'm a lad if I have to. Snort a load of burning bull's hair and make my voice hoarse and deep for the trip. Be like that wan Grace O'Malley, the Pirate Queen from Junior Cert History. Wear a big stupid GAA jersey and shorts with piss stains on 'em. Whatever. They'd get all the publicity in the world off me, imagine me slicing throats and talking English into cameras for them? Sure that's ideal. He's a coward. Same balls craic as Pádraig with the blade, doesn't believe I have it in me because I'm a girl.

Typical shit. I knew if I was to get what I wanted, I'd have to work harder, waste my time putting in a load of extra effort, just to prove to stupid fucking lads that I'm right for the job.

So the day in question, I battled on after a long ould stint in Bradley's hangar. We'd done a load of the Zimbabwe Zebus, the small bulls. They're like little balls of muscle when they dangle and thrash around by the trotters. Pádraig gets freaked out that the knife will go through his wrist, so then Bradley has to come in and steady their legs when the puncture is made. Pair of fools, pure thrilled with themselves when they need the two of 'em to do a one-man job. Then sticking their heads in over the partition, telling me to be careful with the torch, when I can blast a full hide in under two minutes. I have it down, lads, relax. So we finished up anyway, and Bradley and Pádraig went up to the house for jars of the homemade pressed cider, flat shite. I stayed behind, washing down the killing floors with borax. Normally I'd hop for the bus straight after, but that night I stayed around. I'd say I was realigning the bone-saw blades if they asked. After three jars of pressed cider, the two apeshits would always get pathetic, and order a taxi into town to stare at seventeen-year-olds in tight tops above in Neary's Lounge, arriving in with hangovers the next day and acting like they're doing a great job.

After two hours, I stuck a head out the hanger and saw the lights of a taxi up the drive of the main house like clockwork. When it fucked off, I got to work. Dusk was bothering me so I'd to act fair quick. There were too many Dexter calves birthed last season, and they hadn't been inventoried properly by Bradley. He'd never know if one went missing. Lazy prick. They're worth about 800 quid in meat. The evening had nice warmth to it, and the coconut smell of new gorse flower came down off the hill on a breeze, settling the tang of sour cow-shit. So I rocked on over to the Dexter pen with a bucket of grain and started shaking it over the fence. They all came over. They're the ones that only get fed pears, so they were gagging for a bit of grain. I spied one of the untagged calves, ushered her over to the gate and unlatched it. Had the wire noose ready and placed it around her neck, but she was a calm ould bint, in fairness to her.

The sun was low, but clear. It nearly had that desert quality, could have been in Jordan. I had an area prepared against a gravel pile, and a load of bright orange curtains that my nan threw out. I tied up the cow with a chain so that she hadn't much movement, and secured her good to the inside window of an old Ford Cortina carcass that was scrapping in the dirt. I was using the camera on my iPhone 6, which was full HD. I had it on a selfie stick, to get that professional feel that ISIS had. Nice and steady, no shaky wrist shite distracting from the action. I was going to use my arm to steady it and pull it back and forth like a pool cue. I'd spent the last week fitting out my nan's curtains into a basic cow-suit shape, with a few stitches on the sewing machine. I wrapped this over the chains on the calf, who was calmed by the pile of grain in front of her. She was looking great. Full orange jumpsuit. I had an ould brown wig too that I got in the joke shop, lobbed that on her head.

The sun was at a slanty angle, giving a nice mood to it. Then I lashed on the petrol and lit her up. I had the microphone up full to catch her screams, bawling and howling she was. She was tied down good, trying to run from the fire, but she could only thrash on the spot. Rearing her front legs up like cattle don't, jocking like a mare. The flames ripped through the orange curtains, and I was getting right up close with the camera to capture her eyes. She was only a suckling, but she still knew when she was being ended and couldn't escape. She gave all her power into that camera lens. Perfect stuff, it had that passion. I hadn't the memory on the phone to capture the full char. But I got the best bits. Stink of Sunday roast and petrol off my hair. I covered over the black pile of bones with the gravel and disturbed the earth. Bradley wouldn't miss her and he wouldn't check either.

After I washed the evening out of my hair, I sent the file to Malik on WhatsApp. Let's see the fucker turn this down, I thought. This is art. This will show him that I'm ready for Syria. As good as any lad. I watched the screen for three minutes while it uploaded. Malik was online. I waited more for him to watch the six-minute video. I was sick of his shit at this stage, and felt smug as fuck.

Malik: What is the meaning of this? I don't know what this is? Why would you send this?

Me: It's me showing you I'm serious you apeshit. I'm ready for Syria. Make arrangements because I'm booking flights to Jordan as soon as I get offline. You get me hun?

Malik: Please don't. Please leave us alone.

Me: ...

Dickhead fucking blocked me. ISIS fucking blocked me on WhatsApp? Is he for real? What did I do, like?

I didn't sleep a wink with the fury. If I was a lad, they wouldn't give a roaring shit. Why would he block me? I was almost drifting off at about half five, when there was a loud kick on the downstairs door and my room lit up with blue. Malik, you fucking rat.

LACKLAND CANDLEWAX

When leather hasn't been tanned properly, the stink of just one man's tunic can clear an entire chapel. The smell has a peculiarity about it that distinguishes it from all others, in that it has layers and dimensions. The first of these to offend the nostril is a faint cheesy tang of vomit, but with a sweetness, as if the person getting sick has just gorged on Refresher bars. The second is a large wall of meaty dung, like the shit of a sick old sow. And the third is the bang of a recently defiled crypt, when a body has been there a week and the worms are young and the round corpse, bloated, bursts open and purges bowels that have turned iridescent turquoise, with weepy beige fat melting off them. Leather is tanned when the skin of an animal, usually a cow, is scraped of all its hair and flesh, has all its salt content removed and is soaked in its own piss for several days. The skin is then pounded with a mixture of dogs' shite and battered goats' brain. The correct procedure is to dry it slowly; the incorrect procedure is to dry it hastily near an open fire. That's what the dodgy tanneries do, to produce more leather in less time. This is that pure cheap leather sold down underneath the stilt-bridge. A flame-dried skin hasn't been aired, the natural processes that allow the hum to subdue haven't occurred. Instead the stink festers and gets more acrid. Even worse is that the dry smoky leather traps the wretched malodour in. You can't smell this when you buy it, that's the point. But when a man decides to wear his brand-new badly tanned tunic to somewhere warm, somewhere sweaty, somewhere close and moist with the collective breath of a large crowd, a well-to-do crowd with rosemary sprigs under their armpits and down their arses, then the trapped rancid piss-skin stink rapidly emanates from the leather and into the ensuing surroundings. When this happens in a chapel, the stone floors, the walls, the seats, the altar and the statues have to be washed down, the relics removed, the vestments burned, the misericords buried, the tapestries aired. The stone has to be deodorised with a strong milky solution of chalk-lime that'd suck the skin off your hands. If the mason has snaked his patron by using acidic quartz or feldspar as a lampoon for pricey marble, then the chalk-lime wash releases an effervescent humour and discolours the stonework. Eventually this eats away at the masonry, rendering it burnt. If the sculpture is an effigy of a saint, or worse, a king, then the offending mason had better have a great escape plan to avoid getting sliced up and fucked in the river. And that was exactly the threat when King John Lackland visited Limerick in 1210, unreal chaos.

The bishop was so upset at the aftermath of the stench he scarpered on an ass and was seen bawling in a nearby woods, kissing an old black ankle-bone said to be previously owned by John the Baptist, but Fonsy Slattery with the dogs says it belonged to a prostitute who served the Dalcassians of the Shannon Mouth. Saying this out loud also meant getting sliced up and fucked in the river. The archers were on call to oversee the protection of the airing tapestries from the few Norse lads left on the other side of the island, each volunteering their bodies to shield the woven fabric from the rain. Even a slight wetting could shrink a tapestry to the size of a small man's hat. The ordinary people of Limerick were thrilled to see the increased demand in white rocks of lime, with every boy in the city legging it to the quarry to dig them up, grind them down and sell it to the merchants by the punnetful.

Two men, pair of tight-arses, had caused this uproar, one a stonemason and one a king. John Lackland, King of Piss, Lord of Ireland, was a baby burly cunt, with a head of hair like Tina Turner and the eyes of a gannet, disliked by the Gaelic chieftains because he once said he'd like to wipe his hole on their long beards. The common people yurted in disapproval of him for divorcing his wife on the sly, in favour of a continental young wan. The nobles found him to be an unpredictable and unmerciful gowl with a fondness for flap. He gambled like a Spaniard in gammy backgammon caskets that popped up at four in the morning after the soldiers had feeds of bent titmilk, dripping gold from his paws like drunken piss, spilling it all over the game-table. Whether he won or lost didn't matter, because he'd pure throw filthy eyes at bowsies who naysayed. Any prick fuck-acted and they'd have a blade wiped across their wrists and be lobbed in yonder Shannon with the eels. John hid coins in his jocks so no one would put them in their pockets. There was a stink of sour wine off him most of the day. He talked with an apologetic mumble, like a drunk father sitting on the end of an eight-year-old's bed telling them how sorry he was for missing their birthday party.

John was taller than God. He was the one who wore the manky tunic to the unveiling of his own statue in the chapel, a cheap bastard who bought bad leather. It was about twenty minutes into the service before the crowds eventually had enough of the acrid bang and dispersed, leaving the whole gaff empty except for John, who was raging and looking for someone to blame. A knave scraped the tunic off the king's back and it was paraded outside to be burnt, with all the cunty Paddy nobles looking on and throwing sly eyes at each other, mumbling a quiet tune of ridicule at the piss king who'd embarrassed his crown again. John hadn't been to Limerick since 1185, a good few years ago. That's why he sent the money ahead for the nobles to have a statue made of him. He was over for a short visit to get a squint at his massive newly built castle and to scoop loads of free drink and a get few rides in. Mostly he was in Limerick to escape the anxiety of the scenario he'd created for himself over in England. You see, in fairness to John, his dead brother Richard the Lionheart was considered a legend to end all legs. Him and a gang of lunatics rode horses bareback over to boiling Jerusalem and murdered Muslim boys with thick lumps of lead on the ends of chains. They shoved the Muslims' heads on poles and did rave dances on the holy sand in the name of bould Christy nailed to the beams. There were songs and poems written about Richie Big. There were women who said he'd visited them in their dreams and they'd gotten pregnant off his thoughts. John was a crotch full of wet farts by comparison, and could never live up to a dead legend. Being labelled a rat from the start burnt his chest, so he'd get mouldy off a skinful of angels' water and respond to the critics by becoming worse than what they thought of him in the first place, pure passive-aggressive self-fulfilling prophecy stuff.

Over in England, this led to a queer baronial situation where the country's nobles were up in arms and ready to take John down. However, they were doing it in a novel fashion that hadn't been seen before. The way it'd been done for years was that if a king was acting the prick, then a gang of nobles would pal together to tear his head off and fuck a puppet-king in his place. But this time they were doing it very differently. This time, they were drawing up a piece of paper with a set of rules and regulations on it, Magna Carta they were calling it, regulations that even a king had to obey, and if he broke them, then he was agreeing to get his head torn off. John was fond of issuing harsh taxes and pocketing the proceeds, and he loved sending rich lads to jail just so he could suck their wives. If he bowed and signed this Magna Carta, then there'd be no more of that carry-on. He felt intense shame about this development. His anxiety caused him to experience this as a form of castration. So he came over to Limerick, away from his barons, for one last mad session of uncontested power. He had his enemies here too, but they were more eccentric than brutal. The Clan Sweeney, for instance, once raided his wagons, kidnapped a tamed monkey gifted from the Alhambra palace in Granada and shaved off the poor animal's nipples with slate, in response to the long-beard comment.

The night after his ignominious visit to the chapel, the king slushed around on his own in the swampy shit mud, clad in green copper boots, with a waster's pace on him. His brow took on a Jack Nicholson quality as he fecked his tiny black eyes around the courtyard of the castle keep. Most of the tall walls were built with the local limestone. Too young for lichen growth, they had a pious paleness about them that was set off nicely by the odd fire lit here and there. He let out a snappy fart, which rose up to meet his face and smelled like burning chocolate bog-turf. In the centre of the courtyard, the new statue of John temporarily rested agin an ash barrel, where it was being deodorised of its leather bang. It was a daycent enough effort at a likeness of the king, considering the mason had only ever heard him described. Mad hair and small eyes, but a better set of shoulders and nicer arse than the real king. John had strong drink taken at this stage and it was the arse that drew him over for a more discerning gape at his replica. He involuntarily massaged his langer while looking at the lithic representation of his butt, which had clearly been modelled on the arse of a woman. John was impressed by this. His thoughts marvelled at the physical impossibility of trying to fuck his own hole, if his hole was as nice as the hole on the statue. The drink and thoughts of riding brought a small wave of calm across the king's chest, and he felt an optimism he hadn't thought possible after such an embarrassing day. Reaching forward with fat fingers and eyes closed, he traced a soft palm across the stone arse in front of him. He slowly moved the tonne of his body to the rear of the statue, and landed crotch first on the hard, peachy butt, with his belly resting on the shelf of the tail-bone. His entitled fists accosted the front of the bust, and for a moment he regretted that the mason had not represented his likeness with a set of fat milky tits too. He began heavily kissing the statue's neck from behind, breathing like a sick Labrador with his tongue out. His fingers found their way to the facial features and he grasped passionately. To his utter disgust, the stone began to crumble in his digits. He could hear them plopping in the soppy muck below. John was no eejit, and knew well that this meant the earlier alkaloid chalk-lime wash had reacted with and eroded the acidic stone. This was evidently a cheap marble lampoon. A bastard stone had been used, a lower mineral of inferior moral density. Some prick had been robbing him deaf. John lost his sponty and he screamed into the ether. His regal wail slapped the attention of a nearby sentry who was resting in a doorway. He approached his king with enquiry.

John: What unmerciful cuckold etched me from a lump of gurrier's quartz? This is an effrontery. Whose tools orchestrated this excommunicable sin? What hand has committed burglary on my likeness?

Sentry: One of the de Lacys of Cratloe, sir. The third brother is a mason. He received the royal commission. This is his statue.

John: A de Lacy, the dirty bowsie. Have him brought to me immediately. I'll shit on his children.

John had been locked in a feud with Anglo-Irish leader Hugh de Lacy for as long as John had been granted Irish land. He smelled a yurt of deliberate sabotage against him.

Hugh's nephew, Spanner de Lacy, grew up in the hills of the Cratloe Woods, a place a day's walk north of Limerick city with its piney trees exposing their sticky turpentine trunks and needles that pinch your feet when you walk. Spanner was a lanky boy with mouse's back hair, long arms and legs sprawling. He was 24 with a dead wife and two children: two girls, Jaffa and Sully. A third had been born with skin like a trout and only lived a week. His wife died of a broken heart soon after, the way a mother sparrow dies when you touch her eggs, so Spanner sold his children as sex workers to the Dalcassians of the Shannon Mouth. Spanner trained with the St Leger family of Cork as an apprentice stonemason from the age of twelve. He was shit at being a stonemason, and was mostly given the task of cutting square blocks, rather than any finer work that required detail and skill. Spanner's father, a brother of Hugh de Lacy, had been banished from the clan for living his life as a woman. Gearóid de Lacy was transgender, and her suffering was such that she mutilated her own genitals in the mangle of a water-well to free himself of her male pronoun. Spanner's biological mother, Aisling, was old Gaelic and belonged to a druidic people from Sligo, known for curses and necromancy. She left when her husband Gearóid began to transition gender. The Gearóid and Spanner sect of the de Lacys were officially forbidden from using the de Lacy name, by order of the patriarch. They technically had no family name, and were thus prohibited from owning property or engaging in any contract under Irish law. But Spanner said, 'fuck that', and used his de Lacy surname to get a foothold in the Limerick guild of stonemasonry, which is how he came to carve John's statue.

Spanner was langers at the back of a whorehouse in Thomondgate when he got dragged away by soldiers from the castle, who pulled him by his hair all the way across the bridge. They tugged him up the windy stone stairs, past the murder-hole, and lobbed him in the cell. He'd been eating his money earned from the statue commission, but the rest was fecked by the soldiers. John had the horn for Spanner's death, because of the statue but also to send a message to Hugh de Lacy. Spanner was battered from all angles. King John was waiting for him in the dark like a father whose sixteen-year-old daughter had come home late with a smell of vodka naggins off her.

John: Are you the mason who made the statue from the bad quartz?

Spanner: I am, sir.

John: And you thought you'd get away with it?

Spanner: I did, sir, quartz is a fine stone once you get used to it. But prone to wear if it comes in contact with hard water, I warned ye about that.

John: You were paid for marble.

Spanner: I was, sir, but the marble comes all the way from Carrera over in Italy. It would never make it past the hordes of Moorish highwaymen that line the route. Quartz was my only choice. You'd be looking at empty space if I'd have gone with the marble.

John: But you still charged for the price of marble? You cowboy!

Spanner: I did, sir, I'm pure sorry about that. I'd pay you back only the soldiers robbed my dollars.

John: And the fine fat arse on the effigy?

Spanner: The arse is from a different sculpture, sir, one I'd made years ago. 'Tis granite. I stuck your head on the statue in quartz.

John: Robbing my fucking money at every step of the process. Do you know why you're still alive?

Spanner: I do not, sir.

John: I want to find the model who posed for my arse. I need that arse on my face within the next few hours. Get her to me and we'll forget about the rest, I'll let you walk. Who is she?

A flash of white terror imposed itself across Spanner's brow as his introspections navigated the anxious quagmire the king had just presented him. Before his father Gearóid had attempted to physically remove his male sexual apparatus, she had lived as a woman for the majority of Spanner's childhood. During this period, she consistently gorged on donkey's quantities of alfalfa and flaxseed, as both of these crops contain vigorous accumulations of oestrogen. This regular dosage acted as a crude hormone replacement therapy. It had been moderately effective, with varying desired outcomes. It reduced the size of Gearóid's voice box and gave her puffy nipples, but mostly inspired the germination of a gorgeous big round arse. Gearóid had modelled for the arse on Spanner's statue when her son was just a young apprentice. The arse statue remained in storage for some years, sans cranium, where it was often used for the hanging of jackets or gowns. This year, Spanner finally put it to use by altering the granite body slightly, then sticking King John's head on top, to save money.

Now he sat in his cell as a single ailing paraffin lamp lit the side of John's rasher-like face. The king had a noticeable erection. He was crouched in a squat, boots flat, hands crippled under his bearded chin in a gammy clasp, while his rear bobbed like a whippet with an itchy hole on a yard of burlap. He was pensively waiting to attain carnal knowledge of the statue's model. Spanner weighed up his options. His father was now an old woman, so he could present her to the king and hope for the best. But King John, with his penchant for face-sitting, would no doubt discover the scars of Gearóid's mutilated testicles and have father and son killed. The other option was to come clean, let the king know that the arse belonged to his father and hope that His Highness was sexually liberated enough to lie with a transgender person. Spanner had no insight into John's opinions on gender politics and had no reason to believe John to be sexually conservative – after all, John was openly admitting his libidinal entrancement with a hermaphroditic statue of himself. However, despite any potential sexual liberalism possessed by John, it was certainly not retained by society at large, who posited gender in strict binary terms. Trans people, like Spanner's father, were outcasts, viewed as inhuman demons, stripped of title and rights. Were John and Gearóid to engage in consensual coitus, it was certain that both Spanner and his father would be personally murdered by John afterwards, to safeguard the secret. To say that King John having sex with Hugh de Lacy's transgender brother would be a scandal was an understatement.

Spanner felt the sour curtain of dread that drags across a person's body when they realise they are definitely going to die. It starts as a thumpy leaden dinge in the chest that ascends to the forehead, where it is expressed as a helium dizziness. He fell back. The cell was filled with a freezing north wind and he saw his breath catch some candlelight. His thoughts lay with his mother Aisling, who he had not seen since he was five. His memories stirred back to that calm time, when he felt a real happiness. Sweet waves of warm August sun broken by the thresh of long flax stems darted like tiny white moths across his mother's face and illuminated her blonde hair, making it translucent. Butter-yellow flax flowers, pregnant with seed, hung their oily promises on the odour of the summer breeze. Aisling the pagan was whispering stories of the Sligo faeries, of the changelings by Knocknarea cairns and the Aos Sí Púcaí who drink graves. She was weaving flax fibre in intricate little bows and staining each with opaque earthy powders, teaching her young child Spanner of the casting of spells and how to speak with the world of spirits so that he may grow to become a conjurer or mage. Even at a young age, Spanner called bullshit on this, and knew his mother was just a mad Sligo hippie. He found her magick and stories entertaining, but that was where it ended. But despite this cynicism, he still carried with him the small goatskin pouch of charms she gave him when he was born, more for love and sentiment than for any supernatural radiation it might contain. The memories of his mother's nonsense inspired a hot pang of inspiration that animated Spanner's face, and a potential solution began to hatch. He would ask to be untied, so that he could perform a dazzling pagan magic trick for John. While the king was mesmerised by it, he would bash the king's skull in with a chain and escape, rob him of his gold and jewels while he's at it, win–win ... Spanner began to speak to the king.

Spanner: What if I could get you an eternal harem of women with arses like the one on the statue? I mean, I could have a lash at getting you the model I used, not a bother. But to be honest, the rest of her is in need of renovation, and the last I heard she had contracted TB from badgers, sir. What if I could get you arses like that from all over the world? Several plump bints with greased-up olive skin, whose only purpose in life is your pleasure, all at the same time? How about that?

John: You're codding me, cunt. Where would you find that in Limerick tonight?

Spanner: I come from a druidic people of the northwest. I can act in vicarage of the gods, who'd be honoured to bestow such fuck-victuals on a king. I myself would be honoured to do these deeds in your service.

John: I've heard stories of that but is it blasphemy or witchcraft?

Spanner: It's divine knowledge, Your Highness. The Vatican keeps this type of ritual under lock and key, so they can have it to themselves. But I can place you oxters-deep in foreign flap if you'll let me do it for you ...

John the greedy prick began to imagine himself in an exotic orgy with multiple wet, tanned butts, each detached from their personage and humanity in an ebbing sea of hoop infinity. The type he'd read about on the walls of Pompeii when he studied Latin as a lad. The type his dead brother Richard probably had over in Jerusalem. He agreed to untie Spanner, who then lit candles in the cell, so that he could better see the words and symbols he was etching on the limestone walls with a lump of bright red burnt sienna that he produced from his mother's goatskin purse. As Spanner began to carefully remove each little charm from the pouch, his scepticism about the ritual subsided and was replaced with a homely glow of love for his mother. These were her things, her memory fragments loitering in present reality. He could hear her voice in the shadow of his mind as he laid each separate item in a circle on the floor: 'Crow's bone suppository from the trees of Diarmait Mac Murchada's orchard, Saint Brendan's ambergris, Frankish hair gel, pigeon piss pig fist, gullet of Costner's cockerel, darling bastard parcel, fluffy guff.' This ritual gave Spanner a look of intense concentration, which did not escape the attention of John, who was surveying him in full entrancement.

Spanner instructed John to kneel, in anticipation of the sideways ceremony. John complied. Spanner took notice of his own hold on the cold brown iron chain that dangled from his wrist to his shin, tactile in his hand, smelling like blood when blood smells like metal. He became aware of the soft spot on the top of the king's head that presented itself like a boiled egg before him. The ritual space in front of the king was an accoutrement of mad-looking trinkets and hurried pagan scrawls, of markings, numbers, letters, suns, moons, angels and ghouls, with fat wax candles fecked around the floor for full effect. All frivolous fart logic devoid of import. If you were a bird watching from a ledge, you'd have seen Spanner making John look like a pure eejit. Spanner dropped a palm-sized brass thimble in the centre of the letters and numbers and beckoned John to position his hand on this. Spanner's intention was to pretend to conjure a sexual elemental who could transcend John to a far-fetched arse harem. He would do this by placing his hand on John's, then subtly forcing the thimble towards the desired letters and numbers to create the illusion of divine communication. Fairly standard trickery of the gullible.

John: If this doesn't work, I'll have your head left on a pike at the gates of Limerick.

Spanner: It will, sir, just focus on the breathing, keep your eyes straight ahead at the symbols.

Spanner was positioned behind John, both men on their knees.

Spanner: Oh large tawny púca, I come here before you to present the Great John, King of Ireland and England, Prince of Angevin, son of Aquitaine, father of Anjou, His Greatest Highness in this mortal dimension. Can you hear his call?

Spanner gently pushed John's hand so that the thimble spelled out 'yes'.

'Fucking hell,' said John. 'Ask him who he is.'

The board spelled out, 'Declan Tent, managing director of the world's attic.'

Spanner: Oh marvellous and glamorous Declan, what gifts have you for the king?

Thimble: Loads of girls' arses, man, loads.

John: How many?

Thimble: A fortnight worth of hole, arse-lottery stuff.

Spanner: Oh Declan, what must great King John do to achieve communion with your arse farm?

Thimble: Close his eyes and stick his fingers in his ears for a small while.

John expeditiously responded to the instruction of Declan Tent with a servile obedience never before seen in a king. Spanner stood at his shoulder, grasping the heavy chain with both hands like a hatchet. He raised it behind his neck and gritted his teeth, his muscles tensed with adrenaline, his eyes were a fox watching a lame hare. His concentration was fixed on the cracky part of John's head, while the potential force built up in his bones. As he prepared to splatter the king's head open, John's fingers left his ears and began to move wildly on the thimble, which appeared to be behaving autonomously. Spanner recoiled in shock and did not strike him. The thimble spelled out 'yuge'. This was not Spanner's doing.

In a separate shimmer of reality's spectrum, a fat-fingered man with stained skin sat at a mahogany desk. The sun had set, the offices vacant except for a loyal few confidants. His lumpy suit whimpered in its leather swivel-chair. It was the colour of clouds that ruin barbecues. His terror-sweat rose like hot swamps and greeted the palates of others as fresh cat's-piss pourri. The desk had many beautiful telephones, but the man was wiping an upside-down shot glass off an ouija board, surrounded by tea-light candles lit in desperate pentagrams. His desk was flocked with papers.

In Spanner's wet cell, the thimble spelled out, 'Anybody there? Please help. I need to speak to King John. Really sad.'

John flooded with adrenaline and fisted at Spanner's shins like a scolded cat. Spanner, speechless, transfixed, placed John's hand on the thimble and directed his attention back to the ritual, before retracting his own hand from John's.

John: I am King John of Ireland and England. Is this Declan Tent?

Thimble: This is not Declan. I'm reading about you. You are a loser. Very low-energy king. Brother Richard Lionheart is best king, TBH. Sad.

John: Reading where? Who is this? Are you with my brother?

Thimble: On the internet. Reading about constitution. History. Wikipedia. Magna Carta. Real loser.

John: Who is this, damn you? What know you of Magna Carta? Is this the French? Are you a devil?

Thimble: You are responsible for this constitution stuff. Terrible idea. Needs new plan. Very difficult to progress. Needs better words.

Spanner: What is Wikipedia?

Thimble: It is a book of all known truth that anybody can change at any time.

Spanner was addled. His mother's sacrament appeared to actually work. John was in contact with a very aggressive demon or jinn who was speaking in words they did not understand. Spanner tugged John away from the space. John could not understand how the thimble knew about the Magna Carta, which had not been signed or even spoken about outside of a confidential circle. Neither could fathom the dark force they had touched. They returned to the thimble to ask more questions. A shaking John gulped his enquiries towards the scrawls and trinkets.

John: Who are you? Where are you?

Thimble: I'm just like you but far away. I want to talk about Magna Carta.

Spanner: What time is it where you are? And what do you want from King John?

Thimble: 1.15 a.m., Nov 2019. I want to know how to beat a constitution. King John is a loser, his brother Richard is much better king. King John is a low-energy leader. Sad.

John erupted in snarling anger and kicked the candles and charms. He grabbed Spanner by the cuff of his gullet and gartered the chains around his neck. With bulging eyes and spit jumping from his teeth, he screamed, 'Who is this futuristic prick? Where are my brown arses for riding? You fucking did this, you Cratloe cunt. I wanted to get my hole and instead I've to listen to this black-magic bastard tell me about how brilliant my brother is, from 2019 no less. They're still talking about Richard in 2019. I'm not listening to this shite, you pagan gowl. You've signed your own death certificate.'

Spanner's eyes darted around the room, searching for a solution: 'I think I might be able to sort this but if you kill me you'll never know what it is. I've a solution much better than arses.' John let go, and Spanner continued: 'Hear me out, sir. This lad we're talking to seems fairly powerful. Maybe we can give him something he needs and he can give you something you need. If I did that, would you spare me?'

Fat John ran his tongue around his mouth as if searching for trapped meat in his gums. 'What can this future eejit give me?' said John.

Spanner knew that the only thing bigger than a king's horn is his ego, so he looked at John and said, 'This lad is a king from the future. I bet he can make you a legend and your brother Richard a gobshite.'

A lofty smile landed on John's face that looked like it had been shot at him from a cannon. He eagerly returned to the ritual.

Spanner: You mentioned a week-a-pee-day-ah earlier. Tell me this, can you scribe John as a legend in this tome up above in 2019?

Thimble: Yes, I can get all my great men on it, make sure never changes back. I want King John to help me beat this constitution. Need to beat Islam like his brother.

John: You need monarchy, absolute monarchy. That is how you beat Magna Carta. You must prove that you and you alone have a blood-right to the throne. The right to a throne comes from God, no man can challenge it.

Thimble: Where can I buy this monarchy? You give me monarchy or else I will edit your Wikipedia to say that you are even more of a loser.

Spanner: I have a plan, lads. Describe to me exactly what you look like, in great detail. Spell it out on the thimble.

The man from the future began to tell Spanner about his wonderful golden hair and pouty lips, his beady eyes and Saxon chin.

'Fetch me my tools please, Your Highness,' said Spanner. King John produced the leather sack of chisels and a hammer that had been confiscated earlier.

In the corner of the cell, Spanner noticed a heavy block of limestone being used to secure a chain belonging to the door. He began to chip at it with a chisel, precise and careful, carving out the details of the future man's head. Before long, he had masoned a full limestone bust that fit the dimensions of the thimble's description. That night King John and Spanner replaced the head on John's fat-arse statue with the new head of the future man. Under cover of darkness, they took this by donkey and cart to Thomondgate, beyond the castle. They dug deep and buried the statue where it wouldn't be found for many years to come. They parted company, each agreeing not to speak of the events of the night. King John feared that Spanner could contact the man from the future who controlled history with his Wikipedia, and this ensured Spanner's safety. Shortly after, the barons enacted Magna Carta on King John, stripping back his power, and the power of all leaders, from that moment forward. The next year, John died of dysentery. Spanner died by an honour killing, contracted by the de Lacy clan, and dumped in a north Clare bog at the age of 44. Their buried statue lay underground for centuries, as battles raged overhead, as Limerick was besieged, as famine ravaged the land, as Black and Tans trampled above, as Limerick became a free soviet.

In December 2019, the statue was excavated from Thomondgate by a team of US archaeologists by order of president Donald Trump. Its uncanny resemblance to Mr Trump was used as proof that he had a longstanding blood lineage to the kingdoms of Ireland, England and parts of France. The woman's arse was shaved off by the CIA with an angle-grinder. The scheduled 2020 US election was cancelled as the United States army invaded Ireland through Shannon airport. President Trump was declared absolute monarch of the ancient Kingdom of Ireland, England and France. America was absorbed into this territory. Richard the Lionheart's Wikipedia page was edited to read Richard the Loserheart.

LOOK AT THAT CLASS BOAT. BOATS
ARE UNREAL. WHY DID THEY STOP USING
THEM?
ONLY PRICKS HAVE BOATS TODAY

'DID YOU READ
ABOUT ERSKINE FOGARTY?'

There's a three-par golf course in the demilitarised zone between North and South Korea that has active land mines on it, and if you ever played a game there you'd have a 70% chance of dying. This single golf course makes golf one of the most dangerous sports in the world. Just this one course, and another in Florida that has alligators in a lake off a sand bunker. There's a town in America called Centralia that's been on fire since 1962. There's a Catholic chapel in the Sedlec area of the Czech Republic made out of human bones. There's a ski resort in Bavaria that has no snow; the slope is made out of a type of fluffy sand, an industrial silicate, and people ski on that. In 1518 in Strasbourg, there was a plague of dancing that lasted one month, and 400 people died from not being able to stop dancing. In 1858, the River Thames smelled so badly of shit that the British government had to shut down. In Ancient Greece, the most elite fighting force was made up of 150 pairs of gay male lovers. They were ferocious in battle because they fought to protect the person they loved, and not themselves. There was a 17th-century leather-seller from England named Praise-God Barebone whose full name was Unless-Jesus-Christ-Had-Died-For-Thee-Thou-Hads Been-Damned Barebone. There's a Dutch socialist politician named Tiny Kox. The last black person exhibited in an American zoo was in 1906. His name was Ota Benga. Schrödinger's Cat is a theory in quantum physics which states that a cat poisoned in a box is both alive and dead if no one is around to observe the cat's demise. Quantum suicide is the theory that claims it is technically possible to achieve immortality by committing suicide. This theory came about by looking at Schrödinger's experiment from the point of view of the cat. There's a three-inch aluminium sculpture of a spaceman on the moon. It's the only sculpture not on Earth. The only reason it's there is because the Americans gave 1,600 Nazi war criminals secret identities and they founded NASA. Human male infertility is tested with hamster eggs. Medicinal cannabis was introduced to western medicine by a doctor from Limerick. An American doctor called Stubbins Ffirth used to cut himself open and smear the blood, shit, puke and piss of yellow-fever victims into his cuts. He'd also pour shit in his eyeballs. His research was fruitless. Thousands of toads exploded in Germany in 2005 for no apparent reason. Hens have empathy for other hens. Cows are fed rubber-covered magnets so that accidentally consumed metal doesn't slice up their insides. There's a tree in Athens, Georgia, that legally owns itself.

These are just some of the 1,138 facts that I'm writing on the individual pieces of wood that make up my Facts Ark. Noah had his ark, full of animals. But I have my facts, and they are going in my ark. That's all I have left. How did I afford the lumber for this ark? That looks like an expensive afternoon in Woodies DIY, you say? I was able to afford it because I sold the American fridge-freezer for 300 quid to a liquidator's auction and used the cash to buy two old sheds that I'm now taking apart. A Fisher & Paykel RS7667FHCL fridge-freezer. 2007. Retail value of €2,300 including delivery, when I bought it last year in Arnotts. Seven imposing feet of double-door stainless-steel sublimity and virility. A towering behemoth of achievement, a monolithic signifier to any dinner guest that states unequivocally that 'I HAVE ARRIVED'. Would you like ice in your San Pellegrino, Dr Carolan? And then I'd waltz over to the Fisher & Paykel, and it would cough out crushed ice from the left door, shattered crystals of filtered purified water careering into his glass and fizzing up the fucking San Pellegrino. And I'd stare Carolan down while I did it too, the smug Dublin Leinster rugby cunt.

That was before the recession. The fridge-freezer was the last thing to go. Yesterday I threw the keys back in the letterbox of the six-bedroom semi-d in Glasnevin. I've sold the apartment in Smithfield for 68% less than what I bought it for. I've taken Daniel out of Trinity College. I've removed Megan from her school, and cancelled her dressage. Their mother Catherine is thinking about Fás. I've sold my jet-ski, I've sold the Audi. I owe €862,000, count it. When I threw the keys back in that Glasnevin letterbox, I genuinely grieved, as if my possessions were children or pets, truly suffered for everything that was left inside that door that I could now no longer access or call my own. The 50-inch Samsung plasma, the Blendtec blender, the Baby Gaggia coffee machine, the wood-burning stove, the fucking Aga, the Shun Japanese kitchen knives, the Denby mugs, the Dyson steam-cleaner. But they weren't taking the fucking Fisher & Paykel American fridge-freezer, on principle, not a hope. That one was coming back to Limerick.

Catherine waited in the driveway in the Punto when I dropped in the keys. Megan was refusing to speak to me, and the little bitch had been posting photographs of herself in lingerie on her Myspace to get at me. Daniel stayed in Dublin with the Carolans' son and will likely go to Australia – he's nineteen, it will be good for him.

'Mum, I don't want to go to fucking Limerick and be a culchie,' Megan whimpered in her well-spoken Dublin tongue.

'You'll get to see Granny, and Buster, Megs,' Catherine said, with her very tired purple set of eyes sinking into her bitter ould puss.

Catherine was wearing several layers of clothes to save space. Megan was stuffed to one side of the rear seat with the suitcases on her. The Fisher & Paykel fridge-freezer was in the other side, up against Catherine's seat as far as it could go. We silently drove for three hours down the freezing December motorway with the boot open until we got to Limerick. Do I feel bad? No, Megan needs toughening up now that she'll be going to Scoil Carmel, and Catherine deserves it for fucking Dr Carolan and God knows how many of his rugby pals. I've been no angel. There was Alice, Deirdre, Becca and Susan from the office. But the difference is I had the decency to not get caught. And also I didn't fuck people who eat at my dinner table and ask if I bought my wine from Tesco, while side-eye winking at my cunting wife like it's their personal in-joke. Elitist Dublin prick.

We pulled up outside Catherine's mother's house in Corbally. The mother crawled up the driveway puffing a fag, and Buster the half-blind fat bastard terrier behind her, panting like he smoked twenty Rothmans a day too. His stupid arse wriggled when he saw Megan. The mother didn't look at me, or talk to me. Catherine and I didn't even have to speak about it beforehand. But this was the end for us. The Glasnevin house and our jobs were one thing, you keep up a charade for that. But not when there's nothing. Then you're really faced with the void between two people, the lies, the hatred we had, plotting against each other, getting one over on each other. All that toxic shit is tolerable when there's a boiling-water tap in the sink and a heated towel-rack in the en suite. But this was a mutual decision that did not need discussion or thought from either of us.

Herself and Megan took their things from the Punto, and the door on the mother's house was shut. I'd given the few grand from the Smithfield sale to Catherine, to pay for Megan. That's fair, so long as Catherine doesn't decide that she wants some Spaniard's dandruff up her nose. Oh ya, I know about that. The Punto was Catherine's too. I had €268 in my pocket, my Paul Smith suit on my back and the Fisher & Paykel fridge-freezer. I had no plan.

It was already dark at 4.30 p.m. as I wheeled the fridge-freezer down Athlunkard Avenue towards the Corbally Supervalu. Young lads won't rob a seven-foot fridge-freezer, so I left it outside the shop and got a hot chicken roll, which only cost three euro. Not bad, that would be six in Donnybrook Fair. I could smell a rain in the dark ether. The coal chimney smoke from Lee Estate hung low as the cold air above the Shannon River pulled it down into smog. I was definitely back home. Dragging the fridge-freezer to the area underneath the Corbally Overpass was difficult, as there were large stones in the way that the rollers would get caught in. When I tilted it, either the door would open, or the hot chicken roll would fall out of my jacket pocket onto the wet ground. But I eventually made it. I set the fridge-freezer on its side, just underneath the bridge, on the canal. Plenty of space as I got inside and of course, an aluminium fridge-freezer of this calibre has a spectacular energy rating. Anything designed to keep cold in like that is equally as effective at insulating heat. After fifteen minutes, I was toasty and dry, no mean feat considering that it was mid-December. The roll made me do onion burps, however, so I had to open the fridge-freezer door a bit every so often to let them out, which would then leave cold air in, which was frustrating.

I tried to sleep, and that's when the facts first came rushing into my head, jumping up visually when I'd close my eyes. The phrase 'Iron Dobbin' was the first. It was a type of petrol-powered metal horse designed by Italian fascists in 1933. The second was 'Great Stork Derby', which was an unusual situation in Canada between 1926 and 1936, where many women became pregnant because a wealthy man named Charles Vance Millar wrote in his will that he'd leave his fortune to the Toronto woman who could have the most children in the ten years after his death. I don't know why the facts just started jumping up at me. I hadn't thought about them in years. I'd been on *Blackboard Jungle*, you see, when I was seventeen, in 1992. *Blackboard Jungle* was this TV series on RTÉ, Ray D'Arcy used to host it. It was a general knowledge quiz, and every secondary school in Ireland would enter. Our school won, in 1992, and I was the one who won it for them. It was a question about volcanic activity that did it.

I just have this ability to remember facts, it's not an issue for me. I hear a fact once, then it's stuck in my brain, that simple. Winning *Blackboard Jungle* is what got me a scholarship to study

Economics in Trinity College in Dublin. There was no way my parents could have afforded that. Trinity was also the first time I had the pleasure of meeting elitist Dublin cunts. When you're from Limerick and live in Dublin, you get the unique privilege of being considered both a culchie and a skanger. When the jokes about cow shit were made, I got a mention. When the jokes about northsiders were made, I too got a mention. Trying to please elitist Dublin cunts is a losing game. Get a new set of Dubarry deck shoes like the lads from Malahide, and they ask you where your knife is. Pour a sixty-euro barolo into the glass of Dr Carolan, the wife-fucker, and get asked if I bought it in Tesco. You can never win … Unless you get the American fridge-freezer. There's no arguing with that. The American fridge-freezer is the signifier, 'I HAVE ARRIVED'. I should know, I thought, as I lay in one.

I got about an hour's kip, and decided to return to my old neighbourhood in Caherdavin to show them all what a big shot I was with the Fisher & Paykel fridge-freezer and my Paul Smith suit. It was 7 a.m. I pulled her up the canal path. The Corbally Canal, by the way, is another invention of elitist Dublin cunts, I thought to myself as I battered the rollers of the fridge-freezer off the cobbles, which were laid in 1843. Limerick used to have three breweries, in the 19th century, and they were run out of business by cunts. The Corbally Canal was built by the Guinness family. Before the canal, that black Dublin shite had to come down to Limerick on horse and cart. The bumps on the road would destroy the taste in the barrel, so they gave up. And Limerick, fair play to her, brewed her own porter. Then Dublin cunts built the canal to bring the Guinness down, and put hundreds out of work. Just like they did to me.

A group of children on the way to school stopped on the canal to look at me with the fridge-freezer. I felt like smacking them. I carried on. As I got to the lock-gate near Baal's Bridge, an old man with his dog roared at me, 'I thought you were a train, sir.'

'Excuse me?' I retorted.

'The noise, sir, I thought there was a train coming up the canal, with the noise the fridge was making, sir. I couldn't believe my ears, I thought I was near the tracks, thought I was going stone mad altogether, ha,' the wrinkly sarcastic coffin-dodger said.

I immediately grabbed him by the collar and asked, 'Are you fucking calling me a train?'

His skinny-arsed greyhound leapt up and latched on to the arm of my fucking Paul Smith suit, which knocked me straight on to the wet footpath. Coffin Dodger took this opportunity to start belting me into the face and forehead with his black-thorn stick, which split my eye and lip open as his mongrel made tatters of my suit.

After they left, I returned to the fridge-freezer. This was only a minor issue. Myself and the Fisher & Paykel proceeded up past Barrington's Hospital, built by Joseph Barrington in 1829 to offer free health to the poor of the city.

Limerick city centre was barren, stony and grey. It looked like how people describe Glasgow but worse. Unpicked litter assaulted the streets, as pigeons and crows fought over a spilled-out bag of takeaway containers by Arthur's Quay. A cold mire of smoky curtain-fog hung on top of the distant traffic lights. You could hear them beep from a thousand yards, because no engine disturbed their sound. They battled on like chirping mechanical birds, unaware that they no longer served their purpose of moderating heavy morning traffic. The effects of last year's economic downturn had hit Limerick hard. Worse than Dublin. O'Connell Street was a fiasco of unit after unit of closed businesses. Their harsh metal shutters bore down on me as the fridge-freezer and I made our way up the centre of the street. Clearly, there were no morning commuters en route to their trusted jobs because the few cars that passed easily moved around me, and it was 8.30 a.m. Most of the factories and businesses in the city had shut down in a year, because of the actions of Dublin cunts. The young were leaving, or killing themselves. The middle-aged were queuing for the dole. But the big brand flagship stores remained open.

I knew I'd have to do something with the wounds on my face from Coffin Dodger, so I walked into Brown Thomas. It was utterly empty, except for two vapid-looking girls who guarded the expansive retail floor, which had been a hum of customers and make-up women when I visited last year. It was cosmetics I required, not medical attention. I fully intended to complete the visit to my old neighbourhood, so it was imperative that I looked smart, and successful. My lip had inflated to twice its resting size, and there was a large bump above my forehead. The wounds had closed but my face was covered in congealed brown blood. I knew this because I watched my face swell in the immaculate reflection of the stainless-steel fridge door along the way.

I'd left the Fisher & Paykel outside so I made a confident beeline to the Mac counter.

'I have arrived,' I said.

A girl of 22 named Aisling wiped the blood off my face with cleanser. 'The best I can do is hide it under a full face of make-up, love,' she said. Her breath smelled like instant coffee.

A lavish amount of dark foundation was required to fully conceal the bruise above my left eye. This had to be applied all over my face for a convincing finish. Aisling quite cleverly applied blue eye-shadow and a bright red lipstick to reconstruct my face and fully camouflage any evidence of injury. I was quite happy with the results, and did not regret handing over €150 for the procedure. The Paul Smith suit was still ripped, and my starched collar was bloody so I purchased a new shirt from a dandy in the menswear section downstairs. I now had €48 to my name. I was ready to bring the American fridge-freezer to Caherdavin, for envious perusal by the people I grew up with.

The fridge-freezer held its own as we travelled over the Shannon Bridge. The paving of the footpaths was quite kind to the wheels underneath, and we made decent time, reaching the suburb of Caherdavin just after 11 a.m. The Fisher & Paykel and I presented ourselves on the tarmac of Blackthorn Drive at 11.17 a.m. The road where I spent my youth. The kerbs that I threw soccer balls off, the schoolyard where Ernie Kendal chipped one of my teeth with a conker. The bins at the back of the church where Emma Donlon let me feel her tit. The mounds by the community centre where I drank two naggins and needed a stomach pump.

I began a slow march. One hand in the breast pocket of the suit, my posture immaculate, my chest out. The other hand dragged the door of the fridge-freezer, which had come a bit loose from the journey. It was very important that the old neighbours knew that I hadn't been defeated. I was still the big shot who'd made it up in Dublin. Especially after my parents had died and couldn't keep the neighbours updated about the particulars of my success. They needed to be assured that I was doing well. So I began to shout, loudly and proudly, 'I have arrived ... I have arrived ... I have arrived ... I have arrived ...' while championing the fridge-freezer behind.

Godger Canavan's dad was the first to open his hall door. He looked jealous as fuck, the ould prick. He always thought he was better than everyone just because he had a pond out the back. Well, he hasn't got a fucking Fisher & Paykel American fridge-freezer, has he, the lump-faced carp enthusiast langer-nose? Can't even get these fridges outside of Dublin, cunty.

'Is that the Fogarty lad?' said Ms Naughton.

'Why is he wearing a face full of women's make-up?' said Deccy O'Donovan's dad with the lisp.

Before long, the entire rabid road was out in nosey force. Mostly people's mas and das, but they'd report back to their flock. Except for Titmilk Sarsfield, he still lived at home because he had bipolar and was on SSRIs.

'Keep flying the fucking flag, Erskine. Fuck 'em,' he shouted. Thanks, Titmilk.

I dodged through the gobble of codgers. 'Are you OK?', 'Do you need help?', 'Have you taken anything?' were some of the inquisitions. Others enquired as to whether they should ring the guards or get the ambulance. Begrudging old fucks, jealous that I had clearly arrived and was now bigger than this small-town Limerick culchie skanger shit. If anyone tried to speak to me, I just hit 'em with a fact.

'Will you come in and have a cup of tea, Erskine? You look very tired,' to which I'd respond, 'The state of California was once legally considered an island.'

'Do you have a contact number for your wife, Erskine?' ... 'Kangaroos have two cocks,' I'd say.

It went on like this for forty minutes at least. The jealous fuckers following me, as I did eight round-trips from the top of Blackthorn Drive to the bottom of Blackthorn Drive with the fridge-freezer, carrying it like my cross, letting them know that I had arrived. Until they gave up and went back inside.

I had a rest at the bottom of the road, outside Dr O'Brien's clinic, and leaned against the scuffed aluminium behemoth. Titmilk Sarsfield, fair play to him, came over, said fuck-all and offered me a Silk Cut. I obliged. I hadn't smoked in years, but Christ that fag hit the spot. He didn't talk, because he just knew I didn't need talk right now. But then the silence broke.

Titmilk: There's a liquidator's auction out in the old Dell factory by Plassey where they'll take that fridge off you, cuz.

Me: Fair enough.

Titmilk: We'll lob it in the back of my Dyna, and I'll take you out there.

Me: Nice wan, bud.

Titmilk: They'll never take *Blackboard Jungle* off you, Erskine. The boys still talk about that here down in the pub, or when we're playing darts. You're a legend because of that. You're the smartest fucker in Caherdavin. No one's taking that away, man. That's forever.

I burst into tears and cleared the empty fag packets and Lucozade bottles from the passenger seat of Titmilk's Dyna while he loaded the bulky fridge-freezer on to the back. We drove to the auction warehouse in Plassey, and not a word was uttered between us. I smoked half of Titmilk's fags. Then he drove off and beeped the horn several times.

The Dell factory was a gigantic empty warehouse that had once employed half the city of Limerick. I walked through main reception with the fridge-freezer, the negative space of the Dell logo hanging above a desk where the sign had been removed when it closed. Beyond reception was the former factory floor. It was colossal. The height of the ceiling made me feel queasy. Nick Faldo could drive a golf-ball through there, and it still wouldn't reach the back wall. The space once housed hundreds of assembly lines as thousands of workers manufactured all the Dell computers for Europe. This came to an end because of elitist Dublin cunts. Now the machinery was gone, and innumerable household appliances lined the floors. Jet-skis, jacuzzies, office chairs, coffee machines, dentist chairs, wardrobes, Victorian-style gazebos, flatpack decking, full kitchens. This was the pecked-out carcass of the Celtic Tiger, rotting under a wet, dark tree trunk. When you defaulted on your mortgage and threw the keys back in the letterbox, this was where your prized possessions ended up, being sold for about 70% less than what you payed for them. This was a graveyard for the upwardly mobile, a sepulchre for failed businesses and bankruptcy. Like the killing fields of Cambodia, except instead of skeletons littering the ground, it was wood-burning stoves, and instead of bombs causing all the devastation, it was elitist Dublin cunts.

A lump colonised my throat when Fatso Yellow Hair offered me €300 cash for the Fisher & Paykel RS7667FHCL fridge-freezer. 2007 retail value: €2,300.

'It's 2008 now, bud, I'll give you €300. Meowt ... yurt,' said the hawker with the long fingernails.

I used the cash to buy two large wooden garden sheds, a fully stocked tool box and a Dunnes Stores bag full of assorted stationery from the display of a liquidated Carlow art and hobby shop. I took these to the infinite empty car park outside, and dismantled the sheds. Then, like a mother cat with her litter, I carried the wood by hand, piece by piece, until it all lay on the bank of the River Shannon by Plassey.

That's where I am now, building my Facts Ark. There are 1,138 pieces of pressure-treated wood before me on this sand. I've never built a boat, or sailed one, or been on one. But this vision came to me in the fridge-freezer, during my hour of sleep under the canal bridge this morning. The facts in my head were merely a sign pointing to a greater purpose. I haven't arrived, I've never arrived. I can see now that I took the wrong journey. Now I'm taking the noble journey, and I will fucking arrive.

Over the next few days, I will write a fact on each one of these 1,138 pieces of wooden slats with a permanent marker. I will construct a timber raft made of facts, with a simple canopy to shelter from storm. When my ark is completed, just like Noah, I will start anew. Because the flood has come, but this time it has saved the wicked. I will drift north on to the mouth of the Plassey River, adjacent to the pontoon. The current will take me down the tail-race and open into the larger Shannon River. I'll drift past Corbally, through the island fields and meet the Curragower Falls. Then I'll sail on the mighty current that cuts through Limerick city, waving at the people as I navigate the torrent. Finally, out on to the Shannon Mouth and the Atlantic Ocean. Just me on my ark made of facts, getting as far away from Dublin as possible.

DEAD PEOPLE

"The things I take pleasure in, I cant do"

JAMES GANDOLFINI
1161 - 2013
Please rest in Peace James

THE BOURNVILLE CHORUS

The circumstances of this story can't be described using traditional logic. Most stories have a shape to them. This one doesn't have any shape, but it has a shadow, which isn't a projection that's becoming of something sans shape. I can try to describe the shadow of it, but by the time I get to the end, the sun will have shifted position and the dimensions of the story's shadow will be a geometric perversion of what they were at the start. But I'll have a hop off it anyway.

A few years ago, I was sitting down in my granda's parlour watching *Saving Private Ryan*, class film. It was the only thing worth watching on TV coz Granda didn't have broadband, and there's nothing wrong with a war film when it's on. All the boys were on the beach in Normandy, invading, running towards German pricks the way terriers run away from a wheelie-bin full of fireworks on Halloween night. Bang, blart, cuck, cuck, cuck. Bullets flaking off helmets, tearing through chests, bating on rocks. Mortars howling through the sky like injured kestrels. Twenty grand worth of Hollywood blood splashing off the lens every ten seconds. Ould Tinnitus Tommy Hanks with determination in his eyes. Big dirty stinkin grey skies above saying prayers for the ground below. Bit-part actors getting their names in the credits for having guts drooping below their gooches and dragging them off the Frankish sand. Sandy kidneys, speckled spleens, gritty lungs, sullied bowels. Bang of seaweed and raw black pudding in the ether. I bet it was butcher-shop offal too, none of this rubber shit with red sauce smeared on it, real lambs' liver, hanging off their distressed khaki fatigues.

If it wasn't for the banjaxed speakers on Granda's TV, I'd have been fully immersed. There on the beach with all the goons, the slice of adrenaline giving me a mind-horn, but also safe from harm on the couch. I couldn't get immersed though, not that night. I knew that it wasn't the beach in Normandy that I was watching, because they'd shot it down the road on Curracloe Beach in Wexford twenty year ago. Granda used to tell me that that's the beach where the Normans first landed in Ireland, Strongbow *et al*. English cunts but French cunts at the same time. In the 12th century, they weren't fully English yet. They got so cosy in Wexford they never left, like hot-water bottles under a thigh. The Normans had their own language, he'd say. 'Twas called Yola, a pidgin of Gaelic and French, lasted 800 years. The Normans were sound, they joined in on the craic, they became our own. Then he'd keep repeating the word 'quare' and looking off in the direction of Normandy. Coz quare is the only word we've got left from the Yola language. I wondered if Steven Spielberg was having a snakey chuckle with his beaches. Did he choose Curracloe to shoot Normandy because that's where the Normans landed? Did the word 'quare' ever march across Spielberg's tongue?

I snapped out of it, and gaped back at the TV. Tom Hanks and his battalion had managed to breach the Nazi defences at the top of the beach.

'Have you the Bournville?' It was my aunt calling.

'I'll have it up to ye,' I said. The Bournville chorus meant that my poor ould granda was awake and needed calming.

I walked through the tiny dark hallway, which smelled like Fairy liquid and the cider-vinegar tang that piss can get when you don't drink enough water. The kitchen was bare, with a blackened stove and wax jackets piled against a corner. They made the room honk like old smoked bacon for some mad reason. Marble-effect lino draped the floor like a slab, with those grey patches of guff around the areas that see the most footwork. Clear menthol moonlight snaked through the single-glaze window, distorted by the pane of glass that had concaved in the centre from years of being eroded by mountain rain. On very hot days it concentrated sunlight to a beam and discoloured the wood on the presses, like a magnifying glass. My nan used to say that it would set the house on fire eventually. She said that Dickie Rock's car once broke down when he was in Wexford on the way to a swingers' party, and he called to the house to use the phone. Nan made him tea and billy-roll sandwiches, and she spent the whole time sitting upright on the counter to hide the discoloured wood so that Dickie Rock wouldn't see the sun-stain. She said that's where she first got the melanoma on her ear, from the concentrated sunbeam illuminating her lobe while Dickie Rock talked about swinging with a disabled couple from Two Mile Borris. Granda says Dickie Rock never visited and she was just trying to make him jealous, he said she'd always lie to get attention. She used to claim that tiles fell off the roof any time Gay Byrne mentioned Augustinians on the *Late Late*.

I reached up to the sun-bleached press and took out the Bournville. I fucked a pint of milk into the pot on the black stove. I thought about Nan as I stirred the bitter cocoa into the mug, the skin of the hot milk on the shaft of the spoon like a child wrapped around its ma's arm. No sugar, Granda likes it plain.

'Bring it up, will you?' My aunt's voice from the bedroom above.

'I'll be up now, have it made,' said I.

I hated walking up the stairs to see him, it was always like when Archie Jordash took me to the back of the creamery to watch the crow that had gotten its neck caught in the blades of the thresher. The thick velvet blood shimmering on his feathers, barely able to muster a caw, his eye was a button on a leather couch staring up at me in bemused anguish. I wanted to free the crow's wings from the blade, but Archie said to leave him be.

'Crows get caught in thresher blades when they're greedy for worms, it's his own fault.'

Archie took out his eight-year-old cock and pissed on the crow. The piss washed off the blood and the poor ould crow felt a moment of strange relief.

We watched for another few minutes while his life left his eyes. I always wanted to take the crow from the blades, sort out his wings and the cuts to his neck. Wouldn't have mattered if he couldn't fly, I'd have bestowed on him all the crowly desires he'd have, gave him a life better than any other crow. My nan said that crows can learn to talk like parrots if you slit their tongues down the centre like snakes. But I let the crow die because that's what Archie wanted. Archie died in a fire when he was nineteen.

I was at the top of the stairs with Granda's Bournville and I pushed open the door. There he was, in the bed like a melted choc-ice. His skin was fog on a November morning, taut on his bones. His lips had shrunk, his ivory teeth on display. Bright blue veins protruded from his wrists the way that the biro scribbles of a lunatic jump out from a page.

'You took your time,' my aunt said.

'I was letting it cool,' I said.

I gently raised the mug of Bournville to his mouth. I pressed it against his lips with love and care. I tilted the vessel gently. I negotiated every degree of tilt with a sense of guilt. When somebody you love is dying, everything you do for them is an act of guilt. It reminds you of all the times you snapped at them, all the times you ignored them. One tiny gesture for the dying is an attempt to right all those times you fucked up when they were healthy.

Granda was dying. The shadow on his liver migrated to his kidneys and was creeping up and down his bones. When he asked for the cup of cocoa, it meant that he had a brief moment where he could concentrate on something other than his agony. Doctor Condon gave us a pain chart, for us to use as inquiry for the ould lad, but it was full of words you'd never use when you're in the throes of hurt. 'Bothersome or uncomfortable' called for a handful of analgesics, little green opiates with some paracetamol thrown in, the type your ma would give you if you were scared of flying. 'Severe or excruciating' meant the big lads like oxycontin, and if it was really bad, the nurse had to come over in her purple Ka with the fentanyl lozenges. My buddy Sonya Kinsella said I should have kept the fentanyl, coz she can get fifty quid a pop for them up in Dublin. She'd have gone halves. I wouldn't even risk it though, there was a shade up in Drimnagh who reached into a junkie's pocket and caught a fentanyl lozenge. It melted in his fist, he went into shock ... opiate overdose. It's why all the guards in Dublin wear those little rubber gloves now like burly surgeons. Fuck that, I'm not giving a load of Dublin pricks my granda's lozenges.

That day was a 'bothersome or uncomfortable' day, thank fuck, coz he had the codeine at lunch-time. He was on his little Bournville oasis. Every night had been like this for a month. Either myself, the aunt or mad Uncle Richard would keep watch. If we saw signs of a death rattle, we were to call the fat nurse in her purple Ka, and she'd let the ould lad fade in comfort. We'd often mistake a coughing fit for the rattle. The nurse would arrive, get annoyed, and then walk out of the room backwards, talking about how she used to earn double looking after Maoris with bad hearts in Brisbane.

The wall behind Granda's bed had a patchy black mould that ate at the paint because of the damp mountain air and smelled like fancy mushrooms. The curtains were dark yellow, from when he used to smoke, but if you pulled them open, you could see the original white cotton in the folds and creases. They had a pattern like a giraffe, with gradations of brown, yellow and auburn damage from three popes' worth of fag smoke. Whenever I saw that, it made me want to quit smoking but also want to have a puff at the same time. There was a little resin plinth on the wall beside the door, and on it a statue of Saint Gerald with the gammy leg, the Norman saint. Granda was mad into his Normans. Our family name is Purcell. The Purcells were Norman nobles that came over with Strongbow. I'd always be reminded by the family of my Norman surname, and to be proud of it. Granda used to get called a West Brit in the pub and he'd go apeshit, as he never considered the Normans to be full Brit.

'They integrated, they started the Yola culture, ye shower of ignorant pricks. Read a book,' he'd roar at all the boys at the taps, who'd be wearing pints of porter around their necks like brooches.

When he was 56, my nan died. He kept drawing her pension and bought a partial suit of Norman armour from an antique dealer up North. He consulted illuminated imagery he found in an 12th-century psalter and recreated the missing pieces using a petrol engine to a design worn by the Fitzwilliam clan. He would wear the full suit of armour in all his daily transactions, whether it was putting money on dogs in the bookies, getting prostate exams at Doctor Condon's and especially when drinking in the pub. The other ould lads stopped drinking with him when he started wearing the armour. He was barred from all county GAA matches after his presence caused an umpire to suffer a nervous breakdown. The clattering of his chainmail became well known up and down the town. You could hear him coming towards you before you'd see him. He sounded like a shopping trolley full of knives. Tourists would ask him for photos and he'd threaten them with his *bec de faucon*, which was his lanky French hammer that had the metal beak of a falcon on the end of it. He had it with him when they were shooting *Saving Private Ryan* down on Curracloe Beach in '97. The guards confiscated the weapon after he lashed a caterer across the collarbone with it. Granda had applied to be an extra and was removed from the set for refusing to wear an Allied uniform. He argued that his armour was more historically accurate than pretending the beach was

1940s Normandy. He managed to sneak back on the set and hid in the background when they were filming the opening scene. No one spotted him amid the chaos of the bombs and blood, until they looked back at the footage. It cost the Yanks millions to digitally edit out an elderly man wearing full medieval armour from a World War II film. A journalist wrote an article about it in New Jersey. When he rang on the phone, Granda accused Steven Spielberg of Zionist freemasonry and the Mayor of Wexford had to apologise when the story went to print.

He was a fucking legend in his time, he was. More neck than a gin pigeon in a tinman's bin-bag, a fearless fella. Looking at him in the bed, a lump made its way up my belly to my gob like a furry golf-ball, and I got that stinging tickle on my cheeks and behind the eyes that you get when you're about to cry. The little shot of adrenaline too, the feeling of being really alive for half a second. A few small drops came out my ducts, and I felt the sad heavy breath that leaps out of your chest and carries the bones of everything else you ever cried about. I waited for the tear to reach my top lip so I could lick it and taste the salt. Then I clenched my fists and put the lot away.

Granda lifted the lid of one of his eyes, and threw his jaw in my direction.

'You singing quare tunes? There's to be no quare songs for me! No misery hymns, I'm grand.'

'I'm not crying, Granda, the mould is getting to my lungs,' I told him.

The aunt looked across at me as if I'd committed a crime, and gestured with her head that I should leave the room. We were to protect Granda from acquiring knowledge of the severity of his affliction, he wasn't to know. He was fierce contrary and wouldn't take news of his illness well. Crying and sadness were off-limits in the bedroom. Acceptable topics of conversation were darts, the price of pints, lottery tickets, early medieval history, the music of Neil Diamond and the condition and conservation of the local pine marten. Death was not to be discussed.

I decided to head outside to the back garden as the curtains had given me a fag pang. Down the stairs, through the kitchen, out the back door. The freezing night was fizzy and bit at my skin. The moon had fucked off to the other side of the gaff. I flaked open the yellow pouch of Amber Leaf tobacco that I keep wrapped tight so that the moisture stays inside. I stuck my nose in and inhaled first, to get a lash of that damp, earthy, burnt-chocolate stink. I pinched out a lump and put it in my palm. Under the dark it looked like the huge spider that kept me from sleeping in my room for a whole summer the year of my Junior Cert. I rolled it up into a Rizla and grazed my tongue across the sticky part. A tiny tobacco bristle rested on my lip, and burnt the tip of my tongue with a pointed sting. That's how you really know this shit is bad for you. Whatever mad Mayan bollocks first came across a tobacco plant must have known on first bite that it wasn't for eating, you'd never ate something that burns like that. Unless it's chillies, I suppose, but at least they have a sweetness to them. The Mayans discovered them too, and cocaine, and chocolate. Fuck it, maybe that's what they meant by their calendar saying 2012 would bring Doomsday? How many poor pricks have died from cocaine, fags and chocolate? Millions, I'd say.

I raised the lighter to the flaccid attempt at rolling in the dark that hung off my lip. The familiar flick lit up my hands and the house gable-end with an honest-looking glint of orange. Small bang of sulphur in my nostril. I could have sworn that I saw the outline of a woman standing at the end of the garden. But we're in the middle of nowhere here, so what would some beure be doing out my granda's back garden? I reached in the kitchen door and threw the light-switch on with my right arm, still gaping down to see if there was really some beure out the back. There she was, looking off into the distance. Pure long blonde hair and a dress that was sure to get wet in the tall grass. Who the fuck was she? Was she at a Debs and lost her way after too many naggins? Maybe she was one of the Gay Caseys from the halting site trying to rob copper from the boiler. And all her brothers were going to call around later in the Punto to fleece the place. I started thinking about Granda in the bed, getting his head smashed in with a hatchet by Bowsy Casey while I was locked in the wardrobe. Fuck that.

The fag in my hand had burnt halfway down and nare a pull taken off it. I roared at her, 'Hoi,' no reply.

She kept her back to me, like she was in a daze. She looked like she was singing towards the sky, but not making a sound. I thought she must have been one of them backpacker wans from the continent who picked a load of magic mushrooms from the golf course, and now she was off her tits, wandering around the garden. But what if she needed help? I was ready to go down towards her, then the top window of the house opened and it was my aunt's turkey-skin wrist pushing it open.

The aunt roared at me in a panic. 'Call the fat nurse, he's rattling, he's got the rattle in his throat, his eyes are gone back in his head. Call her.'

'Fuck,' I said. 'This is it. I thought he was grand tonight.'

The aunt closed the window and went back in. I frantically reached into my pocket for the phone to ring the fat nurse, when a hand grabbed my wrist. It was the woman, she'd walked up the garden path. She was in full view of the kitchen light now, and was staring at me. Looked like a startled Taylor Swift, but older. Not too bad to be honest, bit of a MILF. Sunken eyes, but with a body that was graceful and sexy. This beure was after taking something for sure. I couldn't stop staring at her though, I couldn't speak. I knew I was supposed to be ringing the nurse, but this wan's eyes were captivating. She was definitely looking for filth.

'What's your name?' I said, half flirting, if I'm honest.

No reply. She had to be pure some foreign wan who'd lost her way and couldn't speak English. But she seemed fairly steaming for me. I hadn't had sex since I went to Santa Ponza with Claire and Mark. I felt like a fucking gowl, Granda above in his last moments and me downstairs flirting.

She still had her hand on my wrist and moved it towards my chest. I felt a tingle, I felt pure horny. Without thinking, I leaned in and ate the face off her, she rammed her tongue in my mouth. Shifting the minds off each other, we were. Pure dirty wan too, making little moaning noises mid-shift and scraping her nails off my back and playing with the lining just between my jeans and stomach.

'What the fuck are you doing?' my aunt screamed.

I'd to snap out of it. 'Stay here,' I said to the wan.

I ran upstairs, feeling unbelievably horny. I couldn't concentrate. The ould lad was in a bad way, shaking in the bed, eyes pointed at the mouldy wall behind him, teeth chattering, grasping for breaths like they were 50 euro notes on the floor. It was the death rattle for sure.

'I called the fucking nurse,' said the aunt.

The doorbell rang. It was the fat nurse. I brought her upstairs and left her into the room. I ran downstairs, out the back. The beure was gone. The Ford Ka coming up the drive frightened her away, and she on mushrooms. I felt a surge of guilt in my belly. I felt like a rat for shifting someone with Granda dying above. I ran back upstairs, the statue of Saint Gerald with the gammy leg staring me out of it, I avoided his plaster eyes. The nurse had that pissed-off look. She was talking about Brisbane. Talking about cocktails under the brutal sun with her ex, and the tall palm trees, and the giant fruit-bats that fly across the city every Aussie sunset to sleep upside-down under the big suspension bridge with the white yachts underneath and the Korean tourists getting bat shit into their mouths from taking photos. Cursing Wexford, cursing my aunt for calling her out to the house.

'One more false alarm and I'm transferring,' she spat.

Granda was sitting up, he was grand, his eyes were open. Looking better than I'd seen him in a while. The fat nurse left the house. I felt relief. I went out the back garden to look for 43-year-old Taylor Swift, no sign of her. Total gowl, why'd she fuck off? I walked all around the fields, through the bog, over Curracloe where they shot the film. No sign of her. She'd gone. Then I went to bed.

The next night mad Uncle Richard came round to keep watch on Granda, with his friend Pregnant Dennis outside in the shit Porsche that he bought on eBay from a man in Switzerland who was in an accident and couldn't drive it anymore. Pregnant Dennis always steered clear of Granda in case he caught the cancer off him. Pregnant Dennis only ever wore corduroy and would listen to Brian Ferry's solo albums fairly loudly in the car.

Mad Uncle Richard shared Granda's passion for dogs, but contested his views on the Normans, preferring instead the 8th-century Moors of Islamic Spain, to which he had no genetic lineage. This angered Granda, and he wasn't fond of the nights Uncle Richard was on watch. Richard gained the 'mad' moniker after he trained a greyhound to put bets on him. He would race greyhounds himself, in a pair of shorts, and lost his redundancy over the course of eight months. When he got into debt, he tried to get the greyhound to pay it. The greyhound was lost in a wager to the Gay Caseys and studded with a cocker spaniel bitch. Richard had a problem with the drink and would drink naggins of Aldi vodka from a Costa coffee cup. I wasn't too fond of mad Uncle Richard either, so I spent most of that night outside, smoking Amber Leaf and hoping that the Woman with the long blonde hair might return. It was cloudy that night, the type of clouds that hug the valleys like a thick continental quilt and afford the atmosphere a quare warmth about it. Fine fag-smoking weather for the winter.

I scraped a bit of grey alabaster off the wall with my fingernails, and looked off towards the sea. Eating fags. The girl was back, down at the end of the garden again. Part of me wondered where the fuck she slept last night, what was her game? But she was back. Looking better too. She must have had a gaff nearby. This time, she had bright red lips, and cracking cheekbones like she'd spent time looking at YouTube make-up tutorials. Eyebrows on fleek like an Avon seller. I knew she'd come back to me.

She walked up to me, pure cocky, new-fangled confidence, distracted. I was going to have sex that night for sure. She leaned in for the shift, straight away. Not a bother on her, not a word spoken. Lashing her tongue off mine.

Mad Uncle Richard stuck his head out the window. 'Your grandfather is making strange noises.'

She stuck my hand up her dress and I started fingering the box off her. Richard went back inside. But she felt weird. Like when you open a fridge and there's nothing inside, only the cold waft of chilly barren nothingness. I stopped feeling horny and started to realise something. This wasn't a foreign backpacker on mushrooms who couldn't speak English. This wasn't a sister of the Gay Caseys. This woman wasn't even a human. I was fingering the fucking banshee. The night before, she'd come here to sing her shrill scream into the valley, to announce Granda's departure. If she screamed, then Granda was dead, so I distracted her by being pure suave.

I left her for a minute and hurried upstairs. Granda was death-rattling, not a doubt, calling for his mother like that lad in *Saving Private Ryan* who was shot by the Nazi sniper.

'Tell Pregnant Dennis to ring the fat nurse,' said Richard. Granda was moments from death for sure.

I scurried down the stairs and passionately grabbed the banshee by the hair at the back of her neck, started feeling her through her dress, rubbing her inside thigh, getting her hot as fuck. She commandeered my hand and gestured towards the house, like she wanted to get naked with me. I pulled back, took the rollie from behind my ear, pure cool like Samantha from *Sex and the City*, lit the fag and said, 'Sorry love, you're not my type, not interested.' The kitchen light illuminated her shrill face, and tears dropped down past her nose, she was sickened. She turned her back and walked back into the dark.

I legged it upstairs. Granda was fine. Richard was drinking Aldi vodka from his coffee cup. The next night Granda was wide awake and alive too, and the night after that. As I tell you this story now, the fat nurse is gone. Mad Uncle Richard died when Pregnant Dennis drove his car against a bridge. But Granda is still here. He's 109 years of age, with no sign of impending death, just the shitty cancer eating away at every inch of his body. But he's alive, and I'm alive. I broke the banshee's heart, and she'll never return to this house.

BEYOND
THE OTTERS
SAUCEPAN

MONTH SHUNTERS

The smell of Aunt Maura's shit was the only thing keeping me from passing out. My shin was on fire, thumping like a bunny, razors creeping up the hairs on my knee and sliding back down to the ankle, then finishing on my toe with the sting of a trillion tetanus shots. Clasping it with the auld hands was of no use to me either. This pain was foreign; we're not built for it at all. It lashed up my spine and made my head feel expandy, like a hot air balloon on full flame from its bellows. Rising up my stratosphere, testing my pain barriers. Steamy, squeaky sweat.

I could hear Maura bawling in the parlour. From the ground, I squinted and caught glimpses of her figure through the crack at the bottom of the locked double doors. She looked like those YouTube videos of Bobby Sands in his cell. There was shit and piss walked into every inch of the new carpet, and I swear it was that stench that saved me from permanent brain damage. The rumble of ammonia-thunder tugging itself along the threaded polyester into my mouth and nostrils was the only distraction from the vulgarity that hugged my body.

Maura had spent Tuesday and Wednesday night locked in her parlour, no neighbours to hear her roaring, and the mobile still in the handbag on the kitchen counter. Shitting, pissing, pacing and starving, with the family fierce worried for her.

'It was the bananas, Terence,' was the first thing I heard when I kicked the front door in. 'Go to the plastic bags full of messages on the counter, and please be careful, Terry,' was the second thing I heard. When I entered the kitchen, I was so freaked out that I kind of exited my body with the stress. My biggest fear was that Maura had developed Alzheimer's and this current incident was a taste of things to come. 'Twud break Ma's heart. Poor auld Maura, like. But when I gaped up at the ceiling and spied the giant bastard near the lightbulb, I felt fucking relief. Actual relief. I didn't know it at the time, but it was called a golden silk orbweaver. I know that now, of course. This is why Ireland needs to leave the bastard EU, if you ask me.

Crowd: Yaaaaaa!

But put politics aside for a moment. Aunt Maura had been the recipient of a Tesco delivery. They do it in a van, only a fiver. Great service, in fairness, especially for Maura in her eighties. And this tropical spider managed to hide in a bunch of bananas she'd ordered, and he gave Maura a scare when she put them on the kitchen table so she'd locked herself in the parlour with no food or jax.

The silk orbweaver is a mad bastard, by the way. They weave these colossal webs, the size of the gable end of a cottage, and they catch bats and birds and all sorts. You should Google the pattern of their webs when you get near wifi. Their webs are pure postmodern; they really challenge the mechanics and structure of other spider webs. A real delight of engineering.

Anyway. It was five summers ago so I was in the shorts. I hopped up on the rickety kitchen table with sweeping brush in hand and stared the bowzy out of it. About the size of a golf ball he was. Hairy boy. With Irish spiders, you can't get a proper gander at their face, but with these pricks you can. He was hanging upside down, creamy white, and all of his little eyes were stacked alongside each other like black pool balls on a table. You'd never agree to a pool game if all the balls were black, sure it would be pointless.

I had a crack at it. It was his pool-ball eyes that had me holding the brush handle like a cue. I was directly underneath him, staring up at his hairy presence. The plan was to aim the top of the handle then crush his stomach, or thorax, or whatever – pure splatter it. It was three in the morning and I'd just done a few cokes with some fat lads. It's worth mentioning that, because I was fearless.

So there I was anyway, brush like a pool cue, ready to smash his stomach. I pulled back my elbow, tensed it, and concentrated intently. I'd one chance. And, of course, I missed. I'd say I got one of his legs in the end, not sure. But he dropped down onto my foot, making a little thud. Irish spiders don't thud, lads. I barely knew he'd had a fair crack at the skin until I jumped off the table to try to get to Maura.

I'd say I got about five feet down the hallway towards the parlour when the legs went from under me and I was on the ground. I hadn't a clue where the spider was; I thought he must have crept over to the Feeney's farm a few fields over that way. Maura was still inside, roaring: 'Is he gone, Terence? Can I come out, please?' I tried to open my mouth, but my tongue felt too fat in my gob to answer her. I stared up at her yellowed photo of Pat Kenny above the light switch, in the plastic frame that used to belong to Padre Pio before she turned against the Church over all the sexual abuse.

'Twas then I felt the all-encompassing vigour of the glorious rush. A bite from a spider of that calibre is a spiritual experience. The possession is so slimy, so transcendent, that your brain releases all the goodies, all the milkshakes: the serotonin, the endorphins, the full complement. I was coming up.

While I was blindly writhing atop the polyester carpet, suspended in the entrancement of my agony and the spider's ecstasy, my consciousness bounded frontways from my skull, all wet and dream-like, and pondered the politics of bananas. This dandy arachnid had snaked his way over from the southern hemo of America. Snuggled into a bunch of bananas that was pumped off a branch out of a plantation, he had smuggled himself in from Ecuador, Peru, Colombia or Honduras, boys. It was in this moment that I pure knew anarchy was my only salvation. This single serum which introduced purpose and meaning into my veins was the revelatory toxin of a golden silk orbweaver. His communion with my being revealed my true path: he carved my illuminated life with his eight curly legs.

Did I ever tell ye that the scourge of contemporary colonial capitalism all started with the banana? Well, I never even knew that I knew it myself until the agony clambered on my wagon with that spider bite.

Through my greasy, sweaty brow and the tang of Maura's shitpiss, I considered the banana wars of the 1890s. The United

States made a balls of the tropics, lads. Made a balls of Latin America. While Europe was laying the logs that became World War I, the young auld Yanks, quiet as mice, drew their dirty navy nappy blueprints for US imperialism on the poor workers of South America. For what? Land? Precious ores? No. For bananas. Specifically, cheap bananas. There are bananas being sold for 10 cents each, lads.

I'm going to ask ye now to all hold yer bananas and get a good look at them in yer hands. Look at them. Are ye looking? This plump, waxy, yellow herb from the other side of the world. It's packed in its own waterproof case and all. Incredibly filling and sweet. Portable as fuck. Great source of energy and potassium. Look at it. It's fucking perfection as a single food item goes, isn't it? Hold it in yer hands now, just above the shoulder. Do ye feel that? The weight of it, like. This exotic tumescence. Very heavy to be transporting on a ship all the way here, like. You'd think they would be a few quid each at least. No, they're not, and there's a reason, and it's the same reason that the Middle East is being ridden up the hole without a condom for crude oil. Put down yer bananas for a minute till I expand on the point I'm trying to make, and the reason we're all here today.

In the 1890s fruit was the commodity of choice. The post-Industrial Revolution bourgeoisie middle classes across the world all wanted their tropical bananas. So the Americans secured them with 'democracy and freedom'. They militarily 'intervened' in the internal conflicts of South America to lower the price of bananas in their favour through a dirty shower of cunts called the United Fruit Company and the Cuyamel Fruit Company and General Lee Christmas the mercenary, now known as the Chiquita Banana Corporation. They got together a private army and performed a coup d'etat on the civil government of Honduras, and installed a military junta that were puppets for the fruit companies, aided and abetted by the US government. Not long after, gigantic plantations of bananas were built and the Honduran economy came to rely solely on the production of bananas. Almost the entire population was reduced to slaves of a corporate-run banana republic. This pattern was repeated throughout Latin America. That's why bananas cost fuck all today, lads. Will ye stand for that?

Crowd: Nooooo.

Aunt Maura's banana spider was sent to me specifically to give ye this message through his fangs, I'm convinced of it. That's why he took my toe.

Crowd: Yaaaaaaaaaaaaas, the toe. Praise the toe. Praise the toe.

Not yet, lads, I'll get to the toe in a minute. We've all had a few sherries. I'll tell ye about the toe. Don't worry.

Crowd: Tooooooooe.

When the ambulance arrived, they thought I was gone. Sure they'd have no antivenom for golden silk orbweaver spider bites in Limerick Regional Hospital. It turned out that the venom wasn't even that dangerous, but I had an allergic reaction to it and went into anaphylactic shock. I'm taking that as a divine sign. If it wasn't for the smell of Maura, and my brother Archie finding me the next morning, I'd be gone. But, after five hours of surgery, they had to take the toe in the end. It was the build-up of potassium in my calf muscles from lying on top of them that cut off the blood flow. Feckin' potassium. What's in bananas? Potassium. I'm also taking that as a divine sign. We'll get to the toe.

Crowd: The toe, the toe, the toe.

They chopped it off, lads.

Crowd: The toe. Tell us about the toe!

Now, a fair chunk of ye have heard this all before, but as I'm glancing around tonight I'm seeing a few new faces this year, and I'm glad to see ye attending.

I digress. So, after the surgery, I stayed in the hospital for observation for about two days. I suppose I was a bit worried about having trouble walking or starting a motorcycle with the big toe gone. I'd a cousin by the name of Gant who used to have his appendix in a jar on his mantelpiece, and I said to myself, fuck it, I'll take the toe back home with me. So I did. They told me to keep it in a vessel with a pickling solution, but I just threw it bare into my breast pocket instead.

After a few weeks it went mushy and started to smell colourful, but after the sixth month, it was more or less in the condition that it's in now, five years later. Look at it there beside me, like a little lump of bark.

Crowd: The toe, the toe.

One night, after a feed of jars in Leeson's of Kilfinane …

Crowd: Raaaaargh.

… I hopped into bed with the jacket on. I reached into the pocket for one of the Hamlet cigars I had and popped it into my mouth. I barely had the lighter out and sure didn't I fall asleep. As I went off, I became aware that I was dreaming. It was lucid: I was in a dream but I knew I was having the dream, if you get me.

I was up a big palm tree and it was fierce hot. I was small as well, and I could see all around me without turning my head. Left, right, up, down, all at once. I couldn't possibly imagine this in a waking state. This was beyond human perceptive abilities, and that's the best way I can describe it to ye now. Smell as well. The air smelled like what tweed feels like, and flowers smelled like a handful of rocks, if your hands were wet. Before long, it became apparent that I was a golden silk orbweaver up a banana tree in Honduras. The moment I realised that, a big machete cut the bunch of bananas I was on and I woke up. I was back to my human perceptions.

Sure, of course, it wasn't a Hamlet cigar I'd put in my mouth before I drifted off at all, but the toe. The toe, through chemical or spiritual means, had the capacity to offer me narcotic visions, nay, the very memories of the golden silk orbweaver that bit me. As the night went on, I stayed awake, sucking the toe and drifting off for spells, glimpsing the history of the spider's life as he made his way from Honduras to Tesco. I even experienced a panoramic view of Maura opening the shopping and I watched as I bit my own foot in the kitchen.

There's many grinning faces here tonight in this crowd. I can see ye now: Eddie Long, Liam Flag, Constance Naughton, Colm Ovens. Ye were the ones who stood by me, ye were the first true believers that night, here in Leeson's public house, in the very spot we're gathering around now.

I'd always had an idea there was something special about the toe, and I suppose that's why I kept it in the breast pocket initially. The night after the spider vision, I brought it to the pub in an ornate jewellery box belonging to the granny. The people of Kilfinane thought I was mad, of course.

'Hear me out,' I said to the bar, 'I challenge any man here tonight to place his lips on this toe I have here. Report back to me and tell me the visions ye receive.' I offered it around the pub and was met by rejection and shame.

'I'll have the bouncers flush it down the jax if you don't put it away, Terry,' said Knickers Doyle. Do ye remember? And from the disgust and distrust, my four apostles – Eddie, Liam, Constance and Colm – came over to me with curiosity and kissed the toe as it lay in my palm. And then we got shitfaced. We got fucking shitfaced. Give yerselves a round of applause, lads. And didn't ye all close yer eyes and each of ye receive separate visions of building webs and climbing trees?

That night, ladies and gentlemen, that night this day five years ago is when the first procession of the Legion of the Camino del Toe began.

Crowd: Raaaaaaaargh.

And each year the numbers have grown. I see before me twenty-six followers of the toe. We've local people here from Kilfinane, of course, but I see some faces from Croom. Deccy Puck in the corner has travelled from Milford, and we've a representative from East Clare over there. All for the devotion of the toe. We've been jeered at, we had a Fanta bottle full of piss thrown at us last year, we've been accused from the pulpit of everything from idolatry to paganism. But I tell ye this, we won't be stopped.

If this is your first year as a member, I'm going to outline how the celebration will proceed. First order is, ye'll eat the bananas ye have in front of ye. That represents the abandonment of everything our capitalist society has taught us up to this point. After that, we start consuming the sweet poitín from the caves of Conor Pass in Kerry. That represents yer embrace of arachno-anarchism.

Crowd: Yaaaaaaaa.

Ye'll each don yer ceremonial robes to signify yer rebirth as members of the Legion of the Camino del Toe. The toe itself will be placed in the ceremonial chariot and carried aloft on the shoulders of Eddie, Liam, Constance and Colm. I will lead the procession of the toe down the main street of Kilfinane. We're to disrupt as much traffic as possible during this, so move for no man, beast or vehicle. Not even Fecky Barry's tractor. We'll walk at our own pace up Chaplain's Lane until we reach Ballyorgan. We'll commence worship of the toe for a further six hours up the hill. When we reach Condon's Bóithrín, there's an area set aside, a marquee, with a bite to eat and plenty of drink. And we'll all get a suck off the toe and get off our tits on spider venom. Are ye with me?

Crowd: Yaaaaaaaaaa.

*

That was the last procession of the Legion of the Camino del Toe in Kilfinane. Listening back to the recording of that speech sends the chills up me. It was so innocent, so harmless. How did it get to this? How did a bit of fun between friends turn into this?

Living in the jungle is like being handed a plate of pig tripe from your grandmother. You've to force yourself to eat it; you've to convince yourself you want it inside you, want it bad, for fear of causing offence. Everything in the rainforest eyes you up like a garlic cheese chip. Fucking everything, including the climate. You must never offend the jungle. When your neck isn't tired from scanning vines for a starving wet jaguar, it's the auburn boar behind the bonnet of an abandoned petrol generator that snakes a lash at you. Or scorpions. Or fire ants when you're resting against a moss patch. Or a brown recluse when you reach for a branch to stabilise your feet in the stinky mud that wants to swallow you down. In the rivers it's piranhas and snakes. If you chance a slash, there's a fish that will climb into your dick and stick spikes up your piss hole.

And that's only the danger you can see. There's trench foot from slopping in the constant shitty black mire underneath the tree canopy. The rust from your own machete will give you tetanus if it skims your skin. Parasites in the water, if you dare chance a sup. Yellow fever. Dengue fever. Malaria. Diphtheria. Cholera. Where we hide out, the only food is insects you can catch yourself. Beetles and cicadas, dried in the heat, on the end of a stick. You can't even roast one, as lighting a fire will give your position away.

The coca leaves keep me going. The bitter, numb cottonmouth dance of a mouthful of coca keeps the hunger away. Keeps my mind sharp. Ya, I'm paranoid, but that's no harm when I've reason to be anyway.

The toe processions from Leeson's pub, they were only an excuse for a drink. Tunes and mushrooms for the more 'subversive' elements of Kilfinane to avoid the fucking summer novena. We'd hold up the toe, we'd kiss it, we'd all pretend to have a trance and make up fantastic stories about the visions we'd have. All shite talk. Then we'd do rounds of poitín shots when someone thought up the best story about being a spider. Followed by singing, dancing, yokes, riding and raving out in the country under the summer stars, not a guard to be seen. The sesh, man. We were about as radical as Jedward. And fuck me I'd love to be back doing that. Sure when the spider bit me, it made the local paper. 'Man in Kilfinane bitten by a Tesco banana spider'. Nothing ever happens in Kilfinane. I ran with it for the laugh. We were just a bored people, inventing our own craic in the arse end of nowhere.

How did it all end up with me in this fucking boiling jungle with a rifle in my hand? I blame Constance. The night of the last procession, she pushed me on the banana rant, the politics of it, the systemic oppression. I told her I'd read it all off Wikipedia and was talking out my arse. But she scorned me for not taking the politics bit seriously. She called me a performative radical. I'd forgotten about her uncle Pat, the IRA man, who trained the FARC guerrillas in Colombia. I'd forgotten that she had that streak in the family, that she had those connections.

I suppose you could say I was in love with Constance. She was fucking gorgeous. I did my First Communion with her, my first naggin, my first yoke, my first ride. I'd have followed her to hell, and that's what I did. She convinced myself and five others that we needed to go to Honduras. That we'd be of better use as a FARC cell in Honduras, taking out the overseers of the banana plantations. Proper instigators of radical leftist revolution. I used my silver tongue to convince those five – now three – that we needed to become real revolutionaries. For that, I am deeply, deeply sorry.

This past year I've seen unthinkable things. I've done unthinkable things. I've slit a man's throat in front of his family. I've burned acres of farmland. I've seen young Conor Quirk dragged apart and tortured by mercenaries, spying it all through night-vision binoculars. He didn't give me up, God rest his soul. I've watched the stoic Eddie Long from Croom rape the fifteen-year-old daughter of a Chiquita Banana Corporation solicitor during a tropical storm. I watched a bullet from a Honduran soldier enter Constance's shoulder and exit her throat as blood and bile splattered a vine. It became difficult to care about anything after all that.

Most nights we'd just wait, as the hot rain slapped the leaves above with a rhythm to it. Your eyes learn to see in that jungle dark. The most successful raids happened during the thunder-storms. With enough coca leaves livening up your senses and perceptions, you can taste the static in the air, and the insects go quiet. When that sharp white lightning crawls over the hills of a banana plantation, you'd leave your position and strike hard and fast. To the big house. Leave no person of any power behind. Send a message to the banana magnates that they are no longer safe. Heads in bin bags, bodies in trenches, family dogs hung from doorways with their guts pulled out. Record it all, post it to LiveLeak. Disappear back into the jungle, and move fast and quiet to the next plantation. By the end, the overseers had left, knowing we would come for them, and the banana lands were ours.

But I'm in now. I've had my souls. I'm the most wanted man in the jungles of Tegucigalpa, and I will bring a reign of justice with me. A reign of blood. If anything, to avenge the death of Constance. This was her struggle more than anyone's. Fuck the banana magnates. There will be a new regime in Honduras tonight.

I have the bulk of 1,600 armed people behind me. At every plantation we liberated from the banana capitalists, we'd take the able-bodied people of the villages with us. I'd use a trans-lator to tell them about the events. The same rant you just heard: Maura, the shit, the spider, the toe, the procession. They ate it up. They were as bored as the people of Kilfinane and needed something to believe in.

They followed the toe; they worshipped the toe. Guns drifting in from Colombia into each of their hands. We are a militia, and not even the Mexican cartels dare fuck with us. The People's Army of the Arachno-Anarchic Toe. We don't need to smuggle cocaine to fund this war, we have the procession of the toe to radicalise anyone. We are the AAT. Our logo is a spider web with a toe in it. I am known as 'El Sin Punta' – the one with no toe. The yanks are too worried about the last bit of oil in the Middle East to be sending aid to the Chiquita Banana Corporation.

I'm taking too much credit here. This was all made possible because of Constance. Her granddad fought with Tom Barry's flying column against the Black and Tans in West Cork. She knew the intimate mechanics of guerrilla conflict. Hit and run, take out the ones at the top, and the rest will fall. Now it's just me and a few West Limerick lads, doing to the tropics what we did to the Brits a hundred years ago. Sure, Che Guevara's grandmother was from Galway; he drank in Shannon in the '50s.

The city of Tegucigalpa is orgasmic with the blind chaos of oncoming liberty. The denizens know we are here. Waiting to strike. Lads, half the Honduran military follow the toe. No cunt will stop us. Oh, if poor Aunt Maura knew she had a hand in all of this.

Last night we made our way down from the hills of Santa Lucia. We have columns posted on all sides. Dug out in trenches up in Tatumbla. Snipers in Rio Abajo. Artillery in Yaguacire. The presidential palace is surrounded and in direct sight. Only a hundred men belonging to the president's armed guard are protecting him. They will surrender and join us … or die.

I sit here in a bush, chewing this coca leaf with a Kalashnikov and the AAT behind me. The sun looms orange on the horizon, spitting peachy warm rays on the facades of the high-rise glass of the Chiquita Banana Corporation. The executives have fled on their helicopters. Cowards. My reflection haunts their office windows. There will be a change of regime.

Ye've been raised on bananas, ye won't turn them down when they cost two euro a pop. There will be no Chiquita logo, no blue oval of Fyffes, only my toe in a spider web.

And ye'll eat it up.

BRUCE WILLIS
IS A GHOST
AT THE END